BATTLE HEAT

BATTLE HEAT

BRITT VAN DEN ELZEN

NEW DAM PUBLISHING

First edition

Cover Illustration by Till & Dill
Copy Edit by Cassandra Brown

ISBN 978-9-0832-0963-0 (hardback)
ISBN 978-9-0832-0962-3 (paperback)
ISBN 978-9-0832-0961-6 (ebook)
ISBN 978-9-0832-0960-9 (Kindle)

Published by New Dam Publishing
www.brittvandenelzen.com

For Mom and Dad—
because you had my back when
I decided to pursue my dreams.

ARMY RANKS

‖‖	Soldier	—	First Lieutenant
‖|	Corporal	=	Major
||	Sergeant	≡	Lieutenant Colonel
		Second Lieutenant	≣	Colonel

 Brigadier General

 Major General

 Lieutenant General

 General

PROLOGUE

10 YEARS EARLIER

My legs moved up and down restlessly under the bench I was sitting on next to Principal Green's office. It was the first time I had been called to his office, and I had no idea why.

I pursed my lips and leaned over to look into the hallway. A bit further on, the secretary smiled at me kindly as she held the phone to her ear. I returned the smile, but an ominous feeling ran through my body.

The door to the office opened. A girl I didn't recognize walked out. Her eyes looked puffy, and the corners of her mouth were droopy. The principal stood in the doorway watching her silently depart. He wore a brown-checkered three-piece suit, stylish round glasses, and his russet hair was neatly styled. He casually pulled a pocket watch from his jacket and checked the time.

A heartbeat later, he turned to me and smiled broadly. "Hunter Jameson. Come on in."

I smiled back hesitantly, and carefully followed him into the office.

The office consisted almost entirely of dark brown lacquered wood with golden details: table legs, pens, a clock, a letter opener—you name it.

I sat down in a luxurious brown leather chair opposite his desk and looked at the map on the wall behind it. It was a detailed representation of our continent, Ardenza, whose right side was entirely cloaked in black: the shadow plains. In geography, we'd learned that these shadow plains had expanded over our continent to include a large part of the rest of the world.

"Hunter," he started, and my attention quickly turned back to the principal. "Do I understand correctly that you want to do the medical program after you graduate?"

My heart hammered in my throat. I swallowed. "Yes, that's right."

Principal Green clasped his hands together and looked at me intently. "I understand from your class mentor that you're looking for more stimulation."

I nodded. "Yes, but I just meant an extra class or something like that."

The principal grinned. "Don't worry, Hunter. Wanting more of an intellectual challenge isn't a bad thing. I'm here to help you with that." He cleared his throat. "We are looking for a student who can handle an incredibly *challenging* program, and we think you are the perfect candidate."

"Oh," I replied, dumbstruck. "What kind of program?"

The principal handed me a booklet, and, after reading the title, I quickly looked up in surprise. "This is about the medical program."

"That's right," Principal Green said. "They're looking for serious, talented students who can take the preparatory course alongside their current studies—so that they can reduce the shortage of doctors and surgeons in the military."

Interested, I flipped through the booklet, then looked back at him. "And you think I'm a suitable candidate for this program?"

The principal nodded and opened a folder from which he retrieved some documents. "The first three years of secondary school, you were already far ahead of everyone else, and we know you can easily handle this level of study. I also understand that you participate in many extracurricular activities—time you could also spend on medical school. The program takes a lot of time and effort, but knowing what I know about the students at our school, I can only recommend you."

The idea of giving up my extracurricular activities—not seeing the friends I made from these different groups and clubs a few days a week felt like a weight on my heart.

"Would I stay in the same classes I'm in now?" I asked.

He cleared his throat. "Unfortunately, that will be difficult. We may be able to arrange some of your classes, but we will rebuild your high school education around the preparatory course. You'll probably have to take some other classes."

I took a deep breath. Medical school was my dream, but obviously it would be easier to finish high school first and then start the degree. What did those three years matter?

A lot, said a little voice in my head. *It matters a lot. You're bored at school right now. No one has ever finished the medical program this quickly! Imagine being one of the first.*

My heart started to beat faster just thinking about it. Becoming one of the youngest surgeons in all of Ardenza sounded very alluring.

"Can I take this home to discuss with my parents?" As a fifteen-year-old, I didn't even know if I was allowed to make this decision independently.

Principal Green smiled. "Of course you can, Hunter, but it's ultimately your decision. You should also know that it's a test program, and we can offer this to only one student from our school, which is why we pay the entire preparatory course *for* you."

It was a fantastic opportunity. Everything I'd been working towards, presented on a silver platter. It was true that I obtained good marks with little effort, but that didn't mean that I could also follow an entire course alongside my current studies—which also required me to give up on a lot of fun things. Could I live with that?

"You're the perfect candidate, Hunter," the principal said. "I'm sure you can pass the program. You undoubtedly have the potential—the longer it takes for you to graduate from the medical program, the longer others have to wait for your talents."

Principal Green was well-respected, and seemed like the sort of man that wanted to keep his reputation intact, so I was sure he wouldn't recommend me for a program if he wasn't sure I could handle it.

A shiver ran through my body. This was my *ultimate* dream.

"There's only one condition," he said. "If you enter the program, you must enlist in the military for a minimum of three years after completing full medical training."

I looked up at him and nodded. *I could live with that.*

CHAPTER 1

I wove the needle through the patient's skin and threaded a complicated pattern that I could do in my sleep. My hands worked together like a well-oiled machine, repeating the movements over and over, slowly closing the open wound. I was pleased with the result, and predicted that the skin would heal nicely—even though I wasn't a plastic surgeon.

"Scissors," I said, as the operating assistant was already placing the required tool in my hand. Again, I reminded myself that I didn't really have to say what I needed. That habit had become so ingrained during my training that I still did it out of habit. Working in a hospital with fully trained medical professionals was different from working in the military, where most surgical assistants had a dual role.

I finished the suture thoroughly and meticulously, after which I left the patient in the care of the medical assistants that were present. This way of working had initially also taken some getting used to, as I found it challenging to give up the care of a patient. But after I realized that I could be of more value if I just practiced my profession, I'd been able to let go of this control—not to mention the expertise of the medical assistants who worked here.

It finally felt normal to work independently in an operating room after graduating from my six-year training to become a trauma surgeon. I had grown more confident over the years, which had been difficult, because ever since starting the medical program, I've heard people whispering that I was *the* child prodigy.

So, no pressure at all.

The sliding doors automatically opened as I exited the operating room, and I entered a space where I could undo my surgical gown and disinfect myself.

While I was soaping my arms under the warm water, the door on the other side slid open and a soldier stepped inside. His dark uniform made a stark contrast with the white, sterile space.

"Lieutenant Dr. Jameson?"

I nodded, but continued washing my hands.

"Major General Hawke wants to see you," the soldier said, saluting, as was customary in the military when speaking to someone of higher rank.

"All right. Let the Major General know I'll be there as soon as I'm changed."

I exited the room a moment later and undid my braid, letting my dark blonde curls hang free. After I put my army uniform back on, and got my belongings from my locker, I followed the path to the army base.

Longingly, I looked out of the windows, biting my cheek. Night slowly emerged at the same time as always due to the slowly dimming synthetic sunlight lamps that filled the sky.

Was I finally going to get my first mission?

* * *

I knocked on the office door and opened it as I saluted Major General Hawke, who was sitting behind her desk. The last time I was here had been right after graduation, for my job interview. The only thing that had changed since then was that the Major General had cut her brown hair noticeably shorter.

"Take a seat, Lieutenant Jameson," she said, gesturing with a small smile to the chair in front of her desk. The Major General always seemed to have a peculiar smile on her lips—as if she knew something you didn't.

She examined the paperwork in front of her and clasped her hands together, her eyes fixing on me again. "You've never been on a mission, correct?"

I nodded. *Please, please, please.*

"Right." She regarded me thoughtfully as she paused. "I'm going to make a big exception, Lieutenant, and I expect you to take this seriously."

Underneath the table, I made fists of my now clammy hands. "Of course, Major General."

The Major General put her hands flat on the papers and spread her fingers. "There is a mission under the command of General Zaregova, SSU mission 3B, which is critical to both the world we live in, and that of the future."

General Zaregova's Special Shadow Unit mission 3B was indeed well known—infamous even. There wasn't much known about what happened there, except that they tracked down mutants and took them from the shadow plains for scientific research. It was known as the most challenging mission in Ardenza, the only mission on this continent that let soldiers enter the plains.

Nearly half of the continent consisted of these dark regions called the shadow plains. No sane person would go in there—not while mutants roamed them. Most of the mutants had been ordinary people before a mutation occurred inside them due to lack of sunlight. As a result, they developed abnormal strength and lost the capability to think logically. According to the research group in Barak, it turned out that they could only use their reptilian brain, as the rest of their brain had given out. "Turned off," as the scientists called it.

I'd once seen a mutant during my training, and it didn't even closely resemble a human. Fortunately, he had been dead because an adult mutant had the strength of five average people combined. We learned that they did the same things beasts did: sleep, eat, and mate. Before there was a wall, they even appeared to regularly abduct animals and people from the borders to presumably eat them when the food on their side was rapidly declining. I honestly wouldn't have been surprised if they ate each other—but skin and bone didn't really fill a stomach.

Major General Hawke continued, "Mutant's killed an entire team during a recent mission. One of the casualties included a trauma surgeon. They're now short a surgeon on the medical team, and need a skilled replacement to support this mission." She cleared her throat for a moment, then looked at me sharply. "I'd hate to see you go, Lieutenant, but they asked for my professional opinion, and I can only recommend you. In addition, it makes no sense for a military trauma surgeon to solely work in the hospital.

"You are a fast learner, intelligent and young, so I have

no doubt you will quickly catch up with the pace there. Promotion to major is already on the horizon anyway, so that's a logical—if not accelerated—next step."

Then I can only recommend you. That was the exact phrase my high school principal had said to me when looking for students to follow the medical preparatory course through a double track. The military's demand for doctors and surgeons had surpassed the supply, as most aspiring physicians and surgeons found the military and the shadow plains a waste of time. Over there, 'nothing ever happened anyway.' That's why they wanted to see if they could recruit high school students and reduce the shortage a bit. I knew this hadn't produced the desired result, as I was the only one of the twenty students across the continent who had completed the program.

I swallowed. "Isn't my lack of experience a problem?"

This had been the question I hadn't dared to ask back then. But getting a rare opportunity to make your dream come true as a fifteen-year-old wasn't something you turned down at that point in your life. However, when it came to this crucial mission, I asked anyway. I was willing to do anything for my career, but only if it had a positive impact. Not in a million years did I want to be the person who stood in the way of this vital mission and throw my career—everything I'd worked so hard for over the years—out the window.

The Major General slowly shook her head and suddenly looked much older. "No experience can prepare you for mission 3B, or what it's like to step onto the shadow plains. It would be a mistake to send someone else instead of the one who has the singular potential for such a mission."

I ran my hands over the pants of my uniform and nodded

again. This mission might be very demanding, but that was no reason to doubt my abilities. This mission was my chance to prove myself. A mission like 3B would be a great asset to my career; I would get to go out into the shadows and work in direct contact with mutants—which was a unique opportunity.

The shadows had been allowed to expand for a long time before there even was a wall and an official border. Since then, camps and border guards had been set up all along the wall to keep the shadow plains under control. The walls had halted the expansion of the area, which in theory could be called a success, but everyone knew that the wall was only a temporary solution to an increasing problem. Any person who thought otherwise was naive. The area's growth may have stopped, but the development of the mutant population was still in full swing—if we were to believe the reports.

The Major General took a deep breath, tapping her fingers on the desk. "As you know, the goal of mission 3B is to obtain as many mutants from the shadow plains as possible for scientific research. There are alternating extraction and scouting missions, usually lasting from a few days to a few weeks. The groups cannot go onto the plains with more than a couple of soldiers at a time, and since adult mutants are incredibly strong, they only extract the *younger* mutants."

She meant *mutants born there*.

I glanced at my hands for a moment, then back to the Major General—who was assessing me as she continued briefing me on the mission. "Because the groups can be gone for a long time, and potentially get into danger, they need skilled and reliable trauma specialists, so that *if* something happens, the team has the best chance of survival."

Nodding, I felt adrenaline rushing through my veins.

"There are a handful of alternating trauma surgeons on the mission base. Often, there are a few weeks in-between the missions you go on, because they demand a lot from you. Only General Zaregova goes into the field almost every time. The rest of the days, you work on the base and monitor the soldiers in the field."

My eyebrows lifted. "Why does the general go along almost every time?"

Major General Hawke folded her hands thoughtfully over her stomach. "He knows the area best, and doesn't want his unit in any unnecessary danger."

"And what if something happens to him?" I asked. "Who will take over the mission then? Isn't it inconvenient to be so dependent on one person?"

"The whole situation is inconvenient," the Major General replied. "And if I'm honest, there isn't enough time to get others at the same level as the General. He's the best in the world at what he does. He is an exceptional, distinguished leader. You should take up specific details of the mission with the General himself."

I just nodded.

She gave me another intense look. "So, do you want to take on the mission?"

"Do I have a choice?" I laughed nervously, raising my eyebrows at her.

Nervous, because I knew full well that I wasn't giving *myself* a choice. I had to do this. I'd worked so hard for a chance like this. Now I could finally show myself—and others—that I'm indeed as good as expected. Saying no wasn't an option.

"I haven't told them my choice yet." The Major General narrowed her eyes. "This is a unique situation, Lieutenant. It's your first mission, and the death toll is high. It's not just anything I ask of you."

To restrain and hide my nerves, I controlled my breathing.

This mission mattered to the world—a mission that could really make a difference and change the future, that could change *my future*, in more than one way.

I met her gaze and nodded firmly. "I'll do it."

CHAPTER 2

"It's happening, Mom," I said to the screen showing my parents.

The crease between my mother's eyebrows deepened. "Hunter, are you sure? You still have the chance to come back home now. You don't owe anyone in this world anything. You know that, right?"

My father soothingly rubbed her back.

Unfortunately, I did. After my father became ill twelve years ago, I'd sworn to help other people as his doctor had helped him. It was priceless, and incredibly empowering, to watch the doctor save my father's life. I'd been *so* impressed that it became my dream to help other people in the same way from that moment on.

I smiled at my parents, who only ever wanted to see me happy. "This is what I've worked for—what I was trained for. I choose to do this." My eyes slid to the corner of the screen to check the time, then back to the rest of my room, which I had already tidied up.

"I also don't have much time left to get ready for the flight, so I have to finish up," I said quickly.

"But you weren't trained for *mission 3B*, were you?" my mother asked, shaking her head.

"No one is trained for that," I replied.

My mother looked at my father, and a moment later, she said, "You will keep in touch, won't you?"

"I'm very rarely allowed to contact the home front, but I'll do my best to let you know when I can." My eyes stung, and I bit down on my lower lip.

My father put an arm around my mother's shoulders and winked at me. "Just be careful there, okay? We'd like to see you return in one piece."

My mother sighed in frustration and slapped him faintly against his chest.

At least they had each other. That made it so much easier for me to go.

I blew them a kiss. "See you again in a few months."

They wished me luck, and I quickly ended the conversation. Blinking away tears, I closed the screen and said my goodbyes to the single room I'd lived in for a year.

* * *

An hour later, I walked towards the hover plane with my belongings—which all fit in a single bag.

I'd never had many material possessions: proof that work and the pursuit of my goals dominated my life. People could also conclude that I valued moments more, but I wasn't a sentimental person.

Additionally, I didn't have many people to say goodbye to—which reminded me how empty my life was. Except for a handful of medics I'd worked with in the hospital, no one would even notice that I was gone. The life I had built up to this point was empty—a shell of unfulfilled potential.

The flight went smoothly, and, because of the hover technique, in almost complete silence. I had arrived within hours at an airbase close to the wall. At least, as close as possible to land because of the lack of light. Not to mention the way the communication and navigation systems seemed to fail the closer we got to the shadows.

I was taken to a small pick-up point in a hover heli because they had more control. The pilot knew the path to the destination by heart, and didn't need a navigation system.

There was a large armored car waiting to take me to the base. The ride with the armored car was only half an hour, but in that short time, my eyes had slowly gotten used to a world that was only getting darker.

Fewer and fewer lights lined up along the road, to the point where we couldn't see anything anymore. Only the glare from the headlights made it possible to observe how the normal road turned into a path that could no longer be called a road. I bounced in different directions on the backseat, and had to hold on tight so I wouldn't get pushed into my seat belts at every bump.

There was a reason, of course. Because of the mutants' heightened senses, they were drawn to any sign of life like a moth to a flame, responding to every sensory stimulus they could perceive.

The only reason the part of the world I lived in wasn't shrouded in darkness is that we'd developed the technology to mimic sunlight. I've never seen or felt a real sunbeam in my life, as the sun stopped producing light long before I was born.

My parents had grown up with a sun that weakened each year, but they still *had* experienced the natural sun. According to them, the fabricated sunlight today was very similar. For example, warmth and discoloration of the skin were both qualities that the natural sun also used to have, but with improvements of our technologists who'd removed the harmful radiation.

Despite those benefits, I would've loved to see one of our moons lit up. Or a real rainbow. Unfortunately, we only knew these phenomena through paintings and old photos.

It was also a lot colder here. The car windows fogged up as I brought my head closer to look outside. The headlights lit up parts of the road, and I could spot snow on the trail every now and then. When the driver finally put out the headlights, my eyes slowly adjusted to the darkness, and I could see faint lights in the distance seeping through the trees.

The base of mission 3B.

The driver, who'd been relatively quiet the entire ride, brought the car to a halt, and I got out. I thanked him after grabbing my bag, and he only responded with a curt nod. Then he drove back up the path we'd come from.

"Major Dr. Jameson?" I heard from behind me.

I suppressed a smile at hearing my new title. *Major.*

I turned and saw a man walking towards me from the darkness with an outstretched hand.

Nodding, I shook his hand. "That's me."

The man noted something on his clipboard and motioned for me to follow him. "Let's start the introductions."

I followed him across the cold terrain and looked at my surroundings. There was no paved road—just a hard, sand-covered surface from which solid pieces of rock protruded. There were, however, quite a few buildings whose entrances and exits were dimly lit. The buildings all looked the same, but varied in size and format. They all looked like metal containers: sturdy, static, and movable if necessary.

But everything paled in comparison to the wall on my right, rising above the base. It looked the same as in the pictures of other parts I'd seen so far: a large row of concrete blocks at least thirty-three feet high. The only difference were the steel frames that sporadically supported this part of the wall. And despite already looking majestic in the photos, the wall was a lot more impressive in real life.

A fierce gust of wind swept past my back toward the massive wall, but was cut off abruptly and turned into a sharp *whoosh*, making me shiver. From the wind, or from the idea of what was behind the wall, I didn't know. Probably both.

We eventually stepped into a room that, to my surprise, was pleasantly heated. There were two other soldiers already inside. I took a seat in one of the designated chairs, and the man who'd led me inside took a position at the front of the room.

"Welcome to the base of SSU 3B. I want to thank you for your efforts in advance, because this is not just any mission. Some soldiers who come here don't return home." He cleared his throat. "I don't mean this as a threat. It's just fact. And here we prefer to give each other the harsh reality rather than a sparkling illusion.

"We have already received and processed your information. Your uniforms and other necessities are already present in your assigned rooms. We expect you to wear the designated clothes for the appropriate activities, so that we're always aware of what each person is doing and to what division they belong.

"Each unit: medical, logistics, technical, infantry, and the others all have their own color. Your respective ranks have already been applied to your various uniforms. Never share an item of clothing unless there's absolutely no other option."

He checked something off his clipboard, then looked back up. "Get yourself intensive light therapy during your stay, for at least four hours a day. There's a sunlight lamp available in every room, in addition to the standard lamps, and there are sunlight lamps in the public areas.

"This is extremely important. We don't want you to get sick from lack of sunlight. Light therapy is already scarce here, so please have the discipline to keep yourself to it." His piercing gaze roamed over us. "That doesn't apply when you go into the field. In there, you aren't assured of a few hours of light per day. So do yourself—and us—a favor and make time for it when you can."

Fifty years ago, for reasons still unknown, the sun began to dim, and its rays became increasingly scarce, causing many people to get sick slowly. By the time scientists were working on mimicking sunlight, it was already too late for large parts of the world's population. And since synthetic sunlight technology was outrageously expensive and couldn't be distributed fast enough, much of the world—mainly the poorer parts—went dark.

Ultimately, the lack of sunshine activated a then-unknown mutation gene in people with an advanced sunlight deficiency. After the world's first cities were engulfed in chaos, scientists and doctors discovered the existence of this gene and its presence in humans. *Every* human, apparently. Once that mutation caused permanent changes in the genes of large parts of the sick world population, it was the beginning of the downfall. The more people mutated, the more deaths occurred, and everything around it went to shit. The darkness spread like an oil stain over large parts of the world, resulting in the rest of the world growing aware of the severity—as always, *too late*. Currently, half of the planet is cloaked in darkness, and half of the world's population, mutant.

They haven't discovered a solution to reverse the mutation yet, but the scientists also believe it's no longer about that. They've already concluded that even sunlight wouldn't be able to reverse it anymore, making it a permanent mutation. Besides, the mutants had lived like this for at least twenty years, so even if they found a solution—the people they once were probably wouldn't be there anymore. They generally agreed that the mutants were a lost cause—except perhaps for the children, if the reproduction hadn't resulted in any major genetic modifications.

In addition to looking for a solution to the growing mutant problem, they also focused on deactivating the gene in the healthy part of humanity. Until then, we had to get light therapy without most people being aware of it. Life had simply adjusted to it.

But being here, so close to the shadow plains, you were put back with both feet on the ground. There was still a problem, a *big* problem, that wasn't just going to disappear.

I was ripped from my thoughts as the male soldier finished up his talk.

"That's it for now. You will learn the rest in the coming days and weeks." He checked something again. "In the coming days, the General will invite you for a short introductory meeting. He wants to check everyone who comes in."

I suppressed the urge to raise an eyebrow.

The soldier put down his clipboard and rolled a large screen forward. He tapped the display, and a map appeared. With a marker, he made a dot on the screen. "Currently, we're here." He traced a path across the map to another point, where he drew a circle. "And *here* are your rooms."

He shoved a hand inside his pocket. "These are the passes with your identification number and department on them. They allow you to enter any space for which you are authorized." After he handed out the passes, he turned off the screen. "I will walk with you the first time so that no one gets lost. The dark can be quite uncomfortable at the beginning."

We followed him out of the room and were greeted by the icy, cutting wind outside. I looked straight ahead at the wall and could make out a group of people coming our way. They were all dressed in black from head to toe and held helmets in their hands. I noticed that they were all covered in dust and had a tired expression on their faces—with one obvious exception.

His uniform was dusty too, but he didn't look tired. He walked with a firm stride, his back straight and his head held high. Some people took over a space with their mere presence, and this man was one of them.

He was tall, and his black hair had a faint blue hue in the dim light. His skin was a clear golden brown, even though it'd taken on a grayish glow from a lack of sunlight. He had a strong jaw and defined cheekbones, accentuated by trimmed facial hair, and a sensual mouth with the corners curved downwards. Thick, dark lashes and brows surrounded his dark eyes.

Something about him made me instinctively tuck a strand of dark blond hair behind my ear.

General Nikolai Zaregova.

Of course, I had known what he looked like… sort of.

Three years ago, when he had risen to fame and caused a lot of uproar on the continent, all the media had covered him. They'd published his enlistment photo—in which he'd been eighteen years old—in every newspaper. After that, his popularity had almost skyrocketed. A whole lot of boys and girls—including students from my degree—thought he was incredibly handsome and had constantly speculated about what he would look like now if he looked like *that* at eighteen. After a second photo of him was found, in which he was standing with a group of soldiers, and you could clearly distinguish his side profile, there had been a lot of speculation. *Did he even exist? How could a general be so young, attractive, and skilled? Why wasn't there more information about him?*

He almost became a myth, causing even the military to bother issuing a press release stating that General Zaregova was indeed the General of SSU missions 3B. This statement gave them back some control over the situation.

The fuss had subsided a bit after that, as everyone believed the military and no journalist could get close enough to the mission's base without being stopped. If they even dared.

But now, three years after the press released that first old photo into the world, his presence took my breath away. He'd been handsome in those photos, but the pictures were nothing compared to the real man…

I frowned.

This man was so much more.

We had instinctively stopped walking. *Everyone* on the path had stopped what they were doing and saluted to the

General.

As soon as he walked past and nodded, people went back to business.

My brain finally returned to reality, and I realized that my arms were still hanging limply at my sides. It was out of character to get distracted like that, so I tore away my gaze from his face and looked towards his shoulder, where the General's sign was embroidered. His sign was slightly different from the regular four stars you got as a general: his stars were pierced together by two crossed swords—the swords that were also strapped to his back.

I saluted.

The moment he passed our group, I got an even better look at him. He nodded respectfully. But for a moment, before turning his head back, a pair of dark, inscrutable eyes looked straight into mine.

As he continued walking, I lowered my arm and stared after him in bewilderment.

"He has that effect on everyone," whispered one of the recruits behind me.

Questioningly, I shook my head. *What effect?*

It wasn't until a moment later that I realized the group had already moved on, and I had to run—thankfully without them realizing it—before I caught back up again.

CHAPTER 3

After a restless first night, the pager I carried went off early with the assignment to report for my first day of work at the medical center. I couldn't remember exactly where that was, but I'd seen a map outside my room, so I was sure I would find my way.

After I arrived in my room the night before, I'd almost immediately dropped myself onto the bed. It was pretty large compared to the narrow bed at the army base at home in Barak. I could sleep spread eagle without one limb sticking out.

All belongings had been in the room, as promised. I had gotten a training outfit, a field uniform—identical to what the General's team had worn the night before—and a set of casual clothes in the correct sizes and colors. I noticed that almost everything was in black except for the undergarments—which were white. White, to quickly locate any possible injuries. There were also a few green items of clothing, the color reminding me of olives. These were all clothes I had to wear for work, but outside of working hours, we were allowed to walk around the base in our own clothes if we wanted to.

After changing into the dark green pantsuit with the white tight-fitting thermal underwear underneath, I made my way to the medical center. As I'd predicted, it was easy to locate, using the map, and I could enter the center with my identification card, which I had fastened to a pocket of my suit.

The medical building was small compared to the gigantic hospital in Barak. I'd read that there was an operating room, two examination rooms, a laboratory, and a large monitoring room.

I passed the latter first. A couple large screens showed five names with soldiers' faces, including vital signs and full-body scans indicating physical activity. Two people studied the information on the screens, while three others were sitting at desks, working on computers. They were all wearing headsets, and I watched curiously as their mouths opened from time to time to speak through them. The realization that the people on the other side of the line were on the shadow plains now— that in time *I* would become one of those people—made my stomach flip.

After looking inside the monitoring room from behind the glass wall for a while, a door opened at the end of the hallway, and a man came my way.

He was slightly older than the average age of the people I'd seen so far. Thin wrinkles were visible on his pale face, and he already had gray hairs starting to appear on his beard and temples.

When he saw me standing, he slightly tilted his head. "Major Hunter Jameson?"

I rubbed my hands over my trousers and nodded.

"Colonel Arepto, I presume?" He was, after all, head of the medical base.

"You presumed correctly." He narrowed his eyes slightly and nodded once. "Follow me."

He disappeared through the door again, and I quickly matched his stride. Soon we arrived at an office with several filing cabinets against the wall and a large desk in the center of the room.

Colonel Arepto took a seat behind it and motioned for me to sit in the chair opposite him. "I've read your file from Major General Hawke, and the Major General has a lot of good things to say about you. Almost only good things, it seems."

I suppressed a frown but said nothing as he opened my file and scanned over some things.

The Colonel clearly didn't suppress *his* frown as he looked up from the file. "Are you truly twenty-five years old?"

Cautiously, I nodded and tried to assess the situation.

"First, we lose one of our best trauma surgeons, and then they send *you*." He clicked his tongue and shook his head as he gestured at me. He looked back to the file, clearly irritated. "You hardly have any experience, only graduated a year ago and are *twenty-five*," he said incredulously.

Wait a minute.

"Colonel," I jumped in, "I assure you that the main base is aware of the gravity of the situation here, and they truly didn't send just anyone." I cleared my throat. "I'm of value, and I will prove it."

He raised his eyebrows in surprise. "I expect nothing less, Major Jameson. That's the problem." He was lost in thought for a moment, then looked up again. "Come with me; I'll explain everything briefly so you can start. The sooner, the better."

I stood abruptly to catch up with him as he slipped out of the office. *The sooner, the better?* My brain struggled to keep up with his train of thought.

Major General Hawke had emphasized that being young and inexperienced could become a problem, but if it were up to me, it wouldn't be one for long. I would take care of that.

In the meantime, we walked past the laboratory, where someone was working with great determination. One of the walls consisted of thick glass, which made it possible to take a look.

Colonel Arepto pointed inside. "Our lab technician does everything that the medical staff cannot do. She performs standard analyzing procedures in the lab on various samples from soldiers, but she's also involved in the mutant research. For example, one of our lab technicians was the first to discover that the tissue cells of mutants didn't communicate properly with each other. The older the mutant, the weirder the tissue behaved." The Colonel walked to the end of the hall. "This discovery has given the research team in Barak a major boost."

After throwing one last look inside, I followed him. A few corridors ahead, a door opened automatically, revealing a disinfection hall.

While we washed our hands, the Colonel continued. "Now we enter the operation center. We have one OR that is equipped for all types of procedures."

At the end of the hallway, we walked straight into the operating room.

"How many surgeries are performed per week?" I asked

as I examined the equipment—all of it of the same high quality I knew from the hospital.

"Usually none. The actual operation center is mostly deserted. There are only a few operations a month, on the soldiers here or those coming back from the shadows."

"So, most patients get injured in the field?"

He looked up. "Yes. The most important medical work takes place *there*. All living members of an extraction or scouting group must return. This means either getting the injured back on their feet in a crisis, or carrying the injured back—and taking an injured person back often proves impossible due to the constant threats at a time like that."

The Colonel was silent for a moment. Then he added, "That also counts for the dead, by the way."

He walked out of the operating room and motioned for me to follow. "The groups that don't make it in the field are often the groups that can't get help with medical problems. One trauma surgeon accompanies a group at all times, as well as a few soldiers with dual functions. All other soldiers received first aid training, but the critical health of a group relies and depends on the quality of the trauma surgeon with them."

We left the operation center and walked into the hallway, which led back to the monitoring room. "To guarantee quality as much as possible, you will often be working here." He pointed to the dashboards with different names and live statistics. "During a mission, all group members are injected with a chip that transmits all vital functions and other information back to us. This allows us to monitor a great deal and provide feedback to the group—with which we are constantly in contact."

I admired the influx of information on the screens and watched a full-body scan being conducted for one of the soldiers in the field. The result even highlighted more minor injuries that would be forming bruises. We didn't have *that* in Barak.

Colonel Arepto watched and continued in a softer tone: "When a trauma surgeon is unable to assist or is under a great deal of pressure—for whatever reason—we can assist the others in the field remotely with procedures or surgeries. Everyone has a body camera with a night function that we can always turn on, if necessary."

The room's sliding doors opened, and a girl about the same age as me walked in. She wore her brown curls in a high ponytail and had friendly russet eyes. Her skin tone almost matched the color of her hair but was just a shade lighter. It struck me that she was one of the few whose skin had not yet acquired a gray tone due to the lack of sunlight.

The Colonel nodded at the girl, and she saluted him as she approached. "This is First Lieutenant Renée. She will take you along on her shift today."

He shot me one more look and then left abruptly.

"Hi," said the Lieutenant, drawing my gaze away from the Colonel. She held out her hand and smiled kindly. "I'm Raven."

Up close, her brown eyes had a purple sheen, and long, dark lashes surrounded them.

I shook her hand and returned the smile. "Hunter."

"Don't worry about Colonel Arepto. He's going through a difficult time." Raven smiled a little wider, and her cheeks dimpled.

"It doesn't seem like an easy place to be," I replied

timidly.

"No, certainly not." She laughed conspiratorially as she sat down behind one of the desks.

I sat down next to Raven as she clicked on her dashboard. She put on a pair of headphones that she connected to the ones she gave me. She explained everything as she walked through all kinds of programs and showed me the different functionalities.

As she was inspecting something, I looked at her sideways. "What exactly is your function here? Besides…" I gestured to the room.

Raven kindly turned to me. "I'm a dual function soldier. Infantry and medical. That means I do both, and also have both functions in the field—whichever is needed most." She pointed to the monitor in front of her. "I'm scheduled here when I'm not in the field."

"What's it like being in the field?"

"Hard." She sighed deeply. "I had to go out on the plains in my first week, and have now been inside twice for a few days. We alternate as much as possible so that we won't have to go too often. I would say everyone goes once a month on average. But most of the soldiers don't stay here for more than a few months either, because it's mentally and physically too taxing and dangerous. With a few exceptions, of course."

"Like the General?" I asked as casually as possible. "Back in Barak, I heard that he goes more often."

Raven snorted. "Yes, but he's the exception to the exception. The General goes in half of the time and has been doing so for three years."

My mouth fell open. "He *really* goes inside that often?"

She nodded gravely. "And hopefully for you, he will join

your group, too. The groups he joins seldom had something serious happen to them." She briefly lifted her finger at me as she listened to the headset and gestured that she was needed on the line.

Raven turned her microphone back on. "What do you mean?" she asked the soldier on the other end of the line. "No, you can do that."

I looked at the statistics of the soldiers now busy in the field, without General Zaregova, and I couldn't help but wonder how they felt. How they *really* felt in there.

* * *

When Raven's shift ended, she explained that dinner was split into two groups. This was arranged so that the active shifts could be taken over without having a major collective break.

The canteen was large and spacious, and completely full during the meals. The food was served as a buffet, but several soldiers had kitchen duty and scooped the food onto your plate. Everyone was only allowed to get food *once*, but I wondered if everyone followed this rule—and whether the soldiers on duty even cared.

After dinner, my whole body had become stiff from all the sitting during the day—which I wasn't used to—and I had to stretch quite a bit before I could get up properly.

"By the way, Hunter," Raven said as she poked me. "I'm going to the bar with a group later tonight. Would you like to join us?"

Surprised, I looked at her.

"Sunlight therapy is still a requirement, and at least that way we'll make it fun." Raven raised an eyebrow in question. "And you'll also get to know some more people on your first day."

I felt my lips tug into a smile. "Yeah, that would be nice," I answered. I couldn't remember the last time I hung out with people just for fun.

"Great." Raven gave me a thumbs up and walked away, adding, "Catch you later!"

* * *

During my short but wonderful shower, I'd stood with my face upwards under the jet for a while. I did this often when my head was full, as if the water could cleanse me from all my worries and fears.

After that, I changed into black cargo pants with a black turtleneck underneath, as it was ice-cold here at night. I let my wet, dark blond curls hang loose, hoping my hair wouldn't freeze as I walked through the chill air.

Arriving at the heated bar, I noticed that it was almost as big as the canteen, but still had a warm and cozy feel. I took off my coat and walked towards an already waving Raven.

Three other people sat at her table to whom she introduced me, "Guys, this is Hunter. She's the new trauma surgeon."

She gestured to the boy with the dark red hair next to her, who looked vaguely familiar. "This is Kelian, First Lieutenant. He also has a dual function, as operating assistant and infantry."

Raven pointed to the girl at the head of the table, who had an arm full of tattoos and dark hair in a long braid. "This is Tania—Lieutenant Colonel; she's coming from the Secret Service to reinforce the mission."

Tania smiled at me.

"And finally, we have Cardan, also Major. He's in the infantry." The guy I sat next to gave me a nod, then took a sip from his beer with a slanted smile.

I smiled back at them. "Nice to meet you."

"Likewise." Tania winked and threw her dark braid over her shoulder.

I smiled back and cast my gaze to Kelian, the operating assistant. "Didn't you return from the shadow plains with that group yesterday?"

He nodded. "I'm glad that's over with. I've never walked around the shadows as much as I did last week."

"You're such a whiner," Cardan said with a laugh, moving his legs as Kelian tried to kick him underneath the table. Then he focused his gaze on me. "Do you already know when you will go into the field?"

"She's only been here for a day, man. What do you think?" Tania huffed.

I nodded in agreement. "I just learned what the monitoring room looks like, so that'll probably take some time." I bit my lip, and Cardan's eyes followed the movement. "But I would like to."

There was a burst of collective laughter at the table, and Raven gave me a compassionate look. "That's what everyone says in the beginning."

"Ah," I responded, grinning and rolling my eyes, "just let me start on a positive note."

"That's the spirit!" Cardan nudged my shoulder and gestured to Kelian. "You could learn something from that, Kellie."

I laughed as Kelian finished his glass and bent over the table to slap Cardan in the face, after which they started hitting each other.

Raven shook her head, and Tania rolled her eyes. "Boys will be boys."

I stood slowly and tucked my hair behind my ears, making the boys look up from their struggle. "I'm going to get something to drink. Does anyone want anything?" I asked.

They shook their heads, and I walked away towards the bar—followed by a 'goddamnit' from Kelian, who'd been hit again by Cardan.

It'd been a strange feeling talking to the group in such a casual way. Not that I only had serious conversations in my life, but because this was new to me—having a group of friends. Obviously, I'd dealt with groups, but none of them had actually involved me this much before. I didn't quite know how to behave myself.

Closer to the bar, I started wondering what to order. Beer maybe—or something stronger? I'd stopped drinking alcohol after graduation, but the short time I'd been here had been pretty overwhelming. Nothing I couldn't handle… But still, it might be nice to relax a little. During my studies, this had sometimes resulted in a trip to the room of someone I'd met when going out, but I didn't particularly felt like ending up in someone else's bed here.

I grabbed the bar with both hands and looked at what they had to offer. Alright, *one* glass, that certainly couldn't hurt.

The bartender, who was a soldier too, walked over almost immediately and grinned at me. But as I was about to order something, his attention shifted to someone who'd come up next to me and had put his hand flat on the bar.

My head abruptly turned, and I looked up, straight into

33

the General's face. It felt like my throat was being constricted as I stared at his side profile, and I shifted my gaze just as abruptly back to the bartender.

His face and hands were no longer covered in dust, and the frown had disappeared. I heard blood rushing through my ears as I thought about *how*—

I was abruptly pulled from my thoughts when the bartender promptly stepped aside and waited for the General to order.

Shaking my head in confusion, I brought myself back to reality. "Excuse me?" I exclaimed and cleared my throat.

The bartender and the General both turned their heads towards me. I wasn't small, but I felt myself shrinking as the General's gaze landed on me.

As if he could hear my thoughts, he leaned his forearm on the bar and turned his body to me. He wore a slim-fitting, long-sleeved black shirt, rolled halfway up his muscular forearms and tucked back into black cargo pants. His presence seemed to shrink the space, and I grew feverish as his eyes focused on me.

"Yes?" he asked in a deep, lilting voice.

I looked straight into his dark eyes for a moment, but quickly hooked my gaze back to that of the bartender, who was also looking at me expectingly. "I'd like to order something," I said, as if it were the most natural thing in the world, and I thanked the universe for not hearing a tremor in my voice. The tremor that I felt so very clearly.

The bartender forced a smile on his face, then looked almost quizzically at the General, who was silent, and whose eyes I could still feel boring into the side of my head. I suppressed the urge to squeeze my eyes shut as I felt the blood rush to my cheeks, and wanted the ground to swallow me whole.

A moment later, the General averted his gaze and looked at the bartender. "You hear her." The General nodded in my direction, and his voice vibrated through my bones. "She would like to order something—and we wouldn't want her to start seeing men in the wrong light of day, would we?"

The bartender looked from the General to me and raised his eyebrows.

I ignored the General and said, "A beer, please," while watching the bartender open the bottle and hand it to me. And because I couldn't resist, I met the General's gaze and lifted the bottle to him. "My image of you remains intact."

He raised a dark brow, and I could swear one corner of his mouth followed the gesture before he looked away to order his own drink.

Back at the table, the group had fallen silent, and four pairs of eyes were looking at me.

"What is it?" I asked, slowly lowering myself back onto the couch next to Cardan.

Raven bit her lip and fiddled with her hair nervously, looking at me in shock. "What was *that*?"

I frowned. "What was what?"

Raven shook her head. "That, at the bar with the *General*, Hunter. Everyone was looking at you two."

"Oh." I took a sip, notably smaller than the last, and felt my cheeks burn again. "Did I break an unwritten rule or something?"

Kelian laughed. "That depends. Why was he looking at you so intently?"

"Tania was afraid you were flirting with him," Cardan

added, pointing his thumb at Tania, who punched his arm.

"I don't mean that in a bad way," she explained.

I laughed nervously and glanced around the table. "It *certainly* wasn't flirting. It was about ordering a drink."

Cardan laughed again. "Good thing, too."

"How so? What's going on?" I asked, trying to keep the curiosity out of my voice.

Tania looked toward the General's table and leaned forward with her arms on the table so I could hear better. "There have been a few incidents where people have tried to hook up with him. Flirting, showing off—whatever," she gestured wildly. "All those people were on their way home the next day."

The others at the table all nodded in agreement.

I pursed my mouth and frowned at the General. "It doesn't seem smart to me anyway, whatever the outcome might be," I muttered. "As the other party in that situation, you're always losing."

Cardan grinned and looked at me over his drink with a twinkle in his eye. "It's indeed better to focus on your peers." He winked at me, and this time Raven bumped him on the shoulder.

"Hey!" a dumbfounded Cardan shouted. "Everyone's rather eager to hurt me tonight."

"That's because you're a fool," Tania replied sweetly, blowing him a kiss.

He pretended to catch the kiss and crushed it between his hands.

I shook my head, grinning alongside Raven. "I'd be careful if I were you, Cardan," she said. "Who knows whether Hunter has to patch you up someday."

36

Laughing, I took another sip and looked out into the room. On a platform at the back was a table where the General and a few other men sat. Someone at his table was speaking while *he* casually leaned back in his chair. I observed the General and took a deep breath. Now that I witnessed him here, he suddenly became real—a man of flesh and blood rather than stories. I was forced to face reality and couldn't help but agree with everyone who had ever praised his looks to the heavens. He was really, very attractive.

The subject of the conversation at my table changed and turned to one of the missions in the shadows. I tried to listen to what they had to say, to learn from their experiences, but throughout the conversation, my eyes kept drifting to where the General sat in the corner, drinking with his men.

Not because I tried to keep an eye on him.

But because he looked back.

CHAPTER 4

The next day, while on duty, I was told to report to the General's office. I had to confess: I was a little nervous, especially thinking back to last night. But I was a professional—just like him—and that's how I would behave.

The medical building was close to the wall, so I had to walk over the grounds for some time before arriving at the main building, where the General's office was located. I greeted the soldiers there and asked for directions to my appointment. When I finally arrived on the correct floor, I quickly knocked on the door twice that had a metal plate with *General Zaregova* on it.

"Come in," I heard him say from the other end.

I opened the door and saluted, waiting for his nod.

His outfit was all black again: a tight black sweater, black cargo pants, and black boots displayed on the long legs sticking out from under the desk. Strapped around his shoulders and torso was a gun holster, minus the weapon.

He looked up, and a brief amused expression crossed his face. The General's mouth twitched and a slight glint formed in his eyes. *"Major Jameson,"* he murmured. "I figured you were one of the new recruits." He nodded to me and gestured to the chair in front of the desk, and I sat down.

I continued to look at him as neutrally as possible, folding my hands tightly in my lap to keep them occupied. I noticed that his black hair was neatly styled, and that he looked well rested.

The General didn't look away either and said, "Is that your excuse for forgetting your place and undermining my position yesterday?"

It seemed to become a force of wills—staring at each other.

I gathered all my willpower to keep going and blinked once. "Sorry?" Had I been in the same situation as him at all? I'd been talking to the bartender, *not* him.

He nodded approvingly. "There are your manners," he muttered, breaking eye contact.

The bubble we'd been in burst, and I took another deep breath. When I finally registered his words, I opened my mouth to contradict him, but he forcefully tapped the paper with his pen, making me clench my jaws, and I felt my ears turn red.

"Major Jameson, the thing is, we don't have time for games here. What we need is a good addition to the trauma department. And as I read here," he held up a few papers, scanning the information, "you're exactly what we need right now, and you have the right qualities."

I sat silently in my chair, staring at the paper, trying to suppress the urge to cast my gaze downwards to my hands.

He let go of the document, put his fingertips together, and leaned back in his chair as I felt his gaze burn into me. When he continued speaking, I met his eyes again and reminded myself to keep breathing. "You were by far the youngest and *best* in your class, got stellar recommendations from everyone you've worked under—which gives me hope that you do indeed know your place—but you have no field experience. You don't know what it's like to work in extremely critical situations, making it a big gamble for us to bet on you. Especially for a mission like this."

I swallowed and felt my cheeks warm. He was right, of course. I *was* young, I *was* inexperienced—and perhaps I was indeed a big gamble. Here, I had yet to prove otherwise.

The General crossed his arms and gave me a piercing look. "If you find it difficult to follow directions, frequently undermine authority, or don't take this mission seriously—you should let me know now."

After a brief silence, I realized that he was waiting on my answer. My heart pounded. "No, General. I take it seriously," I quickly blurted. "I take *this* seriously."

He raised an eyebrow, and I cleared my throat. "Of course, I know my place, both in the military and on this mission. I have no trouble with that."

"You have potential, Major Jameson." He nodded firmly. "A lot, in fact—if I'm to believe the reports. But to fulfill that potential, you have to be open to learning."

I bit my tongue and forced myself to nod.

The General stood, and I mirrored his movement. He was tall, at least one head taller than me.

He walked around his desk and grabbed the door handle. "We can't afford to make mistakes, Major. Mistakes cost lives here," he said as he opened the door.

I walked around the chair as he extended his hand. I grabbed it adamantly and felt the calluses of his hands scrape against mine. The hard cusps tingled with friction.

"I trust that I'll only save lives," I replied, bravely meeting his eyes, because this regarded *my* specialty—*my* talent.

One corner of his mouth lifted as if it had a life of its own, and before I could fully register it, his gaze returned to neutral. I saw the wheels twist and turn behind his eyes *and* get stuck.

After letting go of his hand, I saluted him once more, as I was supposed to—and because I knew my place. "General."

He stepped aside and held the door open for me. "Major," he replied as I exited the room, his eyes burning a hole into my back as I walked down the hall to the stairs and left the floor.

* * *

At the end of the workday, I accompanied Raven and Kelian to the canteen, where we were greeted by mouthwatering smells, making my stomach grumble by the time we'd grabbed a tray and joined the back of the line.

"It smells *so* good," I sighed.

"It *is* good," a voice responded behind me.

I turned, and a blonde man behind me grinned. When he saw my face, he tilted his head a little, examining me. "Hence the surprised undertone. You're new, aren't you?"

"I am." I nodded and smiled back. The man was tall, with ash blonde hair, blue eyes, and a jawline that could cut through paper. "After everything I heard about the mission, I only dared to dream about delicious meals."

He held out his hand while holding my gaze. "Jordan," he said, eyes sparkling.

He didn't mention a title, so neither did I when I shook

his hand. "Hunter."

The line moved, and we got closer to the food, which made my mouth water even more.

"How long have you been here, Hunter?" Jordan asked, and I saw Raven and Kelian exchange glances ahead of me in line.

I ignored them and turned around to get another look. "A few days now." Something about him seemed vaguely familiar to me, but it could also be because he was the picture of a typical jock. "You?"

"A while." He laughed, causing dimples to appear in his cheeks. "What's your specialty?"

He was incredibly handsome, I decided, and replied, "I'm a trauma surgeon."

"Really?" He raised his eyebrows in surprise. "You're very young."

"Tell me about it," I sighed. It's been said too much already. "Accelerated program."

He grinned slightly and shrugged. "If you're good, you're good."

"My thoughts exactly," I said, nodding at him approvingly.

The line moved again, and it was finally my turn. The soldier on duty handed me a plate full of food, and I smiled at the man behind me before I left. "Nice to meet you, Jordan."

He winked. "Likewise."

A warm feeling spread through my body as I watched Raven wave to me from across the room. I sat down at the table with her and Kelian.

She laughed and tapped me on my forearm. "You really know how to attract them, don't you?"

"I don't know what you mean," I said, taking a bite of my food. "But he did look familiar to me."

"Yeah," Raven laughed and looked at Kelian, who shook his head and tried to bite back laughter. "He looks a bit like delegate Kenneth Locke, don't you think?"

My eyes widened, and I gestured to her in agreement. "Exactly!"

Delegate Kenneth Locke was a popular figure in politics, and an outstanding member of the government. One of Ardenza's thirty deputies, elected by the people every five years. They represented the people, made decisions, and chose the army's chief general.

"What are the odds," I muttered. I took another bite.

Kelian was now shaking his head. "Pretty high—it's his son."

"*Major General* Locke," Raven added, nodding.

I choked on my food.

"What?" I asked when I had put myself back together and took a sip of my drink. *How many* generals were here? I was hoping Major General Locke—Jordan—hadn't minded that I hadn't addressed him as the superior he was. And I hoped even more that the incident wouldn't reach the ears of General Zaregova… He already had enough doubts about me as it was.

Contemplating, I watched as Kelian started to eat, but Raven nodded gravely. "Major General Locke is Kenneth Locke's son."

I felt my cheeks burn and put my hands over my face before looking up again. *Goddamnit.*

My eyes scanned the dining room, looking for Major General Locke. I found him sitting at a table on the other side of the hall, and, as if he realized I was looking at him, he met my gaze. Smiling, he dipped his chin in recognition, and I answered it in despair. A frown accompanied his dimples, and he shook his head with a laugh—as if he thought I was an idiot. Which I was.

Someone else caught his eye, and Jordan looked away from me. General Zaregova had come in and sat down next to him. During their conversation, Jordan's gaze drifted back to me, grinning a little. The General followed his gaze in my direction, realizing that I was watching them.

Like a moron, I immediately looked away and pretended to poke my food. *Shit.* I couldn't hit myself in the head while the General was looking, but I still struggled to suppress the urge—which I'd become talented at during the short time I'd been here.

Raven chuckled at my pained expression. "Don't worry, Locke's nice. He treats everyone the same and really isn't going to make an issue out of this."

The General, though, had acquired a somewhat distorted image of me in the last couple of days. Especially if he thought I was flirting with his generals too. *That* provided something to talk about when it came to knowing your place. I thought about yesterday's conversation and remembered that he had sent people home because they'd flirted with *him.*

I suppressed an internal groan and actually started to put the food into my mouth.

There was only thing to do. I had to prove how invaluable I really was.

CHAPTER 5

A few weeks passed, during which I gradually mastered my duties at the base. The only thing missing was a chance to finally prove myself. Except for a few critical moments in the monitoring room, I hadn't been allowed to enter the field yet.

I also hadn't crossed paths with Major General Locke and General Zaregova again. I'd only seen them from afar a couple of times, which had given me some relief. It gave me space to focus on my tasks, and get to know everyone and everything in the medical center.

Besides me, five other trauma surgeons were part of the medical rotation, and all of them had entered the field since I'd arrived at mission 3B. They were nice, but our shifts were rotating too often to really get to know each other.

Luckily, I had Raven and Kelian, who also worked in the medical center half of the time, which made me run into them a lot—when they weren't out in the field themselves, of course.

When my shift ended for the day, Lieutenant Colonel Nigel Kent approached me. He was the trauma surgeon who would take over my shift for the night.

"Hunter." He nodded. "Could you talk to Arepto?"

I cleaned up my things and raised my brows at him. "That depends. About what?"

Nigel was the least pleasant colleague I had here, as he constantly gave the impression that he knew better and felt superior to the rest. The other soldiers shared my opinion, going by their expressions, but Nigel was a person who didn't even realize how much he irritated the people around him. The world revolved around *him*.

He sighed deeply and hung his tunic over the chair. "I heard he's going to send me back into the field the day after tomorrow," he glanced at me, "and that would be the second time since you arrived."

"For real?" I frowned, putting on my coat. "Did he give a reason why?"

Nigel shrugged. "Didn't ask, you know how Arepto can be…"

It was a bullshit excuse, of course. Taking a deep breath, I looked up at him. "I'll talk to him," I said curtly and walked away.

Not for him, but for myself. I'd already planned to talk to Colonel Arepto if I couldn't join the next group. Obviously, I wanted to go into the field myself—to gain the experience needed to complete this mission successfully. I wouldn't get ahead by just sitting in the monitoring room.

A few seconds later, I'd gathered my things and was standing in front of the Colonel's office. I knocked on the door.

"Yes?" I heard him growl on the other side.

Warily, I stepped into his office. "Colonel, could I discuss something with you?"

He nodded and put down his pen, folding his arms together. "What's the matter, Major?"

I cleared my throat and sat down. "I heard that Lieutenant Colonel Kent has been assigned to go into the field on the next mission, and I was wondering why I can't go this time, so we can all take fair turns?"

"I knew this was going to happen." The Colonel shook his head.

"What?"

"That Kent would get you to do his bidding."

I opened my mouth in shock. "No—oh no, I'm not."

"Kent has way more experience."

"Exactly!" I proclaimed. "I *want* to be part of the rotation. So that I can gain experience, too."

He turned his chair so he could look out the windows. "You *want* to go out onto the shadow plains?"

I nodded. "Everyone here puts their lives on the line again and again, while I haven't contributed anything yet."

The Colonel cleared his throat as he continued to look out the window. "The trauma surgeon whose spot you filled—who died last month—was Lieutenant Colonel Célina Arepto. My wife."

My lips parted, and a moment of stunned silence stretched between us.

"I'm sorry," I offered softly.

Shaking his head, he turned back to me. "It's not your fault." He swallowed, and I could see the sadness written in his eyes as he looked straight at me. "It's the fault of those bunglers in Barak, who still haven't found a solution, and send the best soldiers to their deaths time after time."

I said nothing.

"I recognize her fire in you," he continued, "and I don't want any more people of your potential losing their lives to this nonsense."

My gaze softened. "But that's what I'm here for—I considered everything, and made the decision to come anyway. I understand the risks."

"I know." Reluctantly, he nodded once and turned his gaze back to the paper in front of him. "I'll let Nigel know. The briefing is tomorrow, straight after lunch."

* * *

During lunch the next day, I struggled to focus on the conversation. My mind kept wandering to tomorrow's mission. The alarm had gone off that morning after a restless night's sleep, and the realization that I was going to enter the shadow plains had slowly crept in.

After lunch, I walked to the briefing with Kelian, who was scheduled in the same group, and focused on my breathing. I hadn't been able to swallow much because nerves constricted my throat. Kelian also didn't offer many words as we walked together. He did walk a little closer, though, and squeezed my shoulder, pulling me out of my thoughts to look at him.

He gave me an encouraging nod. "Everyone feels that way the first time."

"That doesn't really reassure me," I replied with a laugh, but I was grateful for the fact that he was in my group.

The nerves were always the worst beforehand; with surgery, before a fight... The moment before taking action was always the most nerve-wracking. Once I was inside the room, the nerves would subside, and when I step onto the shadow plains tomorrow, the nerves will give way to concentration. Unfortunately, that thought didn't make it much easier now either.

We walked into the room, and I saluted Jordan in surprise. He smiled briefly and nodded, tapping something on the tablet in his hands.

"Major Jameson, Trauma," he confirmed. "Take a seat."

I took a seat beside Kelian, and two other people came in to join us. A man and a woman, both infantry.

Jordan cleared his throat and put away his tablet. "Well, now that you're all here, I want to welcome you." He tapped the screen and opened a map of a site—behind the wall, I assumed.

He gestured at me briefly. "Major Jameson here is from Trauma, and it's her first time going in. She's backed in her tasks by First Lieutenant Rudolfs. Then we have Sergeants Karper and Wellington, who will safeguard the mission as much as possible. I'm Major General Locke, for those who don't know me yet," he said as he looked at me with a sparkle in his eyes. "And I'm your point of contact during this mission. I'll make sure that the entire mission runs smoothly, and that we can complete a successful scouting."

Jordan marked something on the map with a digital pen. "This is the wall that encloses the site, and this is where we go in." He drew a path across the map. "We continue on the path, passing the remains of the other two walls."

I was about to raise my hand to ask about those other walls when the door to the room opened, and Jordan paused. We all turned to inspect the sound.

The General stepped in and waved his hand for all of us to stay seated and nodded to Jordan. "Continue."

My heartbeat quickened as the General walked to the

back of the room and leaned against the wall. I frowned and tried to recall my question.

Jordan picked up where he left off. "When we get past the third and final wall, the forest we enter becomes denser. It hardly ever happens, but the chance that there are mutants there is always present." He continued down the path. "Beyond the forest, we enter at the old city of Elm, which is also the final destination." He marked some things on the map again. "There are several mutant colonies in the city, which we will map out in more detail during this scouting for the upcoming extraction missions."

After going over the technical aspects of the mission and how we would get to the first stop, we got a short demonstration of the equipment that every soldier was given. Our health chips would be connected to the software of the medical center, and we were given an earpiece that would allow us to keep in touch with the monitoring room. In addition, we were equipped with several knives, a silenced gun—only to be used in emergencies—and different types of tools that could come in handy.

Kelian and the infantry soldiers would carry an additional weapon that could be used for coarser artillery should the need arise—including several bombs. I was given the medical bag, along with supplements, in addition to the reserves that Kelian would carry on his back. We would also get a means of detection—a heartbeat sensor—on which we could observe life within a radius of one hundred and sixty feet, except for ourselves and our team, of course.

Jordan gestured to the General. "General Zaregova will support us during this mission. He and I will carry extra ammunition and various weapons with us. We will focus on the mutants in the area so that we can make this scouting mission a success."

He glanced back at the screen, then clasped his hands together. "That's all. Tomorrow at five hundred sharp, we will meet again in this room to set up the equipment and put on the proper uniforms. Any questions?"

After staring at the screen for a moment, I inspected the marked walls again and raised my hand. "Why are there three walls drawn at this location?" I gestured to the drawing. Three stripes were marked, each indicating a wall. I recognized the line furthest in the shadows. That was the first wall, which was built quickly so that the construction of the official—second *and* middle—wall could proceed as safely as possible. The third line was unfamiliar to me.

"That's because a third wall has been built here."

My gaze darted to the back as General Zaregova's voice filled the room.

"The wall we're now behind was built last—but solely next to this mission's base." He pointed to the screen. "The stripe in the middle is the official wall that guards the rest of Ardenza. This mission is called 3B for a reason."

"Behind the third wall…" I muttered when it finally clicked, and the General nodded. I knew the 'B' stood for 'behind', but I'd always thought that the '3' had been the maximum number of months soldiers went on a mission here. Because very few people made it past three months, it was always described as 'the infamous 3B'.

I looked up at him again and asked, "Do we need more protection here because we go out onto the shadow plains?"

He shook his head and continued his explanation, "Before we knew that the mutants were so sensitive to sensory stimuli, we had gone into the field with armored cars. The mutants had immediately been drawn to the sound."

Jordan cleared his throat, causing me to turn my head to him. "Most of the cars couldn't get away in time before being overrun with mutants. The cars that did return left a trail of mutants that followed the sound and broke through the first barrier at this part of Ardenza. That caused the first wall to fall."

"And the second wall?" asked one of the sergeants, Wellington.

Jordan grimaced. "When it became clear that the second wall at this part of the border was partially damaged and no longer provided enough protection, a third wall was quickly put up in front of it—the wall we see here now. The official border wall of Ardenza—the second for us on this map—has been largely demolished on our side. Fortunately, we did receive help from the main base to properly build our current—third—wall and connect it to the undamaged part of the official wall in Ardenza. The time in between was... difficult."

"It was *hell*," the General said from the back of the room. "That's why we don't talk about it."

Thus, along the length of the mission's base, the official boundary wall of Ardenza, like the first wall, was in ruins. That official border wall remains intact a little further on and continues to form a solid wall: the wall that forms the border along the entire length of our continent.

So, the wall that we could see from the base was, in fact, an extra wall. A third wall that needed to be built because the first and part of the second wall had collapsed. This third wall ran from top to bottom of the mission base and rejoined the rest of the official second wall—which was completely intact there.

It was like tape to an open wound.

Why was this information kept secret? The press would've covered this if they had known about it *because* it had been so intense. It also explained why the wall looked different from the one we knew so well from photos.

Major General Locke nodded in agreement but gave me a reassuring look. "Clear?"

"Clear," I replied and also nodded to the General, who merely averted his gaze.

* * *

After the briefing, we had plenty of time to freshen up before heading to dinner. I didn't have a shift this day because I was going out into the field tomorrow, but I noticed that distraction had been welcome.

It was crazy to think that they'd spent the past few years maintaining the wall here while I was completing my education. It gave me a (misplaced) useless feeling. I managed to shake it off by telling myself I'd done it all for this—to come help here.

At dinner, I felt remarkably calm. Almost too serene. There was a chance that I wouldn't return—that was the reality of every mission. I wasn't naive enough to think I was an exception. Only the blind faith that everyone seemed to have in the General brought me some peace of mind.

Still, there was something gnawing at me.

The General made me nervous. When he was around, I became very self-aware. It made me erratic, as if his approval was *crucial* to me. I didn't like the sense of dependency I felt;

never before had I measured my success by what someone else thought of me.

But now, here, I couldn't help but want to prove myself to the General, to exceed his expectations.

I wanted his respect.

CHAPTER 6

A loud noise awoke me from a deep sleep, causing me to blindly swing my arm toward the alarm clock on the bedside table. With all the adrenaline pumping through my body, it had been nearly impossible to fall asleep that night. Apparently, I'd eventually drifted off, and after rubbing the sleep from my eyes, I gathered my things. I put on the right clothes, braided my hair, and left the room without looking back.

On my way to the assembly room, I encountered only a handful of people, as it was still early, and everyone who worked was probably somewhere inside. Soon, the small building came into view, and I let myself in with my pass. With a sinking feeling, I noticed that I was the first to join Jordan and General Zaregova, who were already inside. I saluted them both and received a nod from the General.

Jordan walked over straight away and handed me a bundle of things. "Here you go, Major Jameson."

I smiled at him in the dim light. "Thanks," I whispered.

He just smiled back, revealing the dimples in his cheeks, and then took back his place at the front of the room—where the General regarded me carefully. His eyes were indecipherable.

I quickly shifted my attention to the stuff in my hands and put on the uniform. It consisted of comfortable but sturdy pieces of clothing, which closely wrapped around my body, and because I could wear my long thermal underwear underneath, I just changed in the room. The pants had elastic ankles straps, and an elasticated hem that hugged my waist. The hem clipped onto an expanded holster that wrapped around my upper body and held my suit together—as well as allowing me to store some equipment.

When I had put my boots back on, Jordan approached to bring me something again. It was the heartbeat sensor, which sensed the heartbeats of all living organisms nearby, in a different color from your own group.

I stashed away the equipment and watched Jordan's back as he made his way back to the front of the room—where my eyes met the General's again. He let his gaze drift to Jordan for a moment, then back at me, observing.

I could guess what he was thinking. The General was exceptionally good at drawing premature conclusions. I imagined how he would put it: *When Major Jameson wasn't trying to undermine an authoritative figure, she tried to secure her spot by flirting with one.*

The thought alone made me grit my teeth.

Since when did I let the opinion of others influence my work?

The answer was: *never*.

My rule is that when you have no control over something, you let it go. I have no control over other people's thoughts, only my own actions. But the General promised to be a significant exception to my rule so far.

I lifted my chin a little higher in the air and tore away my gaze from the General.

The other group members had trickled in slowly, and had changed and prepared to leave like me.

We were all handed helmets with night-vision goggles, and I was glad I'd braided my hair that morning. I had once worn my hair in a ponytail under a helmet on a training mission during my education, which had given me a splitting headache after just a few hours.

The General moved through the group and opened the door. "Follow me," was all he said. He wore the exact same black uniform as we did—the only distinction being the four pierced stars embroidered on his shoulders and the crossed swords on his back.

As we followed him and Jordan toward the wall, Kelian joined me in line and briefly tugged on my braid. "Nervous?" he asked softly.

I looked up at him in the dark and saw his wine-colored hair neatly styled. "Yeah," I replied, and laughed nervously. "*Duh.*"

The General turned his head curtly in our direction, and my smile immediately dissipated. I felt my chest tighten as I imagined him adding "*talks too much*" to his mental notes.

When we arrived at the wall, Jordan turned around, and General Zaregova waited a little further on, looking upwards.

"We'll go through the wall in a moment," Jordan said, "and from that point on, we don't talk out loud anymore. If something *really* needs to be said, we say it hushed."

We nodded and lined up two by two. Jordan turned and walked toward the hatch, where the General softly spoke to him.

Jordan said something back, then stepped away from the General and beckoned to Kelian. "Rudolfs, you walk in front, next to me."

Kelian shrugged apologetically at me and moved forward, where he positioned himself next to Major General Locke, as the latter opened the large metal gate of the wall and beckoned us in after him.

The two infantry soldiers walked in front of me, and after I entered last, the General closed the door behind us. This allowed Jordan to open the door on the other side.

"I assume you can handle your weapons?" sounded softly from behind me, where the General stood.

No one had heard him except for me, since opening the door made a lot of noise, which meant he was clearly addressing me.

In my mind, I went through my weapons: two knives, a pistol with separate charge, and a couple of throwing knives. As it happened, I was very good with weapons—which he could have known had he actually bothered to look at my diploma. I'd scored 'excellent' in weapon techniques during the military part of the program. Not that I was going to point that out to him.

I straightened my back and turned my head slightly. "As we already established, General, I've successfully completed the program," I replied quietly but firmly.

In response, I could swear I heard him chuckle—as if he thought my answer was funny.

Almost. Because I doubted that he had a sense of humor at all.

When he remained silent, I turned my head back and bit

my tongue. I didn't want to give him a chance to accuse me of disrespectful behavior again, though it might already be too late for that. Lost in thought, I had put on my helmet and night-vision goggles like the rest, and switched them on. The light at the latch behind us turned red as the light across the room, at the entrance to the shadow plains, turned to green.

The latch opened. Carefully, we walked out, and I had to get used to the sight that the night vision goggles provided. Of course, we had practiced this during training, but you never completely got used to it. Despite the distorted view, I could clearly see that we were in a thinly vegetated forest with many open spots. My eyes slowly focused, and my ears began to ring slightly. At once, I was alert.

We automatically started walking, and I matched the pace without difficulty, walking alongside the General. The silence—save for our steps, which crackled leaves and snapped twigs—made the hairs in the back of my neck rise.

* * *

We passed part of the collapsed second wall that formed the border for the rest of Ardenza. A long time after we had crossed the ruins of the first wall and walked in silence for almost an hour, I heard a noise from the right. I stopped walking, turned my head, and strained my ears to listen again.

There it was—a sound that could be described as howling wind, but it was a tad too shrill for that, more like a sort of distorted scream. I quickly rejoined the rest of the group, who had continued walking without looking up. But every time I heard the sound, I felt an icy shiver run down my spine and turned my head.

The General moved closer to me and leaned slightly

toward my ear. "Do you hear them?" he whispered.

I held my breath. "The mutants?" I whispered back even quieter, as if I was afraid that they might otherwise hear *me*.

"Yes," he said. "Most soldiers don't."

He was so close I didn't dare to look up, but the acknowledgment in his voice satisfied me more than I'd ever want to admit.

After a while, we arrived at the beginning of the old, decayed city—Elm. In many ways, it still resembled the cities I was familiar with. There were regular but run-down residential areas, and, well into the city, I could see the tall buildings of the city center poking out of the horizon.

The General had been silent the rest of the way, except at times when he'd stopped the group to listen more closely or discuss something with Jordan before we continued.

As we entered the first street, the General gestured with his hand for us to split up. The group was divided into two teams, each taking a different route into the city. There were multiple ways to get to the first shelter, and these different ways had to be checked regularly and kept free from any threats.

More routes meant a higher chance of survival, as did splitting up. The different ways into the city were through the sewer, an underground tunnel, and walking the mostly abandoned streets. Walking the street was the least safe option, for obvious reasons, and it didn't need to be checked.

The General motioned for me to follow him toward the tunnel while the others left for the sewer. Approaching a house, he checked his heartbeat sensor before opening the door and closing it silently behind me. Inside, we continued down a stairwell into the basement.

A predominant, vile stench arose after the General opened the door, and I scrunched my nose. I recognized the stench immediately—albeit stronger than I'd ever smelled it before.

The stench of a rotting corpse.

My heartbeat sensor showed no signs of life, and I didn't see anything suspicious through my night vision goggles.

The General held an arm over his nose as he crouched by a hatch in the ground that he tried to open as quietly as possible.

I inspected the room and quickly found the first body, which belonged to a mutant. It lay on its stomach, a knife protruding from its side, in a dark pool of old blood that was caked to the floor. My night vision goggles made it look like a gaping black hole. The blood made its way to the wall, where another corpse—of a soldier—was slumped against it.

It was a dark-haired man with his head resting on one shoulder and his eyes closed. One of his arms hung limply on the floor while the other lay on his stomach, his legs spread lifelessly in front of him. It was clear from the sunken face of the soldier that he had been here for a while.

Cautiously, I bent down to inspect the man and open his tunic. I cut open a piece of his undershirt, which had once been white, and saw a piece of metal protruding from his hollow chest. A loud buzzing noise pierced my concentration, after which the hatch behind me sprang open. I put a hand over my throat, where my heart beat madly.

The overwhelming stench had made me unconsciously hold my breath. I looked backward, where the General continued opening the hatch. He said nothing as I shifted my gaze back to the soldier, my hand wrapping around the metal dog tag that hung around his neck.

Major V. Tehran, the Year 2133. That made him thirty years old.

I put the silver chain back, adjusted his shirt, and zipped up his jacket. There was something very sad about the fact that his body would be left out here until it had completely decomposed.

Stretching my legs, I turned and took another good look at the mutant. He was as nasty as the one I could remember from my training. They all had the same void expression on their gaunt faces, and they didn't look as strong as they really were—with those abhorrent, sinewy muscles and scrawny bodies.

"Major," the General spoke softly. He pointed to the open hatch, and I quickly walked over before lowering myself through the hole. I climbed down the ladder into a musty tunnel, and my feet eventually hit a solid surface.

The General followed me down the ladder and locked the hatch behind him. He let go and landed in the tunnel with a slight thud, flipping a switch, turning on a dim lit tube. The light ran like wildfire through the length of the tunnel— which, as expected, consisted only of sand and rocks. With the light on, I was able to take off my helmet with night vision goggles and strapped it to my bag.

General Zaregova had already taken off his helmet and spoke through the microphone of his earpiece. I noticed that his hair was now a little flatter than usual—which somehow made him look even more handsome. *No,* not handsome— damned attractive.

And I was staring.

He looked at me expectantly as he wrapped the strap of

his night-vision goggles around his arm and gestured forward. "The other group is already on its way."

Apparently, we could talk again, as he spoke at average volume—and I clearly had to spring into action if I was to believe his impatient look. When he decided I was taking too long, he walked past me into the tunnel. The hallway was so cramped that he had to put a hand on my shoulder and turn me around a bit before he could pass.

I followed him and found my voice again. "How long has that soldier been there?"

"Two months," he simply replied, but I sensed an edge to his voice.

"Why is he still there?"

"Because taking back the dead is not a priority. It's certainly no reason to send a separate team." He stopped walking and inspected a broken lamp. "Our only focus is on the living." The General looked to the side, his dark eyes intense. "We can't afford anything else."

We walked in silence for a while, and I mentally went through everything I had with me. I lifted my head to his back. "Why are you going through the tunnel anyway?"

He walked on but thankfully didn't ignore me. "The other group of four can stand their ground in the sewer. It doesn't matter whether I'm there too."

"I don't think so. I mean—that seems like a big difference to me." I said it before I could think about it and cursed myself. "General," I added scrapingly.

General Zaregova tilted his head to the side. "We take two routes to keep our options open. When one of two is blocked, we have a smaller chance of successfully completing the mission. We need to keep as many pathways mutant-free as possible—for a greater chance of survival. Both for the way there and back."

"But I thought," I countered, "that you would go with the group that needs you most—because you're crucial to the success of the mission." *It was a fact.*

He laughed scornfully. "Everyone is crucial to the success of the mission."

"Of course," I said.

"Besides," he sighed and ran a hand through his hair, "I *am* with the group that needs me most."

I bit my lip. "I'm not defenseless either."

"No," replied the General, stopping abruptly and turning around. "But you are a surgeon. And I don't know if you've noticed, Major, but we're short of those these days," he said cynically. "So, when *I* haven't been able to protect someone, you're the only salvation left."

I met his gaze and clenched my teeth to keep me from asking another question: *But what if you can't protect yourself?* Instead, I nodded, built up my wall, and decided to keep my mouth shut for a while.

That was probably for the best.

CHAPTER 7

The tunnel was slowly coming to an end, and I couldn't be more relieved. I didn't care that it was freezing above grounds; anything was better than down here. The air was extremely suffocating and moldy, streams of sweat ran down my back, and my lungs felt like they were full of dust.

I opened my mouth again after a long time, and my voice sounded like I felt—dehydrated. "Where exactly does this tunnel lead us?"

The General straightened as if my voice had pulled him from his thoughts. "An old shopping center where we rendezvous with the other group." The irritation seemed to have faded from his voice, and he glanced at his watch. "If everything goes according to plan, they should arrive at about the same time as us."

I could just see past the General into the tunnel and saw a ladder slanted under the next hatch. The General grabbed the ladder high, and I saw his jaw tick in annoyance. One of the ropes was broken.

"*Fucking* rats," he snapped, and turned to me, causing me to take a step back. "The other rope will probably give way if

I put my weight onto it."

I looked up and saw that the hatch had the same kind of lock and numeral mechanism as the previous one.

"I think it would be a good idea if I sit on your shoulders," I said, gesturing at him. "Since I'm smaller."

The General certainly was a head taller and broader, so I didn't quite feel like carrying him on my shoulders. I took off my backpack and propped it against the wall—which made me feel like I could soar into the sky.

He looked down at me for a moment, then nodded and knelt. I stepped in front of him and guided his broad shoulders underneath my thighs before he curled his hands tightly around my legs and placed his thumbs in the crook of my knee. He briefly squeezed one knee and asked if he could get up. Planting my hands in his neck, I tried to avoid his head as much as possible. The whole situation was awkward enough without me having to poke his eyes out, too.

A moment later, I was ready. "You can stand now."

I didn't have to hold on tight at all, as he held my knees in place with both hands and straightened smoothly. With my head, I reached the height he'd gotten to with his arms outstretched.

"One more step forward," I said, keeping one hand in his neck, and reaching for the hatch with the other. He started explaining the steps. The lock clicked open in no time, and I was able to spin the wheel, causing the hatch to open with a sigh. The General had said that the room the hatch opened into had been kept tightly closed, and that he hadn't detected anything on his heartbeat sensor.

I gripped the opening of the hatch with both hands as he gripped my thighs and pushed me up until I could haul myself into the space. It was pitch black, except for the light coming from the hatch.

The General picked up our belongings from the ground and passed them through the hatch. He glanced up, and I held out my arm to him. Before he could think too long on it, I clucked.

"It'll go faster with my help."

He seemed about to open his mouth but instead grabbed my arm just above the elbow. I clamped my hand around his upper arm as he pushed off of the leftover rope ladder. I pulled him up with great effort until he landed next to the hatch, forearm bracing on the floor as he pulled himself out of the hole. He closed the hatch, put his backpack on again, like me, and passed on something incomprehensible to the base through his earpiece.

I put my night vision goggles back on and saw the General hold a finger to his lips. He unlocked the door, and we stepped out into the abandoned mall.

Together we walked through the building and spotted the other team at the bottom of the stairwell. A weight was lifted off my shoulders when I saw Jordan, Kelian, and the rest, which automatically made me feel a little more confident about the mission.

We followed Jordan up the stairwell after checking whether the coast was clear. It was a long way up, and I noticed that we had traded the shopping center for an office building after a while.

The signs indicated we had reached the fourteenth floor when we finally exited the stairs and made our way to the far end of the building, where there was a hole overlooking a large part of the city center. How that hole got there must have had something to do with the last days of the old Elm—before it was overrun with mutants and no one had anywhere to go because of the newly built wall.

Major General Locke stood in the opening and looked outside with his binoculars. He gestured to General Zaregova, who nodded back gravely. After they'd inspected the town for a while, I thought I heard some noise coming from the stairwell. Reasonably far away, but nevertheless inside of the building we currently were in. I walked over to the stairs to listen and heard the sound coming closer.

The General stood next to me all of a sudden and started listening to the sound on the stairs, too. My heart was beating like crazy as I reached for my heartbeat sensor and saw a heartbeat flickering—*no*, two heartbeats, close together. I looked up at the General in horror, who at the same time turned his head towards me.

With the heartbeat sensor in hand, I hurried back to Jordan as fast as I could. Grabbing his shoulder, I showed him the two heartbeats on the tiny screen. I pointed from my ear to the stairwell, where the General was still standing. When Jordan noticed the bright spots on the screen, he cursed softly and walked towards General Zaregova with urgent but silent strides.

The rest followed because the stairwell was our only way down safely.

The noise had left the stairs and faded, indicating that they—most likely mutants—were now on a floor. General Zaregova held up two fingers but added three more a moment later and pointed down. The mutants were somwhere two to five floors below us.

We had to get out of here before they got us on *their* radar.

After a few silent instructions, the six of us started the descent. Three floors down, my heart skipped a few beats, and I suppressed the urge to cover my ears; an unbelievably loud screeching sounded through the building. It was possibly the sharpest noise I'd ever heard.

It was now clear that there was at least one mutant on the floor below us, making a lot of noise. As if… as if he was in pain.

The General beckoned quickly for us to follow him down the stairs. The sound of our footsteps was drowned out by the noise the mutant was making.

When I got to the next floor, I noticed a wet trail running over the ground. It went all the way through the hall and into one of the rooms, where the sound was coming from. The screeching gave way to a painful whimper. Still very loud, but more like a wounded animal than an alarm.

As we were about to climb the next flight of stairs, the door in the hallway slammed open, and we heard a scream that could only be described as primal. Since the stairs connected directly with the corridor, the General pushed us roughly out of sight—into the nearest room. There, we squatted close to the ground, trying to keep our breathing as silent as possible.

I noticed that the rest of the walls in the office were made of glass, and we could see inside all the connecting rooms. I couldn't distinguish color through the night vision goggles, but I did see the mutant move. I forgot where I was for a moment while focusing on the mutant. He had a few long hairs on his head, surrounded by many shorter—probably regrown—strands, and looked utterly gaunt, except for a big lump in his belly.

A big lump, which in my experience could never be just organs.

The mutant shrieked again, and panicked hands gripped the lump. He slumped to the ground and rolled around as he frantically pulled the rest of the long hair on his head. He was clearly in a lot of pain.

She was in a lot of pain—because she was in labor.

CHAPTER 8

NIKOLAI

Nikolai Zaregova looked at the screaming mutant and cursed inwardly. *Could that thing shut its mouth before attracting all the mutants in the area?*

He looked over to the door and knew it was risky to take the team to the stairwell, but they had to get out of there as soon as possible. The safest option was to wait for the mutant to leave the building, but Nikolai had the feeling they didn't have much time left.

His attention was suddenly drawn by Major Jameson, who was gesturing excessively at him with her hands. She pointed to her stomach, crossed her forearms, and moved them up and down as if rocking a baby. Then she pointed back to the mutant.

When he finally noticed the bump under the mutant's hands, his mouth dropped open. He abruptly looked back to the Major and nodded firmly. *She was quick.*

For a while, the mutants were thought to be frozen in time when they mutated, but scientists soon discovered that the tiny mutants were actually 'young'. So, it was commonly known that the reproductive organs of the mutants remained intact and that the populations continued to increase behind the wall.

He turned to Jordan and silently gestured what was happening. Jordan's mouth drew in a sharp line but nodded before making contact with the base as quietly as possible through his earpiece.

Nikolai's gaze fell back on Major Jameson as the mutant shrieked again. She was fully focused on the creature when a dull thud and a slithering sound echoed through the hall. The mutant had now risen to her elbows and reached between her sinewy, bony legs. A small, slippery bundle appeared in her hands, and she pressed it close to her chest. The mutant grunted softly, tearing the umbilical cord with her own teeth.

Nikolai grimaced.

He had seen enough. They had to get the hell out of here as soon as possible—before more mutants followed.

A baby explained the two heartbeats, but this was not the day Nikolai wanted to find out if mutants also stayed with their mating partners.

Jordan met his gaze and was clearly thinking the same as he made his way to the door to see if there was a chance of getting out. But just as Jordan put his hand on the door handle, he was stopped by Sergeant Wellington, who pointed to her heartbeat sensor.

Nikolai reached for his and saw, to his great annoyance, that a third mutant had arrived. They had no choice but to speed up now. He looked around the group and gestured that no one was to shoot, no matter what happened. Up here in a building, with only one way out, that would mean a death sentence.

The moment Jordan quietly turned at the door, it was flung open, and a sinewy hand gripped his neck. Panicking, Jordan reached for the hand that was now clenching his throat but was pulled back hard and flung into the hallway.

There was *one* lethal second where everyone, transfixed, caught sight of the mutant as he leaped back at Jordan and swung his claws at his neck. Jordan hadn't even had a chance to draw his knife before he was bleeding so much that he had to grab his throat with both hands to stop it.

Before the mutant could attack again, everyone sprang into action. First Lieutenant Rudolfs leaped out of the room toward Jordan, as did Sergeants Wellington and Karper—to keep the mutant away from them and distract it. Before Nikolai reached the mutant, he looked through the glass walls at the other one—who still lay exhaustedly on the floor with the child.

Nikolai sprinted out of the room with force and pushed the mutant against the wall from behind, but was unprepared when the creature swung its arms and knocked Sergeant Karper against the wall, who slammed into it and grabbed his head.

To his left, he saw Major Jameson rush forward, and he reached out to pull her behind him before the mutant noticed her. It had been a reflex. She was the trauma surgeon, after all, and they were important to this mission.

"I have to get to Jordan," she hissed, pushing his arm away.

Nikolai looked from a struggling Jordan to the mutant, standing close by, and fixed his gaze on Sergeant Karper, who was still leaning against the wall. When the mutant lashed out,

Nikolai sprang into action and let Major Jameson go. But his effort was unnecessary, as a knife whizzed past his head and sunk straight into the mutant's shoulder—which groaned, gripping his arm in pain.

Behind him, Major Jameson briefly nodded to him and tucked away her other knives before running over to Jordan and bending over his body to work on his neck.

Major Hunter Jameson had scored 'excellent' in throwing techniques during her weapons training. Of course, he'd known that when he'd asked her that morning if she could handle her weapons. He'd just wanted to rile her up and watch her nostrils rise and fall with irritation again.

It had been totally worth it, but now it felt a little... stupid.

Goddamnit, Nikolai thought, shaking his head, and tried to get back to the present moment. An uneasy feeling rose in his chest, but he ignored it as the two of them focused on the mutant.

Sergeant Karper tried to push himself up against the wall, but his legs gave out. Wellington motioned for him to stay put and nodded to Nikolai. The Sergeant was a well-trained fighter, he knew that, but none of them could do much one-on-one against a mutant. The two of them, on the other hand, had a shot.

Sergeant Wellington unsheathed a knife strapped to her leg and sliced it over the mutant's chest, creating a long, gaping cut from which dark blood gushed. She kneeled while he was distracted and ran the knife across the back of his knee as well. Nikolai took a calculated step towards the mutant and delivered the final blow. He kicked him hard in the head, knocking him against the wall like Karper, and the mutant collapsed like a sack of potatoes.

Nikolai looked towards the door at the end of the hallway, where the other mutant hadn't yet appeared. "We have to get out of here, *now*," he hissed.

Sergeant Wellington helped Karper to his feet, and Lieutenant Rudolfs supported Major Jameson, who had already disinfected and bandaged Jordan's wound. The Major looked up at Nikolai, and he knew it wasn't good. Jordan needed surgery as soon as possible.

She abruptly looked into the hallway, and he followed her gaze—only to see the female mutant rushing toward him a moment later.

Nikolai could still see the umbilical cord dangling from her frail body before she jumped on him. The impact caused his helmet to pop off, and he fell to the ground with the creature on top of him. He tried to keep the mutant at a firm distance as she lunged at him with strong arms. Nikolai felt something wet and warm run down his eye and cheek—*blood*. He blindly reached for his knife, struggling to keep the mutant at bay. *They were so damn strong.*

A moment later, a warm feeling spread over his throat, and it took him a second to realize that it wasn't his blood running down his neck. He felt the mutant on top of him go limp, and Nikolai's eyes struggled in the dark to focus on what was happening.

The mutant's neck had been pierced by a piece of wood, and Hunter Jameson leaned heavily on the broken chair leg, grunting, pushing, and twisting some more.

For the second time in a short while, Nikolai looked up at her in amazement. She knelt beside him, placed her fingers lightly on his face, and inspected his eyebrow. He focused on her mouth, which he could vaguely make out, and saw that it was pursed in utmost concentration.

She tilted his head with a slender but strong hand and took something from her inside pocket. He couldn't tell what it was, but when she pulled it, there sounded a loud, ripping noise.

Tape.

"Just for now," she said, wiping the blood from his eyebrow with a piece of cloth and then covering it with tape to stop the bleeding. Nikolai's face contorted. Not because it hurt, but because he knew how much it would hurt to take it back off.

She ran her sleeve over the rest of his face and throat, wiping away the warm blood of the mutants, biting her cheek inquisitively. "That's it," she said, turning her gaze away from him to the hallway.

Nikolai couldn't resist taking her wrist and drawing her attention back to him.

"Good work," he blurted.

She just nodded, got off her haunches, and turned around, after which he sat up and pulled himself up too.

Lieutenant Rudolfs was already supporting Jordan, while Sergeant Karper was able to continue on his own after a check from Major Jameson. She walked over to Jordan's other side and grabbed his arm, pulling it over her shoulder.

The least Nikolai could do for her was to grab the arm and support Jordan himself. Not that she needed it, but he wanted to—which was perhaps even worse.

He had quickly taken over the weakened Jordan and gestured his head toward the stairwell.

"Go," he ordered no one in particular.

Nikolai focused his gaze on Hunter Jameson's back, and

a shiver ran through his body. He knew all too well that he had to retain his full attention during a battle or mission. His father had made clear that feelings for others would hinder him in achieving his goals. And he couldn't afford that. Not when he was responsible for so many soldiers and this mission.

But he wondered if he'd really *seen* Hunter Jameson before. If he had even *allowed* himself to look at all. If he'd noticed how she inspected the rooms she entered, in the same way he did. Or how she also gave herself so fully to what she was doing—that her profession was more than just work.

Nikolai knew at least one thing for sure: he had underestimated her tremendously. And somewhere deep down, he realized it would have probably been better if he hadn't found out.

Because as he'd learned, distractions could be deadly—and he was afraid Hunter Jameson was his.

CHAPTER 9

I could still feel the General's hand on my wrist as I walked ahead of the group.

Not because he'd grabbed me roughly—not at all. It was because he had touched me very gently. The moment his hand had wrapped around my wrist, the space had seemed to shrink.

But the severeness of the moment hadn't escaped me.

Jordan's neck was in terrible shape, and Kelian and I were only able to bandage his neck before he lost consciousness. I knew it was only a matter of time before the blood would seep through the gauze and bandage. We had to operate on him as soon as possible; otherwise, he would lose too much blood.

Jordan's neck had been ripped open from his collarbone to his ear, and in the department store, I'd seen that no veins—except the outer jugular vein—had been damaged. It hadn't been fully open at the time, and by applying some pressure to the wound and vein, I had temporarily stopped the bleeding so we could move Jordan to a safer space.

Sergeant Karper would be left with a severe concussion

from the impact the wall had had on him. The force exerted by the mutant might as well have killed him in one fell swoop. He truly dodged a bullet.

Before reaching the stairs, one more thought occurred to me and, under protest from General Zaregova, I ran back to the room where the female mutant had given birth.

The carpeted floor was soaked with blood, and the small, skinny babe lay in the middle of it. He opened his beady eyes when he heard me enter but remained unnaturally silent. I cut some fabric from the curtains and completely wrapped the child inside before catching up with the rest on the stairs.

When we finally got to the bottom of the stairwell, I checked the heartbeat sensor. It showed one heartbeat: that of the child in my arms.

We left the warehouse and went as fast as the wounded would allow, heading for the nearest bunker, which we reached in less than fifteen minutes. Upon arrival, Jordan was immediately rushed inside a small operating room that held everything we needed, save for the optimal hygiene.

Kelian unclipped Jordan's helmet and night vision goggles as I took mine off, and I could see Jordan's face was white as a sheet. I put the bundle containing the mutant child on a table in the room, where Karper vomited into a trash can.

I turned and saw the General looking at the bundle on the table after he too had taken off his helmet and looked up at me in question. "Is that the child?"

"Yes," I simply replied, washing my hands and arms as quickly as possible before I could start operating. We weren't supposed to bring a mutant back from a scouting—that was where the extraction missions were for. But there had been several things today that hadn't gone according to plan.

The General nodded. "Good." He shifted his attention to the bundle on the table and unfolded it. He just looked at it as it moved restlessly in its cocoon, then wrapped the cloth back around the body and walked past me to Jordan.

Kelian had cleaned Jordan's neck and was standing by his side. He connected the gas bottle to the anesthetic cap, and I walked over to the table. Jordan turned his sweaty face to the General standing at his side, but *he* let his eyes drift off to the wound in Jordan's neck.

"Let's see what you can do, Hunter," Jordan said weakly as I put on my gloves.

I smiled back, straightening my back a little. "You don't know the half of it, Locke."

"Wanna bet?" Jordan whispered hoarsely, as his eyes slowly closed, and he gave me a half-smile, showing off a dimple.

I only shook my head.

The adrenaline in my blood retreated, and I felt the surgeon in me take control as Kelian wrapped the hood around Jordan's head and put him to sleep. I put on a second pair of gloves and waited for him to drift off even deeper.

"He's in bad shape, isn't he?" the General asked, gesturing to Jordan.

"Yes," I answered honestly. But my breathing remained calm, and my heart was beating a steady rhythm. My body knew what I was going to do, and what it needed.

I felt my gaze harden and nodded to Kelian, who removed the first gauze from Jordan's wound. "But I'm going to save him."

∗ ∗ ∗

Jordan's neck was indeed in bad shape, but it was nothing I couldn't handle.

Kelian jumped in at the right times and provided me with the necessary sterile instruments when asked. Even Nikolai Zaregova, the General himself, helped count the gauzes, allowing Kelian to focus on other tasks as well.

After Kelian removed all the gauze from the wound, I could see that the artery was torn deeper than I initially thought. This meant that I had to create a bridge to keep Jordan from losing too much blood. We cleaned the wound as thoroughly as possible before I placed the shunt in his outer jugular vein. This allowed the blood to continue flowing through his veins so that I could focus on the rest of the wound.

Jordan had been fortunate that no other major blood vessels or his esophagus and windpipe had been hit. He'd already lost a lot of blood, but with an injury to his carotid arteries, he wouldn't even have survived the short walk to the bunker.

A few intense hours passed, during which I quickly and efficiently repaired the vein. But when I almost finished stitching Jordan's neck back up, I was pulled out of my trance by a soft sound. The baby began to whimper—the first sound I'd heard it make all evening.

General Zaregova looked up at the same time as I did, and our eyes met.

"Maybe he's hungry," I said, blinking a few times.

Kelian let out a tired laugh but quickly clenched his jaw shut as we looked at him.

The General left the room and returned moments later

with a carton of condensed milk. I wrinkled my nose because that shit was rancid. But the mutant child knew nothing else, and food was food, right?

The General took a plastic needle from a drawer and filled it with milk. He gave it to the baby, who sucked greedily from the syringe without spitting it back out. The small, thin arms moved through the air, reaching for the General's hand—who withdrew the syringe abruptly. I smiled to myself as I saw his eyebrows contract in focus. He let the needle go back to the mutant, clearly finding it more interesting than he'd initially let on. This time, the General left the syringe where it was as the tiny hands rose and grabbed his fingers. Lost in thought, he studied the tiny mutant as it drank greedily.

My hands were sore and trembling slightly by the time I finished the last stitches, and I had Kelian clean the closed wound. We carefully removed the cap from Jordan's face, and I gave him some painkillers so he could heal throughout the night. This new kind of pain relief even stimulated the generation of new cells, causing the wound to heal faster than usual.

I strained my fingers into the rubber gloves and took them off; first the white gloves and then the blue ones, which allowed me to quickly notice any tears or other irregularities in my top gloves.

Now that I was done, I felt all the tension slowly subside, and my head began to pound. I carefully rewashed my hands and forearms with the ice-cold water from the tap, leaving my tired hands feeling even stiffer than before.

I looked at the General and pointed to his eyebrow. "Could you sit down, General?"

The General nodded firmly, and when I walked up to him, I placed a hand on his shoulder as he sank into a chair. I pulled the tape off his eyebrow, making him wince slightly. I tried my best not to let the wound tear any further, which was difficult.

I cleaned his wound with trembling hands and kept my eyes fixed on my work.

He raised his other eyebrow, causing me to hiss at him to relax so I could carry on. I looked around for an anesthetic, but he grabbed my elbow and shook his head.

"It's not necessary, Major. Just stitch it up."

I was too exhausted to argue with him, so I started stitching up his wound without using an anesthetic. It would be just enough to keep it from getting infected.

General Zaregova closed his eyes while I finished my work.

The adrenaline and exhaustion of the day were now slowly catching up with me, and I cursed my hands as they began to tremble.

The General opened his eyes, and after I had to shake my hand a second time, he opened his mouth. "It's all right. Go get your rest."

I swallowed my surprise and blinked a few times. A heavy feeling washed over me as I looked at the suture I'd just made. It wasn't my best work by any means, but it was more than enough to heal.

When I finished up, I washed my hands, and a moment later, the General had left the room.

I lowered my head under the tap and greedily drank a few gulps of water. Sighing, I plopped down on a chair in the room and leaned my head against the wall. For the first time that day, I thought about everything that had happened and took a good look around the room. It was a small examination room with a counter and table, on which Jordan lay. There was a bright white light from the ceiling, which had been nice during surgery, but now it made my eyes burn painfully.

Kelian was cleaning the room and threw all the gauze pads from the floor in the trash. Eventually, he slumped into the chair next to me and sighed deeply as he gave me a tight smile.

"Thanks for your help, Kelian," I said, my voice quivering with sincerity.

He clasped his hands together. "I hope it helped."

"I think he'll get better. It will take some time, though."

Kelian got up after a while and looked at Jordan. Then he turned his gaze back to me and ran a hand through his tousled, dark red hair. "We'll probably have to stay here for a few days, but it's not like that hasn't happened before—so don't worry."

I wasn't worried anymore—not about the mission. When I thought back to the nerves I'd felt about going onto the shadow plains that morning, I almost laughed. It paled in comparison to the fear I had felt for Jordan and the rest of the team today.

Kelian walked towards the door and turned around for a moment. "You saved his life, Hunter; that's no small thing." He nodded at Jordan. "He'll definitely remember it."

I swallowed. "*We* saved his life."

Kelian shrugged. "I just supported you." He pointed to the clock on the wall above the door frame. "Try to get some sleep." And before I could react, he walked out of the room.

It had been a very long day, and I let my head sink into

my hands for a moment in silence—except for the sound of Jordan's quiet breathing.

It wasn't until sometime later that I understood what had happened—realized what I'd done.

Exactly one year after graduating, I'd been given my first assignment. And now that I was finally here, I had actually made a difference in a time of need—saved a life in a crisis. Saved several lives—despite all prejudices and doubts.

My lips curved into a small smile.

I had never been so proud.

CHAPTER 18

After a while, I found myself taking Kelian's advice and walked over to the sleeping area.

There, I woke Sergeant Karper to check his consciousness, which I would have to do a few more times that night to monitor the concussion.

I removed the braid from my hair, washed the grime off my body with tap water, and lowered myself onto one of the cots in the sleeping area. It struck me that the General wasn't present.

When I closed my eyes, only the breathing of the others kept me company. My thoughts went in several directions, despite the physical exhaustion of my body, and I restlessly turned a couple of times to change into a more comfortable position. But unfortunately, my head wouldn't give in, which resulted in me staring at the ceiling, my head still pounding a little.

After my thoughts went over the mutant child for the fourth time, I slipped out of bed and exited the room. The light in the main area was still on, and I realized that only the sleeping area had light switches—for safety reasons. It would be inconvenient to have to turn on the lights everywhere when all hell broke loose.

I pulled the vest I was wearing tighter around me against the cold and felt the coolness of the floor seeping through my socks. There was no sign of the child, even after checking several areas of the shelter.

Where the hell had the child gone? And an even better question: where was the General? He hadn't been on one of the beds, nor had he been in the room, but I suspected that the answer to both questions was the same.

Rubbing my temples, I tried to reduce the banging of my head a little.

I opened the door to the kitchen and, startled, put a hand to my chest.

"*Goddamnit,*" I hissed with a thrashing heart. Speak of the devil.

The General sat at the kitchen table and looked up, brows raised. He lay down the pen he was holding in the notebook.

"Apologies, General," I said, pointing to the fridge. "I'm just here to get something to drink." I hurried forward, glad to be able to stand with my back to him.

As I filled a glass with water, he sighed. "You don't have to leave on my account."

I turned around, glass raised to my lips, watching him run his pen over the paper again.

"And you don't have to be so formal at night, either."

"Formal?" I asked, after swallowing a sip.

He looked up in amusement and smiled faintly. "You don't have to call me General at night."

"I don't?" I didn't look away when he didn't, and felt my cheeks burn. I was happy with the dimmed light that hung in the kitchen, so it wasn't obvious. Leaning against the counter, I continued drinking.

"Hunter," he began, and it was strange to hear my name coming out of his mouth. "You saved my life today, so I think we can speak on a first name basis."

I looked straight at him. "So, anyone who saves your life is allowed to call you Nikolai?"

"Not everyone," he replied, and I swore I saw his eyes gleam.

I averted my gaze and focused on my drink, listening to the sound of pen on paper.

After a while, my eyes turned his way again. His black hair was more ruffled than usual, and it almost touched his eyebrow. He'd also cleaned himself and put on a black shirt, which fitted him rather… nicely. His right arm rested with its elbow on the table, and his hand was spread flat over the notebook. With his left, he held the pen and let it slide gracefully over the paper. Although I wouldn't be surprised if he could also write with his right hand because General Zaregova—Nikolai—was apparently capable of everything if I had to believe the stories. But the question as to why I was concerned with what his hands could do, wasn't one I wanted to answer. I couldn't even afford to think about those things. Those fantasies were off-limits.

Something that *did* matter was this mission.

"Where is the mutant child?" I asked, when I remembered what I'd been looking for.

He gestured his head to where I was standing. "In the kitchen cupboard behind you."

"What?" I asked, dumbstruck, my eyes wide. "Why?"

I turned and opened the cupboard, where the bundle

indeed lay. "Did you kill it?" I asked him sharply as I sat it on the counter and unfolded the rags.

"Of course not," he snorted indignantly, as if he was offended that I even considered it. I heard him put down his pen and close his notebook. He walked towards me while I checked the child for a heartbeat. It was indeed there, but other than that, it didn't respond at all.

It was clearly not asleep—or so I thought. Not that I had that much experience with mutants.

"What did you do with it?" I asked and couldn't keep the skepticism out of my voice while studying him out of the corner of my eye.

He clenched his jaw and frowned over my shoulder at the baby. "I couldn't just let it moan."

"So?" I asked, raising my eyebrows at him, waiting for him to elaborate.

Nikolai tilted his head so he was looking down at me. "So," he continued, "I numbed it."

I folded my lips to hold back my laughter. "How much did you give it?"

Nikolai shrugged. "Just a full syringe," he replied dryly, but I spotted the slight concern in his face as he looked at the mutant.

A laugh escaped, and I put a hand over my mouth. It probably didn't do much good for me to laugh at the General.

"What?" he asked, his gaze moving back to me. He raised an eyebrow in defiance and narrowed his eyes, though one corner of his mouth curved up too. "It will live. Mutants are like weeds."

"Let's hope so," I said, looking at the child. "It's just going to be a long time before we can be sure—if it regains consciousness at all—since you gave it as much as Jordan needed." I bit my lip and muttered, "Maybe I should put it on an IV so it won't get malnourished."

"No," he said abruptly. "That's not necessary. It has already had some milk—and mutants can go a long time without food."

I looked at him for a moment. "Wouldn't we waste a healthy mutant?"

Nikolai shrugged and sat back down at the table. "It's a waste of our stock of medical supplies."

"Yeah," I replied, "like the whole syringe of anesthetic you injected."

He looked up and smiled in surprise. "Touché."

But he was right—it would be a waste of the IV, especially if Jordan needed more in the coming days. I would look at it tomorrow, as I was too tired to do anything else right now. The mutant would last for at least a day, so I closed the bundle again. This time, I made sure the nose remained free and put it back in the kitchen cupboard, after which I washed my hands.

Nikolai yawned, and I decided to sit down at the table with him after filling my glass once more.

"So, Hunter Jameson," he began as I sat down, "how do your parents feel about you being here?"

I looked up and met his gaze. "My parents…" As I thought about them, a smile appeared on my face, and I wrinkled my nose at him. "They don't like it."

Nikolai nodded and smiled, closed-lipped. "I can imagine."

Here I was, having a normal conversation with the General. Who would have ever expected *that* at the start of the

90

mission?

I took another sip. "Do you have children of your own?"

"*Gods*, no," he huffed, rubbing a hand across his throat—as if the idea itself was suffocating him—and looked back at me. "But I can imagine you want to keep them as safe as possible," he stated.

I nodded in agreement. "And your parents? What do they think of you being so…" I gestured with my hands to his person, "famous?"

He lowered his brows and gave me a daring smile. "Famous?" he asked.

Under his gaze, I pressed my tongue against the roof of my mouth and felt a warm sensation run through my chest. Nikolai Zaregova was very attractive when he smiled like that. *Dangerous* might even be a better word for it.

The vest I was wearing had done little against the cold up to now, but I suddenly felt overheated.

"You can't tell me you don't know anything about your own reputation," I said, my face contorted at the thought of having to explain it to him.

He raised an eyebrow and smiled even wider. "I've been here for three years, and I can tell you that no one has ever said anything about my reputation outside of the mission."

A knot formed in my stomach, and I bit my lip. I really didn't want to be the one to tell him. *Damnit.*

"Tell me," he said. The look in his eyes told me he was clearly enjoying this.

I threw him a severe look. "You're avoiding my question."

"You avoid mine."

"That was technically not a question."

He laughed out loud, showing off his straight teeth, and the sound took me by surprise. "All right, you win."

I bowed my head in recognition and moistened my lips. His gaze traveled from my eyes to my mouth, and I saw his throat bob.

Oh, no. *No.*

Wanting to break the silence, I opened my mouth, but then immediately closed it again. If he didn't want to say anything about his parents, he didn't have to. I felt my face heat up as I considered my next step.

His eyes darted back to mine, and he rubbed a hand over his eyes. "My parents were in the military themselves, so they understand," he finally said. "But my father died before he could witness it."

Oh.

I braided my fingers together. "That must have been difficult for you."

He nodded briefly and clearly didn't want to elaborate. "My mother is supportive and, of course, knows what it means, up to some extent. But, every chance she gets, she makes sure I know that she rather sees me coming home than leave. As proud as she may be of my…" he gestured toward me, "*reputation.*"

"Did your parents meet in the military?" I asked.

Nikolai nodded.

I averted my gaze.

My glass was empty again, and I set it on the counter, looking at the clock—nearly three-thirty in the morning.

I turned back to him. "I'm going to check on Jordan." I quickly cleared my throat. "I mean Major General Locke, and Sergeant Karper, of course."

At Jordan's name, Nikolai came out of his trance and nodded.

I rapidly walked towards the door but was surprised by Nikolai, who had come over and put his hand on the door handle before I could do it myself. My breath hitched as I met his gaze. His eyes were grave, and his pupils slightly dilated. I could see that his dark eyes were actually brown, with little specks of gold in them. Like stars in a dark sky.

"Yes?" I breathed.

He glanced back at my mouth, and for a split second, I thought he would bend over to kiss me, but then he lowered his gaze to the ground.

As if he'd burned himself, he let go of the latch and ran a few fingers casually along the collar of his shirt. "I just wanted to say thank you. You were quick on your feet, and it made the difference between life and death today."

A smile blossomed on my face at his acknowledgment, and I gripped the latch a little tighter before opening the door.

I nodded at him in the doorway. "*General.*"

"*Major,*" he replied.

Into the hallway, I deliberately grinned at him one more time over my shoulder, leaving him behind in the kitchen, shaking his head, with a slight smile spreading over his face.

CHAPTER 11

NIKOLAI

Nikolai watched her disappear into the main area, then closed the kitchen door again. Taking a deep breath, he felt a shiver run through his body as he leaned against the door. He settled his gaze on the ceiling, and noticed that there was still a smile on his face.

But that smile disappeared as he thought back to the last conversation he'd had with his father.

"Nik, lad, don't start a family when you're trying to achieve big goals," his father told him with a smile as he buttoned up his uniform. "It's so damn hard to leave them behind."

"What about you and mom?" Nikolai had asked. "I love you both."

His father ruffled his hair. "That's different—you have yet to spread your wings. Mommy and I are here to help you do that."

His mother had pulled her husband into a tight hug and didn't cry, but Nikolai suspected she was about to—or would do so later when his father had left.

His father then got down on one knee in front of Nikolai again and grabbed him by the shoulders. "I would much rather stay with you and your mother, but this is important for the future—your future." He hugged him and kissed his forehead, just like he always did with his mom. *"I will think of you every second of every day."*

His father stood, grabbed his bag in one hand, and gave his mother one last kiss. *"Every second,"* he repeated to her, before walking out the door and getting into the car.

That was the last time he had seen his father.

Nikolai couldn't help but conclude that he hadn't been focused. He'd had a family to think about—which he loved—that he thought about every second, which had led him to make the wrong decision and run in the wrong direction *towards* the bomb. *And that was why it was so damn hard that Hunter Jameson was proving to be such a distraction to him.*

Of course, she'd already surprised him by coming here without any relevant military experience—but that hadn't been a positive surprise; she had been far too inexperienced in his eyes. He'd even been slightly offended that they'd sent her. But that had been unjustified. Not to mention that he'd made his prejudices clear on several occasions—to her face.

Hunter Jameson.

In the past few days, she'd surprised him so completely that she had instantly crushed his misguided beliefs. From the moment they had entered the plains, she had a particular focus that most soldiers here would never master. A focus you couldn't train. One he also possessed.

He'd come to see her in a completely different light, and he'd been so wrong.

She had saved lives—saved *his* life. Never before had he been so humbled by another person. A person he wanted to send back at first if they hadn't been so desperate for a trauma surgeon.

He was so unnerved by her that he could feel his curiosity peak constantly whenever she was around—that he wanted to know more. It'd been dangerous for him to let her call him by his first name, but he had been so curious to hear his name come from her mouth. Then he'd also tried to change her mind about the infant mutant's IV, hoping she wouldn't leave the kitchen yet.

Nikolai rubbed his eyes for a moment and groaned inwardly.

She had gained his respect and more in one day. What she'd done was incredible, how she could keep that focus during a fight, saving his life in the process. So, what he felt now—the respect, the wonder—he could link to his underestimation.

Of course, you feel something for a person who saves your life. Of course, someone deserves respect if they exceed your expectations by *miles*. Of course, you're attracted to a woman who—in addition to showing how intelligent, strong, and incredibly skilled she is against all prejudice—was also beautiful.

Of course.

He was only human.

A growl escaped from deep within his throat. It was enough that she was witty, intelligent, and talented. That she had saved his life and the lives of others. Several soldiers on the mission had those qualities. If that had been all, he would still have had the strength to look the other way—he could have put his feelings to rest.

But she also had to be so incredibly attractive.

He had noticed it the first time he'd laid his eyes on her. There was no way around her beauty: with her dark blonde curls, apple cheeks, and a body that you can't ignore, she had already attracted a lot of attention. But now that he'd seen more of Hunter, he couldn't unsee her anymore; all of her extra layers just made her that much more attractive.

Nikolai had seen beautiful women before, but "being attractive" meant more to him than just appearances. It was in the way the Major watched the world around her, how she took in people and spaces, how she held herself, how she moved her body. Hunter Jameson was that type of woman, and every time she let her amber eyes settle on him, it felt like a slap in the face.

From the moment she walked into the bar that day after he first saw her, his senses had zoned in on her. Of course, he'd done his best to not constantly let his eyes wander to where she was sitting, but he'd been instinctively aware of her location in the room at all times. She'd been noticed by the rest of his table, too, and Jordan had even let out a soft whistle.

The idea that others were also aware of her made his skin itch. Naturally, he didn't show it, as it was completely irrational and unnecessary, selfish, alpha behavior. But he hadn't been able to shove it down completely, as he'd exploded into action as soon as he saw her walking toward the bar—in the middle of Jordan's story—with the excuse of wanting another drink. He'd known no one would come to the bar while he was there, leaving him on his own with the new soldier.

Nikolai cursed his treacherous body that had wanted to get closer to her and cursed the part of himself that allowed it. That night it was clear that he hadn't made much of an impression on her, but something in him wanted it to be that way—that she saw him as she did the rest. Not *exactly* like the rest, of course, but not as 'the General' either.

When he found out the next day that she turned out to be some child prodigy, who'd only been graduated for one year and had been assigned 3B as her first mission, he'd seen that as a shortcoming. A good reason to let go of his slight infatuation with her—why she wasn't as perfect as she seemed. The previous night's events made her look overconfident in this new light, and because the position she had to fill was so crucial, he had formed an instant bias. And he'd made sure she knew.

It'd been self-protection for a large part, sure, because he'd be even worse off if everything in her report turned out to be true—that she was as good as everyone thought. As *she* thought, apparently.

Maybe that's why he'd been so hard on her. Nikolai had been aware of the nerves she felt around him afterward, and that she'd even become a little hesitant. He wanted her to show him her true nature—let the curtain drop—before his brain completely abandoned logic. Before he would disappoint his father by making the same mistake.

As general of this mission, he simply couldn't afford those kinds of feelings. Even though he was deeply annoyed by his behavior—it was for the best. Especially now that she turned out not to be disappointing, but far exceeded his expectations, he couldn't afford to let her get close—*there*, where he wanted her.

But had he thought about trying to see whether she felt the attraction, too?

Yes.

Nikolai had to confess that he'd often encountered dark blonde hair and amber-colored eyes in his dreams. And this had only gotten worse after he'd seen Jordan approach her. Nikolai liked Jordan, and trusted him with his life, but something had stung when he saw the looks and smiles between them. That she'd called him by his first name in such a familiar way.

Had that been a reason to let her use his first name? *Perhaps.* Was he so selfish that he wanted to hear his name coming from her lips? *Yes.*

And had he just wanted to kiss her? *One hundred thousand percent, hell yes.*

Nikolai clenched his jaw and walked over to the sink, where he filled a glass with ice-cold water. He emptied it in one gulp and refilled it while gripping the counter. Nikolai placed his hands on the wooden countertop, dropping his head. For the first time in his life, he didn't want to be the general. Not the person so many lives depended on—not the person everyone looked up to in times of chaos. Not the person who was no longer a person in everyone's eyes but a pawn in this world.

Hunter had mentioned that his reputation exceeded him. That *he* was famous. Of course, Nikolai had noticed how newer soldiers on the base looked at him, so he'd known they were talking about him in the outside world. He didn't care, nor did he find it particularly interesting. How the outside world saw him was a matter of the outside world.

What bothered him was how most of the soldiers looked at him at times—as if everything depended on him. Nikolai put that pressure on himself enough as it was, which was another reason not to get distracted by Hunter Jameson.

He bit his cheek and wearily rubbed his eyes again. As general, he couldn't get emotionally entangled with *anyone.*

Even these thoughts made him untrustworthy.

If there was anything he'd learned from his father's example, it was that to achieve your goal; you had to be one hundred percent focused. There was no room for distractions.

But was there anything wrong with being close to someone purely on a physical level?

No, Nikolai thought, *there was nothing wrong with that.* Especially if that would eliminate distraction. He had often found mutual physical release without either party forming an emotional bond. But the image of someone else with *her* made his stomach turn viciously—that would distract him even more. Another couldn't give her anything that he wasn't able to give her either. If she would even let him.

Besides, this mission didn't precisely provide many opportunities for serious relationships. The time for that would come when they finished the mission. Maybe Hunter didn't even want an emotional connection but wouldn't be opposed to a physical one? It was worth a shot.

Perhaps the tension between them would finally ease.

A little bit of her was better than nothing.

Right?

CHAPTER 12

The following day I woke with a heavy head. My thoughts instantly flashed back to the night before and how the General—Nikolai—had looked at my lips like he'd wanted to kiss them. Of course, I wasn't sure and had tried to stuff the memory far away while I'd spent some time in bed, staring at the ceiling.

After that short night's sleep, I quickly freshened up, tied the overalls around my waist, and pulled my hair into a tight ponytail.

Karper was eating on the couch with Wellington when I entered the main room to check his head wound. When I finished, he thanked me with a "Thanks, Doc."

I walked towards the room where Jordan was lying before I had breakfast myself. I was really curious about how he was doing this morning, so when I heard soft voices behind the door, my heart skipped a beat. If he was talking again, that was a good sign. A perfect sign.

I softly rapped the door and heard Jordan rasp for me to come in. Carefully, I opened the door and saw that the General was sitting next to Jordan's bed. I hadn't been ready to see him again, and gave him a quick nod before letting my eyes focus on Jordan.

He smiled broadly and winked. "The woman of the hour," he said hoarsely.

"Good to see you're awake," I responded, as I walked over to him and carefully checked the wounds' bandage.

I felt the General's gaze rove over me, and I subconsciously looked his way. His dark eyes focused directly on me, and I felt my cheeks warm from the intensity in them. Something had changed between us since last night.

"I need to change the bandage," I announced to no one in particular. The wound had leaked last night, which was to be expected.

When they both waited for me in silence, I looked up. "You're welcome to continue your conversation while I'm at it."

They both let their eyes drift to each other, and the General cleared his throat. "It will probably take another two days before you can start exercising again. After that, we'll stay an extra day so you can regain some of your strength," he said.

Jordan opened his mouth with difficulty. "Did you report everything already?"

"Yes, everyone knows."

"Shit," Jordan muttered and winked at me. "My reputation is in ruins."

"What reputation?" I asked with a laugh, and even General Zaregova smiled, forcing me to take my eyes away from him again and push out the memory of last night.

Jordan mockingly crossed a hand over his chest. "You wound me, Hunter."

Smiling, I shook my head and rebandaged the wound after disinfecting it.

I discarded my gloves and washed my hands, looking back. "Take it easy, okay? I'll check again this afternoon."

Jordan sighed. "Can't you also come by in between for an extra check-up?" I saw him raise his eyebrows at the General, who narrowed his eyes and shook his head with a deep sigh.

"I think Major Jameson has better things to do," he said, raising an eyebrow at his Major General. If I didn't know better, I'd say it was a warning.

"Maybe I'll have some time later," I promised Jordan, looking straight at the General. "Could I look at your wound in a moment, General?"

The General nodded in response, and I left the room.

Arriving in the kitchen, I decided to join Kelian at the table and, like him, have some soup with dry crackers.

"Did you catch some sleep last night?" he asked.

I pursed my lips and moved my head up and down hesitantly. "It took me a long time to fall asleep," I confessed.

He nodded. "You experience a lot on the first day in the shadows—and this was not just any first day."

"Of course that would happen to me." I sighed.

"It only happens to those who are strong enough to handle it," Kelian corrected, as he took a bite of his cracker. "The universe never gives you something you aren't ready for."

"Wow," I said, looking at him. "I didn't know you were the spiritual type."

Kelian shrugged. "I strive to surprise."

I laughed and started my breakfast when the door opened, and the General walked in. He filled up the small space and looked straight at me, but said nothing. I had to remind myself to swallow my food.

The General went to the counter and grabbed a pen. Before walking out of the room, he turned his head to me and said, "I'm in the back room, in case you want to look at my brow."

My attention shifted to his full dark eyebrows—which were beautiful—except for my stitching.

"I'll be right there," I replied, dipping another cracker into my soup, but the door had already slammed shut.

Kelian just raised an eyebrow at me. "What was that?"

"No idea." I took a bite of a soup-soaked cracker and avoided his gaze. "But he can wait a little while."

Kelian chuckled. "If you say so."

* * *

After taking a little longer with my breakfast than necessary, I walked to the back room with my suture kit.

I knocked once and opened the door.

The General sat behind the desk and looked up from a tablet on which he had been typing.

"Major Jameson," he said in a low voice, and I swore his eyes turned darker.

"General," I replied, holding the kit in the air. "I've come to check your brow."

The corner of his mouth twitched. "What else?"

I clenched my jaws and decided to take his question rhetorically, after which I placed the kit on the desk a little more urgently than necessary. His brows raised in amusement. Nikolai turned with me in his chair as I walked around the desk. He sat with his knees far apart and his arms casually resting on the armrests.

I stepped between his legs with the cleaning supplies in hand and tilted his head up towards me. "This may sting a little," I warned him before I started to clean the wound, and he briefly closed his eyes, hissing at first contact.

When he opened his eyes again, and I was still working, I felt his gaze sweep over my face. I gently moved the cloth up and down, my heart beating in my throat. I bit my lower lip in concentration, and felt his attention move there, making me swallow noticeably.

I quickly stopped cleaning the wound and placed my fingers on either side of the suture. "I can redo the stitching," I said, frowning. "It is not done properly and—"

"Will it heal this way?" he interrupted me, grabbing my wrist and lowering it a little.

Glancing at the hand clasping my wrist, I answered, "Yes, but not nearly as neatly."

"You don't have to do unnecessary work—this is fine." He lowered my wrist and weakened his grip until he ran his thumb along the bridge of my hand. I held my breath and suppressed a sigh.

Dangerous territory.

I didn't give in and withdrew my tingling hand. "I can do better—make your skin heal nicer."

He waved his hand dismissively. "I don't care about that—so if the reasons are purely aesthetic, it isn't necessary."

My perfectionism played up big time. I had to bite the inside of my cheek not to push the fact again. The stitching had been done in a hurry and wasn't my best work, but if he didn't want it… Well, then he simply didn't want it.

I met his gaze and nodded as I stepped out from between

his legs and put the tools away. "At least try not to move your brow too much, so it will it heal faster." *And more beautiful*, but he didn't care about that.

"I'll think about it," he said.

I pointedly kept my mouth shut and left the room.

* * *

The next day, I focused my energy on helping Jordan through his rehabilitation. His neck had healed to the point where he could move his head in either direction without hurting the tender spot or pulling the wound too much. I'd also taken on the task of checking the mutant child from time to time.

I did my best to avoid General Zaregova as much as possible after the last conversation we'd had. Except for a few glances and muttered words, this had worked, and the situation returned to normal. At least there hadn't been another we-are-now-on-a-first-name-basis scenario.

The journey back to the base, which followed soon after, went almost without any problems. Jordan was able to walk on his own for the most part, which made everything a hell of a lot easier. Kelian, the General, and Sergeant Wellington took turns supporting Jordan, and I also walked beside him for a while.

On our return behind the wall, a small medical team was already waiting and immediately took Jordan inside to check him. General Zaregova was also taken aside by a Colonel I didn't recognize and handed him a letter. The moment he unfolded the paper, I tore my gaze away.

I placed my helmet and other tools in the crates that lined the outside wall and followed the medical team inside. There, I opened a door with my pass, and someone slipped in after me, matching my stride to walk next to me.

Surprised, I turned my head to the right to see that it was the General, carrying the bundle containing the mutant child.

"Walk with me, Major," he said, without looking my way.

"Okay," I replied calmly. Those were more words than we had spoken to each other in the past two days.

He automatically placed a hand on my back to guide me into a different hallway than the medical team took Jordan. I slightly increased my pace so that his hand stopped touching my back and felt the blood rush into my face.

We arrived at the central area of the medical center, and the General asked everyone to gather together. He handed over the mutant child to someone and told them to take it to the lab. There it would be examined before we sent it to Barak.

The General informed us of Colonel Arepto's early departure, which we took with great—and minor—astonishment. He'd packed his things and received permission from the General to return home and take time to mourn. A collective murmur went through the room, and Raven arched an eyebrow at me.

The General opened his mouth and let any speculation already there go up in smoke. "Until we find a replacement, Major Jameson will take over the Colonel's duties."

I abruptly looked up at him and felt my lips part in astonishment, along with those of many others in the room. But only Lieutenant Colonel Nigel Kent dared to protest out loud. "*What?*"

Irritation radiated from General Zaregova's face as he glanced at the Lieutenant Colonel. I knew from experience that he didn't particularly like people who undermined his authority.

Nigel cleared his throat and tried again. "With all due respect, General, the Major *just* got here."

The General didn't look away. "And in that time, Major Jameson has proved that she's very skilled. I trust that she can keep things in order over the coming weeks, and that you will support each other throughout this period until we find a replacement."

I wasn't quite sure what to make of the enormous responsibility he'd just given me, and it was clear that at least Nigel shared this view. He looked from the General to me and narrowed his eyes slightly. The moment I met his gaze, he subtly wrinkled his nose at me.

But nothing went unnoticed by Nikolai Zaregova, who tilted his head in Nigel's direction and looked at him the way a predator viewed its prey. "Do you have anything to add to that, Lieutenant Colonel Kent?" he asked coolly.

Nigel quickly looked up at the General. "No." He cleared his throat. "Of course not, General."

General Zaregova looked around the room. "That's all." He zipped up his suit and—without another word or looking my way—left the room.

Raven grinned at me and shrugged. She was probably more excited about it than I was.

I glanced back at Nigel, who had now turned his back to me, talking to another trauma surgeon. *It doesn't matter what Nigel thinks*; I tried to convince myself. Being the medical head of this mission, even for a short time, was a significant step in my career.

But why *me*?

I gestured to Raven that I would come to her in a minute

and ran after the General. He had already reached the end of the hallway as I called out, "General Zaregova."

He stopped and turned around. "Yes, Major?"

"May I ask," I asked, as I jogged toward him, "why?"

The General looked down at me and folded his arms. "It wasn't just my decision."

I raised my eyebrows in question.

"Colonel Arepto contacted me yesterday with the news that he was leaving. Not very convenient, if you ask me, but certainly overdue." His eyes wandered over my face. "He indicated that he would like you to take over his duties."

Bewildered, I looked at him. "*Me?*"

He nodded.

"Why did you agree?"

He shrugged. "I could see where he was coming from."

"Really?" I asked incredulously.

"Yes," he replied simply, and gave me a small smile. Then he turned on his heel and walked out of the hall.

Was he messing with me?

Lost in thought, I leaned against the wall, and a crazy feeling rose in my gut. If he and Colonel Arepto thought I could do this, it was the greatest compliment they could've given me. I would oversee all patients and medical cases, and ultimately be responsible for the monitoring room.

However—I believed in myself and my skills.

And I wouldn't disappoint them.

CHAPTER 13

After a long first day of reading documents, updating reports, and attending a meeting with the capital to introduce myself, I decided to visit the bar. There were already a lot of people inside, despite the time approaching midnight. One of those people was Nikolai Zaregova, who sat quietly in the corner of the room, talking to some of the other generals.

I took a seat at the bar and ordered a drink. While I waited, I glanced back to the General's table. Nikolai looked up at me at the same time, and his eyes seemed to absorb the light of the bar, even from afar.

I quickly averted my gaze.

Dangerous, I repeated in my head like a mantra, and thanked the bartender as he put the drink in front of me. My fingers curled around the glass as if it were a life raft, and I raised it to my lips.

Over the rim of my glass, my eyes seemed to drift back to the General. Instead of his usual black attire, he was wearing a high-collared, beige knit sweater that was a shade lighter than his skin. His black hair was subtly styled, and he didn't look like a General. Not as… formal.

My gaze continued downwards, over his muscular arm and along the lean hand clutching a glass, straight back into his dark, inscrutable eyes. Surprised, I held his gaze for a moment while he took a very lazy and deliberate sip of his drink. Time seemed to freeze until I noticed that my breathing had accelerated, and my heart was racing up and down in my chest like a caged animal. The blood rushed through my ears, and I abruptly broke eye contact.

I rapidly downed the rest of my drink and gathered my things in a rush. If I didn't want to act like an idiot any more than I already had, I had to remove myself from this situation as soon as possible—and my bed currently sounded like an excellent alternative.

I put on my warm coat and rushed out into the cold directly after paying. My brain tried to get my mind back on track as I walked back to my room with great strides. If I wanted to recover from the past few days in a normal way— no, if I wanted to recover *at all*, I would have to do it in my own room.

* * *

By the time I'd traded my regular clothes for a more comfortable pair of leggings and a sweater, my brain had regained some grip on reality. To take my mind off the General and his smoldering eyes, I cleaned up my room.

Half an hour later, I was finally tucked in bed, reading, when I heard a soft knock. So quiet that I thought I had imagined the sound at first—until there was a second, louder knock. Cautiously, I put my book on the bedside table and got up from the bed.

My heart skipped a beat as I opened the door.

Nikolai Zaregova stood right in front of my room. And the fact that I already thought of him as 'Nikolai' instead of 'General' made the whole situation even worse. Why had that damned man let me use his first name?

Now he was here. The literal person I was trying to avoid. He looked down at me and inspected the room behind me. He had a severe glint in his eyes, but his energy felt… tense.

"Hey," he just said, his breath warming the air around him.

"Hi," I returned. The cold rushed in through the open door like a sharp wind. I stepped away and gestured inside. "Do you want to come in?"

The General looked at me doubtfully as he clenched his jaws. I crossed my fingers behind my back, hoping he would say no, but made a fist as he nodded and walked inside.

Shit.

I closed the door and immediately felt overwhelmed by his presence. The way he seemed to fill a room was intoxicating. The hair on my arms rose, and I became acutely aware of my body. Not knowing what to do with my limbs, I decided to walk a little further into the room and turned back around to look at him expectantly.

Nikolai cleared his throat and rubbed his freshly trimmed face. He seemed to be wondering, too, as he searched the ceiling in vain.

I studied him. "Can I help you, General?"

"Yes." He shot me an impenetrable look. "Call me Nikolai."

A laugh escaped my throat, releasing some of the tension from my body with it. "Then is there anything I can help you with, *Nikolai*?"

He shook his head, and his gaze was now directly on me. "Listen, Hunter—I can't put my finger on it, especially these last few days."

Everything in me felt in which direction the conversation was headed, and I folded my arms to hold myself together. "On what?"

Nikolai held my gaze. "You." He shook his head again as if surprising himself. "I don't do relationships. Especially not *here*. This is not the kind of place for that sort of... emotion." His jaw tightened. "But I can't get you out of my head."

My eyes widened. I could now actually hear my heart pounding in my ears. "What?" I muttered softly, not sure if I'd heard right—if I'd wanted to hear it.

"And I have a feeling it's the same for you," he continued as if I hadn't spoken, taking a step closer and studying my face intently.

I inhaled sharply and had to do my best not to nod, but everything was perceptible to him. This was General Nikolai Zaregova—who didn't want me to call him General. He was known and celebrated for his achievements, something close to a legend in Ardenza—he had that reputation for a reason.

Nikolai took another step toward me, leaving him only a few breaths away. He tilted his head slightly, looking down at me. It felt like my body was made of lead, and I actually stopped breathing.

Nikolai gently moved a hand to my face and brushed his thumb over my cheek, looking from my lips back to my eyes. "I can't offer you anything, Hunter; no promises, no relationship, *nothing*." His fingers burned into my skin. He might as well have tattooed his name on my forehead since I knew there was no turning back now as much as I wanted to believe otherwise.

But I vaguely realized that he was giving me a choice—it just didn't feel like one at all. The inner voice that could give me all the reasons as to why this wasn't a good idea hid somewhere deep inside my brain—fleeing from the monster that had taken over my thoughts and held the reins to my body. At that moment, it all didn't matter anymore. No consequence would outweigh the moment I was in now.

I moved my hand to cup his neck and gently pulled him toward me while we continued to look at each other. I gave him a choice too, but his answer was written on his face.

Something deep inside me sighed when his lips finally met mine. He responded by moving one of his hands to the side of my head, followed by the other. As he slid one hand into my hair and fisted a handful of it, he opened my mouth with his and let his tongue slide inside.

Slowly.

Lazily.

As if he had all the time in the world to explore my mouth.

The feeling tingled all the way to my toes. I slipped my arms further around his neck and pressed myself closer into his heat before he let his hand wander, wrapping one arm tightly around my waist.

Nikolai kissed me deeper and more insistingly as he lifted me and pushed me against the wall. I hooked my legs around his hips and pulled him as close as possible, forcing him to grab my thighs and grip me even tighter, pinning me against the wall with his muscular body.

He traded my mouth for my neck and throat.

A strong hand moved from my thigh to the bottom of my sweater and found its way underneath. With his hand spread, he continued his way thoroughly from my hips upwards—as if he didn't want to leave a single piece of me untouched. He then cupped my breast and let his teeth scrape along my neck and shoulder. I could clearly feel the evidence of his desire through his pants.

All of a sudden, it felt like a bucket of cold water washed over me, and I created some space between us by pushing him away. Our chests almost moved simultaneously up and down—our breathing erratic.

I put a hand over my mouth. *Had I gone mad?*

The beast in my brain clearly thought so, screaming for me to pull his body back against mine. But the rational part of me knew that I would destroy myself afterward—that I was jeopardizing my career. That this, whatever *this* was, clearly wasn't a great idea for me.

"Why not?" I breathlessly asked him instead.

He shook his head in a daze and frowned. The wave of longing partly faded from his eyes until he seemed to see again, but kept looking at me as if though he had no idea what I was talking about.

"Why can't you offer me more?" I insisted, wanting to kick myself for that question. Whatever his answer was, I would never come out unscathed.

"Hunter…" He took a deep breath and reluctantly lowered me so that I was back on my feet. "I'm the General," he said, matter-of-factly.

"*So?*" I shot back, irritation lacing the word.

And I realized that I *wanted* more—wanted more from him than just a physical exchange. I could have done it with anyone else, but not Nikolai. If I went down that road, I would destroy more than just my career. It would never be enough.

And any promotion I would get from then on would be questioned.

Nikolai ran a hand through his hair and pressed his lips together—lips now a darker shade of red from kissing. From kissing *me*.

He parted them again. "*So*, I have a lot of responsibilities, and I can't afford to be distracted—by no one. That would mean putting someone before everything else: making one person the epicenter of my universe. I can't, and mustn't, let that happen in my position."

I looked at him for a while before nodding. "I understand that your work comes first." That was the case for me, too. It wasn't so much an argument to plead my case, but it wasn't purely factual either. "But defining something or not doesn't change the situation," I emphasized.

You simply couldn't choose what feelings you had for someone, and whether you thought that person was important. Starting a relationship wouldn't suddenly spur feelings—at least not feelings that weren't already there. Just like you couldn't choose not to have any feelings involved when you decided only to sleep together. As much as he wanted to believe he had that control.

"I just can't offer you more, Hunter," he sighed.

A shaky breath escaped me, and I felt my heart pull back behind a wall, which was now rising again, and I stepped away from him—because I, too, knew myself.

"I can't do this." *With you*, but I didn't say the last two words out loud. That would mean I had to expose something. And it was clear he didn't care about that.

I had feelings for him. Nikolai Zaregova had been the subject of my thoughts for the past few weeks. I couldn't let him be the center of my self-destruction as well. It wasn't worth risking my career for someone who wouldn't face his own feelings.

Nikolai looked at me intensely and reached for me with his hand as I distanced myself from him, but he stopped himself and let his arm hang limply back at his side. "Hunter…"

I only raised my brows and looked at him breathlessly. I tried not to focus too much on his eyes, as I would probably drown in them and forget why I wasn't touching him anymore.

After a moment of silence, he nodded. He ran a hand through his hair and walked to the door. A shiver ran through my chest at the realization that he would rather have nothing than all of me.

But somehow, I understood, too. He was a General, and couldn't afford any weaknesses, no matter how much he wanted to believe he could keep his—or my—feelings out of the equation. I was still at the start of my career, and I couldn't jeopardize it for something that might not even be there.

When Nikolai looked back, our eyes met, and I could see he was having a hard time with it too—which perhaps scared me even more. He quickly turned his head to the door and waited with his back to me for a moment before he tensed his muscles, and disappeared through the door.

I slumped backward on my bed and draped an arm over my eyes.

It was better to have nothing of him instead of a little, and be able to lose everything I'd worked so hard for—to lose control and let myself be consumed in the process.

It really was better this way.

Even if it hurt a lot right now.

CHAPTER 14

NIKOLAI

That night Nikolai had gone to bed tired. He felt like he'd been tossing and turning for hours before giving in to the situation—even the cold shower he'd taken beforehand hadn't helped. All he could think about were Hunter's words.

Defining something wouldn't change the situation.

Nikolai knew precisely what she meant. It was why the look in her eyes now haunted him. He could only think of how her dark blonde hair had curled around his fingers, how her lips had glided over his, and how perfectly his hands had fitted on every curve of her body.

After staring at the ceiling for a long time, hands tucked underneath his head, he got out of bed and brushed his teeth again. But Hunter—her essence—lingered in his mouth like a phantom. A welcome phantom in any other situation. But dear gods, not *now*. He couldn't afford a lack of sleep.

Nikolai knew that Hunter wanted him, too. It had been more than apparent from the way she'd touched him. She just hadn't given in to those desires. At least, not *yet*.

All Nikolai could do to ease the tension and fall asleep that night was dealt with his hand. After that, he finally got a few more hours of restless sleep—but sleep, nevertheless.

His dreams went on and on about the blonde Major who had him under her spell. The way she smiled and wrinkled her nose, the amber eyes that resembled liquid honey in certain lighting, and her scent: *mint and basil.*

* * *

Nikolai eventually woke up sweating and decided to take another cold shower. He brought himself to another release with his hand, and convinced himself that it was his body's natural reaction.

Oh, he was going to see her today; he was aware of that. If he had to, he'd make *sure* that he would see her.

While Nikolai changed and put on his uniform, he allowed himself a moment to think about the night before. She'd clearly wanted something from him too. *Clearly.* But she hadn't let it get that far. Probably because he was indeed the General, and she didn't want to jeopardize her career. He couldn't argue with her—*of course, it was a good reason.* But it stung. It stung that his title held her back. In fact, it nagged him so severely that Nikolai was still mulling over it during breakfast. He'd have to figure out a way for her to stop seeing his position as an obstacle, to eviscerate the tension between them, so they could fully focus on the mission again.

But what if it wasn't enough? What if it would never be enough?

Nikolai shook his head as if he could shake the thoughts out, too. He would make sure it was enough. Nothing at all was a worse alternative.

For a second, again, he wished that he wasn't the

General—that he wasn't carrying the entire responsibility of the mission on his shoulders. That the world wasn't a mess and the mutants didn't exist. That he'd met her in Barak.

But that wasn't reality.

Nikolai let his head hang between his shoulders and smiled cynically. When one of his generals asked him what was wrong, he simply shook his head. He knew how ironic the situation was. If they started something, both their careers would be in jeopardy. If they didn't do anything, the tension could cause them both to become so distracted that they would make mistakes… and then their careers would still be in jeopardy.

He drew a clear line between physical and emotional inside his head. A line he wouldn't cross—that he *couldn't* cross.

Nikolai grunted in frustration and finished his breakfast.

* * *

Sometime later, he was in Jordan's recovery room. Partly because Nikolai wanted to see how he was doing, but for the most part hoping to run into Hunter and size up her reaction. That turned out to be fruitful, as his conversation with Jordan soon got interrupted by Hunter walking inside.

She took his breath away, and the line he'd drawn so firmly that morning instantly blurred. His mind seemed to freeze, not remembering what he and Jordan had been talking about.

For a moment, Nikolai was lost.

She was back to wearing her dark green overalls, which hadn't been zipped all the way up, exposing the black turtleneck underneath, hugging her elegant neck. That neck that he'd kissed yesterday and had haunted his dreams. He also noticed—with (dis)pleasure—that the suit snugged close around her waist because of the buckle belt. That her long legs protruded from below her curved hips and ended in black, buckled boots. She'd put her dark blonde, slightly curly hair half up half down in a bun. She looked rested.

At least one of them slept well.

Hunter then walked into the room as if he wasn't even there. This drove him mad with frustration—and *yes*, with desire, too. That always seemed to be the case when it came to Hunter Jameson.

When she finally looked up from the clipboard, she glanced at him and nodded. "*General.*"

But before he could say anything back, she struck up a conversation with Jordan—whose progress was improving so fast that he was allowed to go back to work that day. And then, as smoothly as she'd entered, she left the room again. Nikolai could have sworn it was in a bit of a rush, which gave him more satisfaction than he cared to admit.

"She," Jordan said, pointing to the closed door, "is something else."

Nikolai carefully tilted his head to Jordan, who had a big smile plastered on his face, and continued, "I have to do something for her, don't you think?"

Nikolai's spine locked. "I don't know if she's waiting for…" he narrowed his eyes as he gestured at Jordan, "whatever you're offering."

Jordan rolled his eyes dramatically. "Contrary to what you may think, I can be a real gentleman. Plus, this isn't exactly the environment to start that kind of shit. As lovely as she is."

Nikolai pursed his lips and tried to keep the irritated look off his face. Completely irrational, of course, since he was repeating the exact same argument over and over to himself.

"I just want to thank her for saving my life in a nice, light-hearted way. With a drink, perhaps." Jordan gave him a half-smile and winked. "It's not nothing, you know. The world has kept a great asset."

Nikolai's body lost some of its tension, and he laughed as he got up to leave the room. "She'll appreciate that, I think."

Jordan nodded, then raised his chin at him. "But between us, Zaregova, what do you think of her?" He wiggled his eyebrows. "Would you have approached her in Barak?"

Nikolai snorted. "Go and worry about your recovery."

"That's not a *no*," Jordan emphasized.

"It's a: *I'm not going to answer hypothetical questions since I have better things to do*," he retorted.

Jordan laughed out loud. "Watch out, Nikolai. You'll scare women away with such a serious attitude." He looked doubtful for a moment. "But then again, they'll probably expect that from the infamous *General Zaregova*."

Nikolai grinned and shook his head. "Glad to see you're doing better, Locke."

"General," Jordan saluted with a laugh.

CHAPTER 15

I hadn't been ready to see Nikolai again so soon after our… *encounter* last night. It had been quite uncomfortable, and that was putting it mildly. He'd been watching me constantly, and I'd done my best to pretend not to notice. The moment I saw him sit next to Jordan, the sweat spontaneously broke out across my lower back. I'd left the room as quickly as I was able and fled to my new office. Here, I had quickly closed the door behind me, which I now leaned against, letting go of a deep sigh.

The mutant child had been sent on its way to the scientists in Barak the previous day, and they had informed us that they needed more mutant children for the various studies. I had yet to pass this on to Nikolai, as he was head of the mission.

I was ripped from my thoughts as the door suddenly opened behind me with great force. The only reason I stayed upright was that I could grab hold of the chair in front of the desk to regain my balance.

"Were you standing against the door?" an amused, deep voice asked behind me. A voice that was etched in my memory, most likely for the rest of my *fucking* life.

I quickly turned around and shot Nikolai an annoyed look. "Do you always just blast into someone's office like that?" I snapped back.

He smirked and closed the door behind him. "Were you hiding from me?" he asked with a sly smile, an eyebrow raised defiantly—as if he already knew the answer.

"No." *Yes.* "I actually need to talk to you about something, now you're here." I was relieved that my voice sounded steady.

His other brow raised too, and he looked at me expectantly. "Listen, Hunter," he began.

But I didn't let him finish that sentence. He had started a conversation like that before, and it hadn't ended well. "The scientists said they needed more mutants for their research," I quickly blurted out.

He nodded. "I'm aware."

"Oh, of course," I sheepishly replied. "Well, that's all— besides thanking you for your effort in bringing back a mutant, despite the complications."

His eyebrows dropped into a frown. "Didn't you tell them you were responsible for that?"

"Of course *not*," I snorted.

Nikolai stepped closer. "You should have."

I moved back a little, bumping into the back of the chair. Casually, I let myself slide past it and quickly took a seat behind the desk. "I've noticed that undermining a superior doesn't always work in my favor."

Nikolai followed my movements with a wolfish smile and walked over to the window behind me.

"Do you need anything, *General*?" I pointedly asked him.

He leaned his hands on the back of my chair, then moved

closer to me. "I've told you to call me Nikolai," he whispered, his breath bouncing off my ear and cheekbone, leaving behind a tingling sensation.

"I still retain the right to do whatever I want with that." I slightly turned my head to him and looked him in the eyes. Those endlessly deep, dark eyes. I tried to ignore his mouth— and failed. The lips he had kissed me with the previous evening drew into a little smile, and his eyes twinkled knowingly. He was definitely aware of the effect he had on me.

"And if I ask nicely?" he asked.

I drew my mouth in a sharp line. "Only if you demand it."

Nikolai shook his head as he stalked closer, his eyes fixed on my mouth. "Never."

Forgetting what we were talking about, I felt myself move towards him and part my lips slightly.

He straightened and ran his hands over his black clothes as if smoothing out the creases that weren't there. A second later, he'd left the room.

I swallowed, loudly clearing my throat, as I frantically bent over my paperwork.

Asshole.

* * *

That evening I went to the bar to toast to Tania, who would be leaving the following day to go back to regular living in the civilized world. I hadn't spent much time with her in the past month, but the group invited me along anyway.

As I stepped into the bar and looked around, my treacherous eyes naturally slid to the back corner. Jordan was back, and waved over with a smile when he saw me looking. I returned the gesture. His wound was still a long, red gash across his throat, but it was healing nicely. It certainly didn't make him any less handsome.

Despite that, there were a number of reasons why I could never see him that way. Firstly, because he felt more like a brother. Secondly, because he was a General, which led me to the third: *Nikolai*. I sighed and let my gaze slide past Nikolai, who seemed to have no problem not looking my way.

Tania had ordered several rounds of drinks, which meant we had to stop Kelian from climbing on the table after the bartender put on music for Tania's last night. Raven and I had laughed at the way Cardan had drunkenly stared into nothingness for nearly an hour. And eventually, everyone started yawning a little as the evening came to an end. I had thoroughly enjoyed myself, and even noticed that my mind had been distracted for most of the evening.

I was suddenly overwhelmed with a sense of friendship I'd never experienced before, as I looked at the individuals at the table. After I announced I would pay the rest of the bill, everyone had cheered loudly and banged their glasses on the table, once again drawing a lot of attention from the rest of the bar.

Raven burst into laughter, and had to put a hand to her mouth as she saw me suppress another burst of giggles. But I had myself somewhat under control compared to the rest because I hadn't drunk any alcohol. As head, I could be paged to the medical center at any time and wanted my mind to stay clear.

When the group found their way out of the building, I told Raven not to wait for me, and I walked over to pay at the bar. I saw Jordan rise from his seat at the table, approaching me as I stood there, and I felt an intense curiosity flare-up.

Jordan smiled as he took his place beside me at the bar, and I raised my eyebrows in amusement. "Hunter! How's my favorite surgeon doing this evening?"

"My night has been amazing. Thanks for asking," I solemnly replied, trying my best not to laugh out loud again.

He nodded gravely, a smile still haunting his lips. "The thing is," he started and cleared his throat, "I realized that I hadn't thanked you properly."

I quickly brushed off his comment. "It's my *job*, Jordan; you don't have to."

Jordan rolled his eyes, and the smile disappeared. "I'm serious, Hunter. Thank you. I have no idea how I can ever repay you, but let me start with a drink."

The respect that showed in his eyes for everything that had happened, affected me. I knew he was offering his friendship. "That seems like a great first step," I replied, moved by his words. As emotional as I'd been in the past few days, it was more than in my entire life put together.

His eyes lit up. "Wonderful."

"Don't start expecting too much, Locke," I said in a warning tone, and scrunched my nose at him, making him laugh. I noticed his table silently watching us, and felt Nikolai's eyes drill into the side of my head.

"I wouldn't dare," Jordan said, and I stuck my tongue out at him. "My treat tomorrow night, all right?"

Grinning, I nodded at him and paid before leaving the bar—walking into the chill evening air.

* * *

"Hunter," I heard behind me a moment later, and suppressed a shiver. It was like we were two magnets that just kept attracting one another. Nikolai walked up to me and the frozen surface crackled under his boots. "Wait."

I let out an unexpectedly long sigh, which filled the air with mist. "Yes?" I asked, wrapping my arms around myself so I couldn't do anything crazy with them. Like touching him. Which I wanted.

"Locke can't offer you any more than I can," he just said.

I raised my brows and felt the cold seep through my coat. "I think this falls outside of your responsibilities as a general, Nikolai."

"I'm not saying this as your general, Hunter." He narrowed his eyes and looked down at me, his dark hair falling over his eyes.

"Jordan and I are just friends."

He laughed. "It's naive to assume that's all he wants."

"If I were you, I wouldn't assume *you* know anything about what *I* want," I countered.

Nikolai threw his head back in frustration. "I think we both know that isn't true."

"Why don't you mind your own business?" I growled at him, and started to walk away, but turned around again a beat later with clenched fists and stepped closer. "Not every man just wants to sleep with me, unlike you."

The conversation turned, and his face twisted. Nikolai looked thunderous. "It's not like that, Hunter."

"What is it like then, *Nikolai.*"

He narrowed his eyes. "Why are you ignoring what's so obviously between us?"

"There is no *us.*" I turned away so he couldn't see the

emotion on my face.

"*Please*," he snorted incredulously and followed. Nikolai grabbed me with one hand and turned me around. His face was very close now. "Why are you ignoring it?" he asked through clenched teeth.

"*I* am *not* the one ignoring it," I gasped breathlessly.

I felt too much, and it was too dangerous to allow any of it. I would only want more, and before I knew it, the dam would break and have the power to destroy everything around me.

Nikolai abruptly let go of me, as if he'd burned himself, and took a step back to create some distance. The air around us seemed to crackle with electricity, and his gaze proved that he saw something in my eye that frightened him.

The feelings I had for him were probably all outlined on my face. Only now he realized what had been clear to me all along, but to actually see that he wanted nothing to do with it crushed my heart.

Nikolai turned and started to walk away, clenching and unclenching his hands. After a few steps, he also turned and walked back towards me. Nikolai Zaregova seemed to lose control and was unable to decide for the first time in his life. I didn't know whether he wanted to kiss me or smash a fist through a wall.

"Why not, Hunter?" he suddenly asked, his voice low. The glint in his eye promised war.

My heartbeat betrayed how much I wanted him. "Because you're the General," I replied, trembling.

"I don't believe you," he immediately said and examined my eyes—but he found no lies in them. It was part of the truth, after all.

"Suit yourself," I replied, irritated, and averted my gaze. He should get a medal for his perceptiveness if he didn't already have one.

"What if I wasn't a general?" Nikolai intently looked at me again.

My face grew warm. "Then I wouldn't either."

"*Bullshit*," he snapped at the lie that was clearly visible now.

I didn't want to speak the truth, not if it meant making myself vulnerable.

Somewhere, a realization sparked in me at the tone of his voice. Nikolai wanted me so badly that it made him angry. Angry at himself? Angry at me? Angry at his title?

All of the above, I guessed.

"Sleep well, Nikolai," I said, braver than I felt. I turned and walked away to my room.

A treacherous disappointment swept through my body at the realization that he wasn't coming after me. I found myself holding my breath and inhaled a large quantity of the cold evening air.

I felt his eyes burn into my back, but I didn't dare to look. Afraid of what I would do.

CHAPTER 16

The following day at the medical base, I received news that Nikolai had gone back onto the shadow plains, and something about that didn't sit well. It was always nerve-wracking when a team left, but it felt different this time—because of him. Thus, I couldn't resist walking past the monitoring room and inspecting his data.

Trying to keep those feelings at bay the rest of the day, I decided to take alternative routes through the medical center to not constantly walk past the monitoring room and drive myself crazy. At least, that's what I *tried* to do.

But after a hectic day at work, I had arranged to meet with a nearly healed Jordan for a drink. He was waiting for me outside, leaning against the wall at the entrance to the medical building, and pushed off when he saw me. "By the gods," he responded, nodding to passing soldiers. "Are you *the* Major Jameson?"

"The one and only." I smiled wearily at him as I hid my pager.

He gestured with his arms toward the path. "May I accompany you to the bar?"

I nodded, and took a deep inhale of the fresh evening air. "Yes, please." Taking over the duties as head had proven to be quite overwhelming, especially in combination with the exhausting situation between Nikolai and me. I hoped it would be over with soon, both for the mission and myself.

We were just walking for a while when Jordan cleared his throat and rested his hands on his back. "What did you do before all this?"

"Before the mission, you mean?"

He nodded.

"I worked in the hospital at the main base in Barak for a year, right after I graduated."

He rubbed his throat. "How old are you actually? You must be one of the youngest surgeons we've ever had—here at least."

I inclined my head. "Twenty-five, but it was met with more resistance than praise here."

"I can imagine—not because you're not good, obviously," he quickly added and nudged me with his elbow, "but because we have quite high standards here, and experience is often the most important. But in your case, they were able to assess your talent and potential well."

"Thanks." I looked up at him. "What about you?"

"My position required a good mix of being young, talented, and having a history of incredibly valuable experience."

I regarded him thoughtfully. "But you're still young for your position, aren't you?"

Jordan shrugged and pursed his mouth. "Twenty-nine is still considerably young. It's just not that exceptional. Major generals my age are more common. Not like Zaregova being a General at his age. *That's* rare," he admitted.

I didn't want to think about Nikolai and tried to shove him out of my mind. "Is it difficult to hold such a high position with your father as—"

"Delegate?" His face drew into a pained smile. "So, you connected the dots, huh?"

I shook my head. "I didn't realize it until someone said it, and then it was suddenly crystal clear."

Jordan nodded. "My father tries to keep the fact that his son is in the military out of the news. Mainly for me, because he is very proud. But to answer your question—no, it isn't difficult. It was in the beginning, but not anymore."

"Did they think you became major general because of your father?"

He shook his head. "No, it wasn't that. Now, my position is solid—nobody has questioned it for a long time. I've thoroughly proven myself." He grinned broadly, and I mirrored him. "It was difficult when I just finished high school. At the start of training, everyone assumed that I'd secured a place in the program *because* of my father."

"And you hadn't?"

"No, I even signed up with my last name misspelled. Only after I got through the selections did I have it adjusted as if it were an administrative error."

"Ballsy."

"Well." He winked. "What can I say?"

We arrived at the bar and walked inside. "So, what kind of experience brought you here?" I asked him as we sat down at the middle table.

He held up two fingers at the bartender, then leaned his elbows on the table. "I started working when I was seventeen, right after high school. I soon proved to have a lot of potential, and was promoted to colonel at a reasonable pace—I was about your age then. But as you probably know, the ranking division works differently if you're not specialized."

I nodded. It was almost impossible for me, as a doctor, to ever become a general in the army. Mainly because I was a surgeon first and a soldier second.

Jordan continued his story: "So when this mission started three years ago, General Zaregova indicated that he wanted me on his team, and I got promoted to major general for that reason. He just pushed my title through." He chuckled. "His word is law, and the main base knows it. Though Chief General Domasc would never admit it."

Despite everything, a smile crept over my face. "Have you known the General for a long time, then?"

Jordan took the two beers from the bartender and slid one toward me. "Kind of. We were stationed at the same wall post a few years earlier. We built up a sort of mutual respect there. We always tried to outdo each other in everything until he was promoted after saving the life of Chief General Domasc in an explosion."

"Seriously?"

Jordan nodded. "General Domasc personally ensured that Zaregova was made lieutenant-general after that happened. Probably the biggest mistake of his career, if you ask him."

"Why?"

"Because later on, General Domasc started to feel threatened by General Zaregova's success here." He gave me a crooked smile. "But again, not that he would ever admit it."

Lost in thought, I took a sip of my drink and then gestured

with my bottle to Jordan. "And now you're here."

"And now I'm here," he agreed solemnly.

We drank for a moment, and Jordan ran a hand through his blonde hair before he turned his attention back to me. "Do you have anyone back home?"

I grinned. "No. I never really took time for that. I've always been so focused on my career that I never had the time to commit to a serious relationship. Now I'm glad I don't have one."

He nodded in understanding.

"What about you?"

"Not now," he sighed. "But I did have a serious relationship. The first girl I fell in love with—my *childhood sweetheart* if you want to call it that. We dated for five years, and I always thought we'd get married young—that it was forever, you know. But after a few years of service, I found that I could no longer share my new life with her. Not in the way that mattered or the way I wanted to. She thought it was all too intense and wanted nothing to do with it. Then we grew apart, and I haven't had or felt anything serious since then. Especially not here."

"That must have been difficult," I said softly, thinking about Nikolai. I wondered if he'd ever been in a serious relationship, maybe even had a childhood sweetheart of his own. My stomach knotted at the thought. First loves almost always held a special place in someone's heart, even if that person was no longer *in* love.

"Yeah, it was," Jordan confessed.

I regarded him curiously. "Does the idea of loving someone again scare you?"

Jordan looked up in surprise. "No." He shook his head.

"Definitely not."

"Don't you think it's a scary idea to give up that control again? Exposing your feelings like that?" Because that was what scared me the most. The feeling that I would be losing control—wouldn't hold any power over myself when Nikolai was around. That something could happen to him, and I wouldn't be able to do anything about it. That I had no influence on what consequences it would have for me.

"*If* I meet another woman I'm crazy about, it won't be a matter of giving up control or not." Jordan smiled again, revealing his dimples. "I won't have a choice."

* * *

The following days quickly turned into a week, and when I was woken early one morning, I instinctively knew that the group had returned from the shadow plains. That *Nikolai* had come back.

I'd been instructed to go to a conference room because I had to attend the meeting as interim head of my department. I got dressed in a heartbeat, and made my way to the building, where the other heads were already waiting.

Entering the room, I nodded to the others present and then let my eyes rest on Nikolai, who was still standing with his back to me in his field uniform. He turned, and I could see that his hair was plastered to his forehead—his eyes dark. The sight of him after all this time made me feel short of breath.

Nikolai looked straight into my eyes, and I saw his face twitch as if it hurt him to look at me.

"General," I quickly said and saluted.

His gaze darkened even more, but he simply nodded and began the meeting.

The good news was that they extracted another mutant child and sent it to the capital. The bad news was that the mutants seemed to be getting closer and closer: instead of downtown Elm, a few were already spotted in the suburbs. It was something we should all be wary of.

"Any questions?" he finally asked, but no one opened their mouth. It had been a straightforward story. He'd explained the steps from here and prepared them for us to implement directly in our teams.

But what I did wonder about was why he hadn't looked directly at me once during his talk. So, when everyone got up and left the room, I couldn't help but slow down and wait for them to leave. I looked around the room and pretended to study the information on the various boards instead.

Nikolai gazed out of the window, but when he turned around and found me alone in the room, he slightly tilted his head. "Yes, Major Jameson?"

I approached him. "I witnessed the past few days through the monitoring room, but I still wanted to ask you personally how you're doing."

Nikolai blinked. "Personal questions don't seem to be part of your responsibilities, Major."

Fine, I deserved that. But I knew he'd had a few long days and we hadn't exactly ended it on a light note. I tried again. "How are you, Nikolai?"

He swallowed and looked away. "I'm fine," he sighed.

Automatically, I stepped closer and brought my hand to his face to smooth my thumb over his eyebrow, tracing the suture I'd made. But when I got close to the wound, he got hold of my wrist.

"Does it still hurt?" I whispered. He *looked* like he was in pain.

"If I need your help, I'll ask for it."

I narrowed my eyes at him. "Why do I get the feeling you wouldn't?"

Nikolai let out a surprised laugh, despite his uptight attitude so far. I took another step back and added softly, "I just wanted to make sure you were all right."

Nikolai looked up in surprise, and his face relaxed. Even the crease between his eyebrows smoothened.

Damnit. Couldn't I just shut up for once? As a result, I felt my cheeks burn, and decided that it was my cue to leave. I turned and walked towards the door.

However, before I could open it, Nikolai had placed his hand flat against it and held it shut. I let the latch slip from mine and turned as he towered over me.

"You know, Hunter," Nikolai drawled, looking down at me with his dark eyes.

"Hmm?" I could only utter, trying to keep control over myself.

"I've been thinking," he continued.

"Oh?" I responded softly.

He lowered his head so that his mouth was a breath away from mine. "About what I would do if we were alone in that bunker," he continued, and I felt his breath bounce off my lips. "And I concluded that I still had a bone to pick with you after that conversation the other night."

"Lovely," I muttered, sounding more indifferently than I felt.

Nikolai clicked his tongue and said, "Smartass." After which he slowly wound one of my escaped curls around his index finger. "But that's not all I've been thinking about."

I swallowed.

The trance I was in as he opened his mouth again was roughly interrupted when I felt the latch turn and bore into my side. I veered off the door as if it had burned me. Nikolai took hold of the door and pulled it open a little further.

After an unintelligible conversation, Nikolai said, "Put the Chief General through to my office."

He looked at me for a moment and tilted his head. "We'll finish this conversation later."

Nikolai walked out of the room without looking back, and closed the door behind him. I counted to ten and then made sure I got the hell out of there.

I definitely didn't want to finish *that* conversation.

CHAPTER 17

My mind went over this mornings' events for the hundredth time while I was staring into my glass at the bar. To make matters worse, Nikolai had been sitting on the other side of the room all evening, and I couldn't quite convince myself to leave the bar. Just like I couldn't entirely ignore the excruciating fact that he'd been looking at me all night. He responded now and then to something that was said to him, but other than that, he only had eyes for me.

He had said that this morning's conversation wasn't over yet, but I didn't want to know what else he had to say. It would probably just be harder to stay away from him and not burn my hands. Everything had already become so much less attractive to my brain compared to that one man who haunted my mind. My gaze wandered in his direction again, and I sighed in defeat. He looked *so* good in black.

Nikolai looked over the rim of his glass as he held it between his thumb and middle finger and knocked it back. Then he responded to someone at his table and broke eye contact. That was for the better since I didn't want to come across as desperate, especially since *I* was the one who didn't just want to sleep with him.

Why was that again?

Before he could look my way again, I let my eyes wander and saw Jordan approaching the bar. My grip on the glass tightened, and I quickly let go. I didn't want to draw unnecessary attention to myself because of broken glass.

"Hunter, are you okay?" Jordan asked, sitting down on a stool next to me.

"Yes, why?" I answered too quickly.

Frowning, he pointed to his cheek. "You look a little pale."

"Aren't we all?" I joked sarcastically.

He opened his mouth to say something, but was then interrupted by another voice.

"Where are the drinks you promised, *Locke*?"

My face twisted as Nikolai stood next to Jordan with a sly smile. The other man grinned at him. "You can't blame me for wanting to talk to Major Jameson, can you?"

Nikolai's smile became more devilish. "No, I can't."

My smile faltered, and I felt my cheeks heat up. I pulled my gaze away from the two men and focused on the glass in front of me.

"Let me know if you need anything," Jordan said and gently patted my arm. Then he walked over to the other side of the bar to order drinks.

"We still have to finish this morning's conversation," Nikolai muttered, leaning one forearm on the bar. A smile still played on his lips. The bastard knew what sort of effect he had on me. He knew it this morning, and he knew it now. I hadn't changed my mind, and there came a moment when he just had to accept that.

And that moment—I decided—had arrived.

The blood was crawling to my cheeks, and I trembled with frustration as I stood abruptly. I slammed my money on the counter, and grabbed my coat to get out of there as quickly as possible, leaving a stunned Nikolai behind.

Outside, I walked over the path to my room and irritably rubbed my eyes, which stung from rising tears. Of course, I didn't want to like him, but unfortunately, I already was past the point where I was in control of my feelings—if I'd ever been.

Nikolai had to learn when it was time to quit. He'd read the truth in my eyes days ago and knew damn well why I couldn't sleep with him. That it would damage my career, and—

Fleeting footsteps sounded behind me, and I accelerated my steps without having to run. "Leave me alone," I called back. I didn't care who it was, but I took my chances.

Nikolai grabbed my arm and turned me around roughly. He looked irritated until he noticed the tears streaming down my cheeks, and his face completely contorted. "What's going on? Did something happen?"

"*Yes*," I snapped and pulled my arm out of his grip. I hadn't turned around before he'd grabbed me with both hands.

"What the hell is going on, Hunter? I swear I'll—"

"*You* are what's going on!" I hoarsely interrupted him.

He looked genuinely surprised for a moment, his gaze filling with disbelief. "Me?" He slowly started to let go. "What the hell did I do?"

I laughed bitterly and felt another tear escape. "As if you don't know."

Nikolai frowned, his face thunderous. "Hunter, you really need to explain this to me."

"I don't *need* to do anything," I said as I felt raindrops trickle down my face, mixing with my tears.

He sighed in frustration and held my arms tight, his eyes illegible. "You'll have to do it anyway."

Breathing deeply, I met his gaze and considered my options. What did I have left to lose? *My principles?* I'd lost those from the moment I kissed him.

"Hunter," he warned.

"I'm falling for you, and you're playing a game with me!" I exclaimed. "All you want is to sleep with me, and you know that if you keep doing what you're doing, you'll succeed— but," another tear escaped, "you just don't give a shit that you would hurt me in the process, okay? Now it's spelled out for you." I shook myself free, and Nikolai was frozen in place. "Do whatever you want with it."

"Hunter," he growled as he came after me. "Hunter, you don't get it."

I laughed sarcastically. "I think I understand perfectly well."

"Then why do you think I just want to sleep with you?"

I turned and looked at the man standing in front of me. My eyes widened in annoyance. *Was he serious?* "You literally said you can't give me more."

"*Can,*" he insisted, dangerously low, as he took a step toward me, and I stayed in place, transfixed. "What made you decide I don't *care?*" he asked, more urgently, and took another step forward. "How dare you think I wouldn't *want* more from you, Hunter?"

Nikolai ran a hand through his hair and wearily shook his

head. "I'm the general. I can't afford this. Being the general, I can't give you more—I'm not allowed to give you anything—but when it comes to you, I can't think straight."

My breath caught in my throat.

"Knowing that I would never be allowed or able to have you completely, I hoped that one day you'd at least sleep with me. I knew you found me attractive, and I would have settled for just that. At least that was *something*. I convinced myself that I could leave it at that—because I want it so damn much.

"But in the past few days, I've realized that it will never be enough—that I'd always want more. That's what I was trying to explain this morning, but it's so damn hard, Hunter. You don't want to know how much this is endangering *everyone* here and out there." He pointed a tight finger at the base and clenched his jaws as he looked at me coolly. "So don't *ever* tell me I'm playing a game with you."

We looked at each other for a while, and the icy look started to disappear from his face. The spoken words slowly settled, and I felt my body heat up. My heart seemed to be beating faster as I stared at him. I didn't even feel the rain anymore, which now also soaked his face completely.

Unconsciously I took a step in his direction and looked at him. His gaze was fixed on my every move, and shifted to my throat as I swallowed. And when I tilted my head a little towards his, instinct seemed to take over.

Nikolai grabbed my face with both hands and placed his lips on mine the very moment I opened my mouth for him. One of his hands glided down my throat and nestled into my wet hair as he claimed my mouth as if he'd done it a thousand times before. I wrapped my arms around his neck, trying to pull him closer.

I wanted everything.

Now.

My intention was unmistakable, and he broke the kiss to look at me—seeking confirmation. He grabbed my hand and looked around. "Shit," he snapped and pulled me after him. Nikolai kept looking around, but I didn't give a shit what he was looking for. The only thing I could focus on was him.

We had to get somewhere inside—as soon as possible. It was too cold to stay outside, and I certainly didn't want any spectators. So, when we passed an empty conference room, I pulled him in that direction.

Nikolai stopped me and ran the back of his hand over my cheek. "I'm not going to take you against the wall or on a table tonight. We're going to my rooms."

I stepped closer. "I *want* you to take me against the wall or on the table tonight," I whispered hoarsely. Besides, his quarters were on the other side of the base, and I didn't want to wait any longer.

Nikolai pulled me closer and kissed me as he opened the door and locked it behind us. He flipped the switches, blinding the windows, leaving only the faint glow of the emergency sign near the entrance illuminating the room.

Rain tapped against the windows, and I didn't even feel the cold anymore as Nikolai turned to where I was standing. Slowly, he ran a hand through his wet hair. His entire being screamed war, and he focused on one target.

Me.

We automatically stepped towards each other, and our lips met again. We tried to get rid of our clothes as fast as we could. I threw his wet coat on the floor, and took off his damp shirt and undershirt, bringing me face to face with his muscular torso. I ran my hands over his chest, exploring, and then curled them around his neck.

He was, without a doubt, the most attractive man I had ever seen.

When I lowered my hands and tried to loosen his belt, he grabbed my hands and brought them to his mouth. My thighs touched the edge of the table, and he kissed my hands before releasing them. He took off my outerwear until I stood in front of him in my bra.

Nikolai kissed me from neck to shoulder and ran his broad hands down my spine to my hips until he was on one knee. He took off my boots with great skill, and I unzipped my pants before he quickly pulled them down. I stepped out of them and stood before him in only my underwear.

He rose again as his eyes roamed over my body. "Beautiful," he said simply, and then he captured my mouth with his again. He pushed me further back until I was sitting on the table before he took my bra off. He carefully lowered me back and looked at me from a distance. His wet hair stuck to his forehead and touched his dark brows. His dog tag was the only thing left on his muscular chest, glistening in the dim light.

Nikolai smiled and shook his head as he grabbed my thighs to pull me closer before bending over me and shifting his attention to my breasts. He ran his tongue roughly over the curve and bit it teasingly before taking one of my nipples in his mouth.

I pulled myself up by his neck to kiss him again and tried to get his belt to open. After a while, I left the intricate buckles to him and took off my panties. I ran two fingers over the damp spot between my legs.

Nikolai's attention darted to the movement, and he muttered, "Do that again."

I ran my fingers again over the spot, and he laughed breathlessly.

He gently pushed my hand aside and ran his own fingers over me. Upon contact, I let my hips rise in a silent demand for more. Heading my command, he slipped a finger in, which was soon joined by a second. All the while, he kept looking at me, and in the dark, I couldn't see where his pupils ended, and his irises began.

When he finally seemed to lose control, he bent over me, and his warm dog tag fell against my chest. Reluctantly, I felt his fingers withdraw, and he looked at me. "Are you protected?"

I blinked, then nodded breathlessly. "Yes." Birth control nowadays protected us from everything. "You?"

Nikolai nodded and took off his boxer shorts in a heartbeat. He positioned himself against my entrance and nibbled at my lip for a moment before slowly pushing forward and giving my body time to get adjusted to him. All I could do was focus on my breathing and his mouth, which wholly engulfed mine again. I felt myself slowly spread open as he settled into me.

The moment he was completely inside, he broke the kiss and looked up. He shook his head in disbelief, and I kissed him again.

After what seemed like forever, Nikolai began to move. His mouth grew tighter, and his breathing quickened as he drove into me again and again, his body tightening. Very slow and deliberate at first, but as my breath hitched and moans started to escape, he quickened his pace. Nikolai now claimed me in two places. I frantically clawed my way up to his muscular back with my hands so I could hold on. It was all I could do as he took over my senses.

"Shit, Hunter," Nikolai gasped as he wrapped my legs around him and lifted me off the table. He pressed me against the cold wall, which overwhelmed my senses, and I shrieked. There he continued tirelessly, resulting in me finding release, and I bit my moan into his shoulder.

He let himself move out of me, and I staggered on trembling legs. Nikolai ran his hand over my breast and softly squeezed a sensitive nipple. As I stood on my toes to kiss his neck, I felt his body stiffen. He roughly turned me around, bending me over the table, and seated himself deep inside me again.

His hands clasped my waist as he seemed to go deeper and deeper, moving up and down roughly. I completely lost control over my body, and my moans turned into orgasm after orgasm, until I lost count.

Finally, Nikolai reached his peak, too, after turning me around again and letting us merge once more. A hand was wrapped in my hair, and he pressed his forehead against mine as we recovered together.

I was still dazed as he gently lowered me back onto the table. My legs were limp, and my throat felt like sandpaper. Like I would be permanently dehydrated for the rest of my life, and beads of sweat rested on Nikolai's chest too. His stomach tightened when he laughed, and he planted kisses on my neck.

"*Hunter, Hunter, Hunter,*" Nikolai said, clicking his tongue. He shook his head again. "I've come to the conclusion that I wouldn't have had it in me to leave you alone after sleeping with you."

Still breathing heavily, I ran my finger along the contours of his face. Then my fingers wrapped around his dog tag, and I read what it said. Grinning, I remarked, "I find that those seven years haven't given you any head start where experience is concerned."

Nikolai narrowed his eyes and tapped my nose. "Oh yeah?" He untied his chain and put it on my neck. He placed the metal tag right between my breasts. "That looks better," he said and planted a tender kiss on my lips.

I enclosed the dog tag with my hand and my heart was beating wildly at the intimate gesture. "Is this your way of marking your territory?"

Nikolai came closer and grabbed my face with one hand. "I'll show you exactly how I mark my territory—and how much *experience* I have."

CHAPTER 18

Nikolai had insisted that I stay with him that night, so I ended up following him to his quarters. On the way there, we made sure we didn't encounter anyone. Neither had we spoken a word to each other until he opened the door and his rooms were revealed to me.

"Wow," I said approvingly. The rooms were at least three times as spacious as mine.

Nikolai laughed. "I find it rather excessive." He wrapped an arm around my waist and kissed me on the mouth. "Except for now," he muttered. "Now it's convenient."

Surprised, I ran my fingers over my lips as he approached the wood stove and turned it on. The gesture had felt so natural that its power took me by surprise.

I made a circle around the room and tried to compose myself. "It makes sense that your position comes with better rooms," I said, running my hand across a table. "When you do sleep in your bed, it may as well be extra comfy."

Nikolai got up, and the room filled with a warm crackle. I tracked him with my eyes, wondering how things stood between us. We'd made our feelings known to each other, but what did that mean? He turned around, met my gaze, and came over to me. My heartbeat fastened as he reached me and tucked some hair behind my ears. I traced his body with my hands and swallowed.

My fingers curled in his hair, and I pulled him toward me. It was almost too much, this hunger for each other. My body practically begged to be touched by him.

The veins in his throat were visibly throbbing, and I ran my lips over them, trailing a path from his neck to his face.

"Hunter…" Nikolai whispered as his hands roamed the sides of my body.

I gently bit his lip in response, and one of his hands shot into my hair. He turned my face to his and kissed me. He kissed me deeply, exploring my mouth, as he escorted me to his bed. It seemed that once we touched, a sort of spell came over us, and we couldn't stop.

Though, to get my shirt off, I had to break contact. I jumped out of my pants and only wore my underwear, after which I continued walking to the bed. His gaze tracked me, and did not leave me for a second, while he also discarded his clothes. My hands itched to touch him again, but I could only watch his generously shaped body as the muscles underneath moved.

I felt the side of the bed push against my thighs and lowered myself backward.

Nikolai now only wore his boxers, and the dim light cast shadows which sharply defined the muscles in his long, strong legs. I instinctively touched his dog tag, which hung above my breasts along with my own, and wanted to take them off to put them aside, but he just shook his head.

Nikolai leaned forward on the bed and placed his hands

on either side of my body, forcing me to lean back a little until I lay flat. He slid a strong arm under my body and lifted me slightly off the bed to open the sheets and move us underneath them.

He pulled me towards him and kissed me again as he rolled on top of me, kneeing my legs apart to get in between. I could feel the evidence of his desire pressing through the fabric of my underwear, which was already damp with my own. He deftly took off his boxers and then shifted his attention to mine. His fingers slid under the edges of my briefs and pulled them down. He let his hand travel the same way back and squeezed my side gently on his way up.

I carefully ran my hand over his face as he simultaneously ran his fingers slowly along the curve of my breasts. Then he rested his arms on the pillows at either side of my head, pausing only to look at me.

With glinting eyes, he ran his nose down my cheek for a moment and whispered, "You don't want to know how much I've thought about you in my bed." He ran the crook of his index finger along my face and rested it under my chin, pushing it up. "And everything we would do."

His voice sounded soft and intoxicating. Evidence of his excitement throbbed in my hand.

My throat felt raw, and no matter how much I swallowed, it didn't seem to make a difference. "Was talking part of that, too?" I said, with more control than I had, since I was almost trembling with anticipation.

His chest rumbled with laughter, and he changed position by leaning on one arm, holding mine down with his other hand, and planting a kiss on the knuckles. An electric shock shot through, straight to my core.

I intertwined our fingers and placed our hands above my head. His hips nestled closer to mine, causing me to curl up and wrap my legs around him.

A gasp escaped from my lips as I felt him press against my entrance, and he looked down at me.

"Oh, Hunter," he sighed before capturing my mouth again and lowering his hips too, allowing him to enter. Another sigh escaped him, less controlled now. Nikolai slowly rolled his hips up and down, in and out, a little further each time than the last—until he was completely seated. When he stopped moving for a moment, I opened my eyes and saw Nikolai looking at me again. His gaze was intense, as if he was trying to capture the moment.

A warm, tingling sensation of that same intensity spread through my chest, and he opened his mouth to speak, then closed it again.

I knew what he wanted to say. It was written all over his body—in the way he touched me as if I were the most precious thing in the world. In the way his heart beat in his chest against mine uncontrollably.

Instead of saying it out loud, he conveyed his feelings with his lips. I pushed my hips up pleadingly, and Nikolai withdrew gently before moving slowly and purposefully back again. This was clearly more than just sex, and the tenderness of his movements left a lump in my throat. That was the last thing I wanted as my longing for him raced so fiercely through my body.

With a flat hand, I pushed him away from me and twisted my hips so that I could roll over, leveraging my weight, to get on top. I saw his eyes glimmer, and the corners of my mouth curled upwards as I parted our hands and planted my palms on his muscular chest. Not for a moment did Nikolai let his eyes stray from my face, not even when I straightened up and rode him.

My rhythm was faster than he'd initially assumed, but judging by his lost expression, he wasn't going to complain. My climax soon followed, and after I found my release, I felt him harden even more, if possible. He pushed his upper body off the mattress and pressed me closer to him while he, too, let himself come deeply rooted within me.

I planted my hands on his shoulders and sprang into action to get off him, but he clasped both hands tightly around my hips and held me in place. Nikolai laughed out of breath when I raised an eyebrow at him. It was a beautiful, deep sound, and I was convinced the world didn't hear it nearly enough.

"I don't want to let you go just yet," he said, and rolled us over so that he was back on top. He placed his arms around my head so that I was hidden in a cocoon of his making.

My other brow rose too. "I had no intention of going anywhere."

His hard stomach shook against mine. "I mean," he corrected with a laugh, kissing both of my eyelids, "that I want to hold you in my arms a little longer *while* I'm still inside you."

I smiled teasingly. "How *romantic*."

"Well," he said, looking smug, "I've never given myself to anyone like this before, so… you could say it's romantic."

One corner of my mouth curled up in surprise, and he let his lips slide over mine, leaving a tickling sensation.

"Why?"

He laughed. "Which why do you want to know?"

"Both."

"So greedy." But his look turned serious. "Because it always felt way too personal, and I didn't want to give myself completely like that to someone. And now I do because I've never been in a relationship where it felt right."

"*We* are not in a relationship either," I reminded him.

"Oh," he frowned, and dramatically raised his eyebrows, then thoughtfully looked at me from the corner of his eye, "we aren't?"

I shook my head, laughing.

He nodded firmly. "Then I'll have to do something about that."

"Do I have a say in that?"

"*Of course.*"

"Then who says that I give my consent?"

Nikolai narrowed his eyes, and a devilish look appeared on his face. He let his hand wander to my breast. "I don't think the consent will be a problem, would it?" He caressed my sensitive nipple between his thumb and forefinger, and drew a sigh from me.

"Goddamnit," I said, which made him chuckle.

"Not exactly what I had in mind, but at least it's not a no."

I shot him a sarcastic look. He slipped out, rolled to the other side of the bed, and stood. Nikolai had turned his back to me, giving me the opportunity to admire how incredibly beautifully built he was.

Nikolai turned around, and I wondered if I'd actually made a noise, so I looked behind me, too. He snorted and shook his head before disappearing into the bathroom.

I rubbed my hand over my face. I still had no idea what was going on between us. He had just talked about the future, *a future together*, but I didn't want to—dared to—go there yet. I didn't really know how to deal with it all. But here… where the world was in shadows, and no one was sure of their lives, things were even more complex.

I was so terrified. Afraid of what I might feel for this man—what I already felt for him. Nikolai was everything I'd ever wanted in a man, even though I'd never consciously considered it. He suited me.

He belonged with me.

But as he'd said before, he was the general of a vital mission. I was a part of this mission—important, but far less crucial than he was. And if he got distracted by me or worried about my safety… I could take care of myself, and he knew that, but Nikolai Zaregova was not a man who could just take his hands off something. If anyone had a great sense of responsibility, it was him. Not to mention the scandal it would cause for both of us, from which I wouldn't walk away unscathed.

For a little while more, I didn't want to think about what all this meant. Luckily, I was pulled out of my thoughts by Nikolai calling to me from the bathroom.

"Are you coming?"

"Huh?" I called back.

"It's, '*whatever you say, General*,' for you."

I laughed and clamped my lips tightly shut when I heard the shower start, and Nikolai poked his head out through the doorway. "Will you come to the shower, Jameson?"

"It's *Major* Jameson," I told him, as I tried to slip past him into the bathroom. But the attempt was futile, as he'd already grabbed me in the doorway and threw me smoothly over his shoulder, making me cry out.

Then he shoved my butt straight up under the cold jet—making me scream even louder.

CHAPTER 19

I woke up to feel a hand caressing my spine—*Nikolai's* hand. My mouth smiled before I even opened my eyes and looked at Nikolai, who rested his head on one of his hands.

"What time is it?" I asked as I closed my eyes again.

"Too late."

I opened one eye. "Nik…"

The nickname brought a smile to his face. "It's six o'clock."

"Shit." My eyes opened wide.

I quickly rolled out of bed and began to collect my discarded clothes while he observed the scene with one arm propped under his head, smirking. I had to be back in my own room before anyone saw me leave his. This was not the time to be confronted with questions about Nikolai and me. *Damnit*, I didn't know if that moment would ever come.

When I was completely dressed, and took my coat from the chair, he got out of bed in only boxer shorts. I had to look away. Otherwise, I would end up in that bed again, and I just didn't have that luxury right now.

He walked to the door and leaned carelessly against the

wall. I put on my coat and sighed deeply as I reached for the door handle. Nikolai stopped the door with his hand.

"This looks very familiar to me," I told him, looking at him expectantly.

He wasn't amused. "When will I see you again?"

"I don't know," I replied with a shrug.

"Tonight?"

"I have a late shift." I thought for a moment. "Maybe tomorrow?"

He growled. "I have meetings all day."

"Um, the day after, then?"

Nikolai shook his head. "Then I'll be back in the field."

A heavy weight settled in my stomach. "*Oh*," I managed. The idea of Nikolai going back out onto the shadow plains made me nervous. I knew it was unjust, because he'd gone out into the field countless times—always with a positive outcome.

Nikolai sighed and lifted my chin with one finger so that I had to look straight at him. "I'll think of something," he said, then planted a kiss on my lips.

"Okay," I muttered and nodded, not knowing what else to do. I slipped out into the cold, then walked quickly to my room to change into clean clothes before the day officially began.

* * *

That afternoon, the capital ordered three missions to go onto the shadow plains, one after the other, all assigned with extracting a mutant. The scientists had reached a point in their research where they had to do a lot of testing. And the more test objects, the better. Therefore, three teams were set up, which I wasn't part of as I was now in charge of the medical department. Nikolai, however, had decided that he would join all three subsequent missions, and that there would be only one day between each extraction. Which meant it was going to be very difficult to see him in the coming weeks.

I arrived at the medical center and walked down the hall towards the monitoring room, meeting Raven along the way.

"Major Jameson," she saluted, nodding at a passing soldier.

I smiled. "Lieutenant Renée. How are the preparations going?"

When there was no one else in the hall, her eyes widened, and she sighed deeply. "I just got back from the briefing for the third mission. The different missions succeed one another onto the shadow plains so quickly that all briefings are held beforehand." Raven shrugged dubiously. "Do you know why there is such a rush?"

I shook my head. "Just that the scientists need additional mutants for testing."

This morning, I read the main base reports, which clearly stated that three extractions had been scheduled in close succession. But the question Raven asked had also started running through my head: why *was* there such a hurry?

"General Zaregova will make sure it all goes well, whatever is going on." I knew I would hear something from Nikolai if I needed to. The inclination to ask him was strong, which made keeping work and relationships separate already a challenge.

Raven tilted her head at me in surprise. "Look who suddenly has faith in the General."

I rolled my eyes and decided to ignore her comment. "I would have loved to have gone into the field together,

Raven."

She nodded in agreement. "This will be my last field mission. Crazy to think I'll be back home in a while. What am I supposed to do with my life then?"

Raven followed me to the monitoring room, where we paused in front of the glass for a moment. The screens that hung high on the walls were off because no scouting or extraction was underway as preparations were made for the three upcoming missions. The tables, lined with screens, equipment, and anatomical scale models of various body parts, were unmanned and deserted. Tomorrow, this room would fill with medical professionals again, who would support the soldiers in the field with various matters.

"You are all slowly leaving now. In a few weeks, I'll be the only one left," I laughed, but didn't truly find it funny. I'd gotten a lot of support from the group of soldiers who had slowly become my friends.

Kelian and Cardan were due to leave together in a few days, as they had come in together and had been close friends from the start. After their last mission, they would leave the base. They would go with the first group, in which they were placed together. But before Raven left with the third mission, Kelian and Cardan had promised to have a little goodbye party with the both of us.

Raven put her hand on my shoulder and smiled, causing dimples to appear. "We'll all see each other again in the civilized world in a few months, Hunter."

I wanted to believe that. But in here, it was so hard to see beyond the present day. I didn't dare to think about the future for fear of being disappointed.

Before I could answer, my pager went off, and I noticed

an incoming call from Barak. Adding that to the mountain of paperwork I still had to complete for the upcoming missions, I couldn't afford a lot of free time.

"I'll see you later, okay?" I told her and walked out of the hall before she could see the emotions written on my face.

* * *

The days before the first team was due to go in were stressful. They were long days in which the main base sought a lot of contact, and I had to fill out even more paperwork. Those days had also made me decide that I didn't like being the head of the medical base—that I'd rather do the work I'd studied for. I missed it—being a surgeon.

The night before Nikolai was to leave with the first group, had me restlessly toss and turn in bed. For the past few days, I'd been scouring the rooms I entered, hoping to run into him before he went out into the shadows and time would separate us. But I knew that when *I* was that busy with work already, I could only imagine how much he had to do.

I slowly let go of the hope I held on to because I knew I wasn't able to see him anymore. I didn't even know what was going on between us—let alone that I had any right to see him.

Feeling frustrated, I opened my eyes and calmed my restless legs before getting out of bed. The thoughts of Nikolai intoxicated me, and I had to clear my head if I wanted to get some sleep tonight. I jumped into some comfortable clothes with a thick overcoat and didn't even bother to close my boots after putting them on.

Once outside, I sat against the door and closed my eyes. The cold and silence did wonders for my nerves. A sharp breeze blew across my face and ruffled my hair. I could now focus on my stimulated senses instead of the seemingly endless stream of thoughts.

"Hunter?"

I was startled and abruptly looked up at the person in front of me.

Nikolai had his coat closed high and held out a hand to me. "What's going on?"

"Nothing," I said, stunned, and grabbed his forearm. He pulled me up smoothly. "I just couldn't sleep."

"Me neither," he confessed. "It certainly won't help to sit out here. Let's get inside."

My throat had dried up, and I silently opened the door to let us in.

"Last time I was here didn't quite go according to plan," he chuckled, unzipping his coat.

I was staring at him blankly. "Are you insane?"

"What?" Nikolai raised his eyebrows.

"You have to get up in six hours. You shouldn't be here right now."

Nikolai pursed his mouth. "You're right."

"You have some important weeks ahead of you, Nikolai."

He gave me another half-smile.

I walked over to him, put my hands on his shoulders, and shook him. "*I'm serious.*" But the words didn't sound convincing, as I could only think about how happy I was to touch him again. His scent—blueberries and pine—flooded my senses.

"I know, Hunter." Nikolai folded his arms around me and put a hand in my neck. "Me too."

My heart got distressed by his presence, and I looked up

at him. "It's crucial that you're well-rested for tomorrow. You have three missions in a row! That requires inhumane effort."

His eyes crinkled in the corners as he looked down and stared at me. "Let me sleep here then," he whispered, lowering his head to kiss me before I could protest—which I probably didn't even have the strength to do.

He explored my lips and opened my mouth, working his way in with his tongue. Mine quietly took its time to welcome his before breaking the kiss and sighing deeply.

"I don't think this is smart, Nik," I muttered against his chest.

He tilted my head towards him. "And yet I want it." His lips met mine again, and this time I didn't stop him. His mouth only grew more compelling, and I couldn't think clearly as he peeled the clothes off my body, and I stripped him of his. Until there was nothing between us anymore, and we only touched each other with our bare skin.

Nikolai wrapped his hand around my hair and lowered me down onto the bed. He got in between my legs and went out to explore with one hand. All the while, he looked at me, making me forget to breathe.

"*Hunter*," he growled hoarsely and shook his head in astonishment.

I looked at him and responded, "Just come."

Nikolai leaned over me and placed himself in front of my opening. "A bit impatient, are we?" He pushed my legs a little further apart with his hand.

"Please?" I tried more sweetly.

"Because you ask so nicely," he responded breathlessly, then slid himself inside. He gave my body time to adjust to him deep within me. All the while, he kept looking at me—

with eyes that seemed almost wholly taken over by his dark pupils.

Nikolai bowed his head and buried himself in my neck, planting kisses that scratched a little because of his stubble. He let himself slide back completely until only the top was left and then slid back hard, eliciting a moan. From me? From him? I had no idea.

He let himself go in and out at an increasing pace as I felt him throb deep inside. His mouth traced a path downward, and he took my breast in his mouth. He sucked at the tip, which was already hard, and bit down gently.

He slowly picked up the pace, and I felt myself reaching a climax.

Nikolai hoisted himself up on his arms and roamed over me with a predatory gaze, leaving me on the edge of orgasm. He sat up and turned me with my back towards him, and planted kisses from my neck down to my tailbone. "Your skin smells like mint and basil."

That made me laugh. "That's quite specific." *Said the hypocrite who thought he smelled of blueberry and pine.*

"It's divine," he responded, sliding his hand from my ass to my thighs, all the while kissing my neck.

I felt him press urgently against my butt, and I subtly rubbed my back against him. Nikolai was all too happy to oblige. He guided himself in front of my entrance and buried himself in me from behind.

He filled me even more thoroughly, and his breath caught as he moved roughly inside me, like he was possessed. The quiet lovemaking of before had given way to pure and unadulterated desire. He tightly gripped my waist and let a hand drift to my chest. I ran my hands through his hair and along his neck to hold on while I completely surrendered to him.

He lightly bit my neck and let himself slide out of me, causing me to let out a protesting sigh. Nikolai laughed hoarsely and bent my body forward on the bed, then grabbed my hips and guided me on my knees in front of him. He pushed them apart and buried himself deep inside me again. Still sensitive from the first time, he moved at a fast pace, and I came much faster than I had ever done in my life. The tension made me strain everything together so that he, too, eventually rammed into me and shook with relief.

Nikolai kissed my spine and sat there a little longer, just like last time, before leaving me.

He hooked his arms under my back and knees, carrying me into the bathroom, where he cleaned us. He also carried me back—*which was completely unnecessary*, as I'd told him.

In bed, I turned towards him so that I could admire his handsome face.

"I'm afraid I won't be able to take a normal step tomorrow," I confessed.

He laughed. "Hunter, you know that's what every man wants to hear, right?"

"Show off."

Nikolai laughed again, a deep and pleasant sound that bounced off my bones, and I ran a hand over his face. A moment later, I planted a feathery kiss on his mouth. "Thank you for finding me."

Nikolai shook his head and pressed me close to him. "I'll always find you," he muttered softly, running a gentle hand over my hair.

I slept so well the rest of the night that I didn't even notice

Nikolai slipping out of bed to get ready and head out onto the shadow plains with the first group.

CHAPTER 28

The first time I saw Nikolai again had been from a distance, between the first and second missions. I had been walking towards the medical center and had seen him about a hundred yards away, talking to someone I didn't recognize. As the other person walked away, Nikolai had glanced my way, and our eyes had locked. I hadn't realized I was walking in his direction until someone else came up to him and said something—after which I quickly turned around and changed direction.

The morning after the first group returned from the mission, all I had received was a report saying it had gone according to plan, and I received two living mutant children at the medical center a few hours later. These had been approved and sent to the capital before the second group had a chance to go into the field again.

That evening we had the promised farewell of Cardan and Kelian. It was a welcome distraction from the last few days of uninterrupted work in the monitoring room or attending meetings. Every night I came back to my room and tried to get myself to sleep, doing my best not to let my mind wander off to Nikolai.

The four of us had arranged to meet in the bar, and gathered in a secluded area at the side of the room. We'd been drinking for the return from the first mission and their return home. It was a crazy idea that in a short while, Raven and I would be the last of the group I had met on my first day, who had become my friends.

Cardan walked up with four bottles of beer in his hands, and Kelian clapped loudly. "That's how it's done!"

Raven rolled her eyes at me theatrically, and I pursed my lips as I reached for a bottle.

"Hunter," Cardan began as he slid onto the couch next to me, "I have a confession to make on my last night—a clean slate and all."

I looked at Kelian and Raven opposite me in question, who did their best to look severe and shook their heads. *We don't know what he's up to either*, they seemed to say.

"I think it's a shame that things never worked out between us," he winked.

Laughing, I gave him a hard shove, causing him to lose balance and grab the table.

"What?" He ran a hand through his hair, grinning. "I thought you should know."

Shaking my head, I looked from Raven back to him. "You really are an idiot."

Kelian nodded in agreement. "Say it even louder, Car; maybe the General can hear you."

My head shot up, almost at the same time as Cardan's brows, and he poked his head out of the cubicle inquisitively—into the bar. Raven punched Kelian in the arm.

"What?" he asked her in disbelief, rubbing his arm. "It's plain as day that he wants her."

"Oh?" I responded almost casually. "Is it now?"

Raven's eyes darted to me apologetically. "Yes," she answered immediately, "but that doesn't mean it has to be said out loud." She let her eyes drift to Kelian in warning, who innocently put his hands in the air.

I looked at Cardan, but he just shrugged. "I don't know a thing."

Kelian and Raven exchanged glances before looking back at me. Kelian wanted to open his mouth to ask me something, but Raven got ahead of him and put her hand on his, silencing him.

"Enough about the General," she said. "This is your last evening; what do you want to do?"

"Talk about Hunter and the General," Cardan replied with a laugh, and Kelian gave him a high five.

"No," I snorted, "forget it."

Raven kicked him under the table. "Besides that."

Kelian took a long gulp of his drink, watching Raven absently withdraw the hand she had still on his. He wasn't the only one who could pick up on signals, and when his gaze crossed mine, I raised my eyebrow at him.

Cardan toasted. "Let's drink to good friends, and that we may see each other again in Barak."

"Cheers," I said, raising my glass to him.

* * *

I had spent the day before the third and final mission was due to leave with Raven. She'd told me that she was more nervous than usual because she felt like there was more on the line:

there was an end in sight for her now, and when she would come back from this mission, she'd go home again.

Triggered by Raven's words, I looked up to see if more medical personnel were due to go home soon. People usually didn't stay for more than three to four months, and I'd noticed that the personnel who were to leave after the third mission had not yet been assigned a replacement. Not that it wouldn't be possible later on, as I had been sent to mission 3B rather last minute—but it was strange that no replacement had been assigned at all. That's why I sent a message to several of my contacts in Barak about this. However, three days later, I still did not have a reply.

Unlike Raven, I wasn't quite ready to go home yet. I could imagine it felt different for her now that she was actually about to go back home, but, to be honest, I didn't want to think about home at all yet. There were still too many things to sort out before I was ready to leave. For example, Nikolai and I hadn't even talked about after all this—we hadn't even discussed the situation here. I knew he wouldn't leave until the mission was finished, but what did that make us? Were we together? Would I wait for him? Did *he* even want me to? It wasn't like our responsibilities would disappear once we got back to Barak. Nikolai was still a general—perhaps the most famous in all of Ardenza, after General Domasc. And I was still a major, which made me inferior to him, which meant that my career was still on the line.

I couldn't easily shake it off, and it became increasingly more difficult to pretend that the growing feelings I had for him didn't exist.

The night before the third mission, I ran into him after I locked my office and walked toward the exit of the quiet medical center. I had to suppress the impulse to touch him when I saw him being followed by a group of soldiers. Instead, I stopped to salute him, as was expected. He had nodded indifferently, but I saw the truth in his eyes.

After he exited the hall, I leaned back against the wall and stared hopelessly at the ceiling. It was tough to be so close to Nikolai and not be able to say anything, but it would have been even harder if I hadn't seen him at all.

* * *

The last group had entered the shadow plains that morning and were on their way to Elm. I was the head of the monitoring room, and because the head was always in contact with the general or leader of the group, I knew I was about to hear Nikolai's voice again.

I still hadn't received a response from Barak to my question about the replacements. Even after at least four mutants were sent their way within a week and a half, they'd dodged my messages—as if I'd never sent them. During the meetings, too, they'd talked around it or said they'd sort it out for me—and never came back to it. Although it was incredibly frustrating that they didn't respond, except for a confirmation on the safely arrived mutants, it did make the paperwork a lot easier. Usually, I would have had to do a lot of administration around replacements. But the lack of clarity made me feel uneasy.

With Nigel Kent now in the field as the mission's surgeon, others had to take over his head monitoring shifts, and I had scheduled myself at the start of the mission. I usually had to be available for the capital at all times, but since I hadn't had any contact with them for the past week, I saw a rare opportunity to take over a shift. Working in the monitoring room was a pleasant change from my duties as the medical head. At least I was immersed in the medical field again.

I stepped into the monitoring room and put on a headset as I nodded to the medical staff who had gathered at their monitors and saluted. My headset went live, and I switched to the General—Nikolai's line.

"General Zaregova, Major Jameson speaking. I'm taking over this line this morning. Let me know if you need anything," I routinely said through the microphone, my heartbeat quickening.

On the screen, I could see how far apart all the soldiers in the field were from each other, and I signaled the location of Nikolai, close to that of Nigel Kent.

"Will do, Major," he replied.

I held my breath at the sound of his voice and enjoyed it for a second before looking up again and turning off my microphone. Obviously, I couldn't tell him how nice it was to hear his voice, but I hoped he knew.

Breathing in deep, I looked at the screens on the wall, where information started flashing about the other group members, who were close together in the sewer. Raven belonged to this group, and it was clear that their heartbeats were increasing, which made me frown.

"What's going on there?" I asked behind me.

The Lieutenant who was in contact with Raven began talking hastily through her headset when I noticed Brigadier General Lucas taking a hard blow to his body, and multiple alarms went off at once. Raven's right side also glowed red on the screen, but there weren't any bleedings or open wounds, indicating a different type of impact. My concentration focused on her information, and my heart raced in my throat. *Come on, Raven. You're almost home.*

It was quiet in the room as we watched and waited while the group members were fighting for their lives.

Multiple vital signs flashed: body scans showing multiplying red and blue spots due to internal and external bleeding. Several heartbeats spiked, and loud signals sounded—but the chilling silence on the other end of the line was worst of all. My eyes darted across the screens, seeking clarity, and I forced myself to take a few deep breaths.

After what seemed like an eternity, a soldier in the back left of the room started speaking into the microphone and gave us a thumbs up. There was a collective sigh, and I could see the group members' heartbeats slowly decreasing. That the injuries that had been previously blinking violently were not life-threatening. That everyone was still alive.

"Lieutenant Renée reports that a mutant attacked them from a side corridor in the sewer. The mutant is disabled, and all group members can still move independently," the Lieutenant behind me said.

I nodded in relief. "Once the adrenaline has subsided, we'll check again to make sure everyone is okay."

I was glad my heart rate wasn't hooked up to anything because it had definitely gone through a similar increase. The Brigadier General had been hit in the head, and Lieutenant Renée, Raven, had gotten a hard blow to her side. Judging by the impact on her body, her side was getting pretty bruised. I hoped her willpower to go home was enough to carry her through the pain.

"Do you have contact with the others?" I heard Nikolai ask through my earpiece.

I straightened my back upon hearing his voice. "Yes. A mutant attacked them, but they have the situation back under control."

"Any wounded?"

"Also. But as far as they say, and we can see here, nothing life-threatening."

"Thank you, Major," Nikolai said after a beat of silence.

"Of course," I replied with a tremor in my voice, and clicked off my microphone again.

Silence fell on the other end of the line, and it remained for the rest of my shift.

CHAPTER 21

NIKOLAI

It had made a difference, Nikolai decided after Hunter had gotten on the line and he'd heard her through his earpiece. Hearing her voice had empowered him in a way that was new to him. Not something he could overthink right now, because a mutant in the sewer on the first day…

He'd been walking down the tunnel with Lieutenant Colonel Kent when he'd lost contact with the other group for a moment. When his Brigadier General hadn't answered, Nikolai had known something was up.

Fortunately, they had resolved the situation and met that first evening in the bunker. The damage had been minimal: Lieutenant Renée, among others, had a severe bruise on her side that would undoubtedly turn blue, and Brigadier General Lucas had received a hard blow to the head. But the monitoring room had told them not to worry—so he tried not to.

Now they were walking through the deserted, dark streets of Elm, heading for the nest of mutants they'd discovered on the previous mission and left alone. They had gone to other nests during the first two missions, as there wasn't much known about the mutants' intelligence or animal instincts. It was too risky to go to the same nest every time and hope the mutants couldn't spot a pattern.

Nikolai glanced at his sensor as they arrived at their destination—an old, run-down office building on the corner of a major intersection—and spotted a group of six mutants inside. During the second mission, he'd seen two smaller mutants among them, and they had to separate them from the rest of the group.

He motioned for his team to split into two, one of which would distract the mutants, as discussed during the briefing.

His Brigadier General's group knew what to do, and settled down a short distance away to fire flares at a building in the distance. They crackled and left a trail of white sparks as they cut through the air, before hitting their target and softly continued to hiss. It was enough noise to grab the attention of the older mutants in the group and draw them away from their nest—just enough not to attract the attention of other groups.

Three of the mutants left the building and went to investigate the sound.

Nikolai motioned for Lieutenant Renée and Lieutenant Colonel Kent to follow him so they could get a direct view of the mutants he could now distinguish: the remaining full-grown mutant and the two smaller ones—just as expected.

At best, they could take both the little mutants with them. They'd brought back two mutants each time thus far, and had long since reached the goal of the capital, which had only requested three. But Nikolai didn't want to leave anything to chance, and he was confident he could take both smaller mutants with him and reach his goal faster.

Cautiously, they walked into a ruined building directly opposite the mutants' nest, while the other group still distracted the rest of the mutants with flares.

Lieutenant Renée took a gas bomb from her backpack and began checking it. They would throw the gas bomb at the mutants' residence. It would go off silently and render the smaller mutants unconscious, after which the large mutant would realize what was happening, and he would also—due to the threat—start exploring the area. Nikolai would then fire another arrow in the opposite direction, luring the mutant away from his whereabouts.

In theory, it sounded perfect.

But just as Lieutenant Renée gestured to Nikolai that she was ready to throw the gas bomb, they heard a loud crack behind them. Nikolai spun around at the sound and saw that Lieutenant Colonel Kent had sunk with one leg through the old, gnawed floor and was trying to pry his leg free—resulting in even more noise.

He raised his hand to Kent, who immediately stopped moving.

Nikolai looked back to the hideout and saw what he feared: the sound of the creaking had been enough to lure the mutant out of its lair—to them.

Nikolai's heart began to pound wildly as he and Lieutenant Renée crouched to free Kent's leg from the floor.

The mutant already figured out where the noise was coming from, and Nikolai heard him enter the decaying room, pulling his knives from the sheaths on his back.

"Retreat," he said in his earpiece to his Brigadier General

and absorbed the force of the mutant's attack with both blades crossed high in the air. The move only slightly grazed the mutant, and Nikolai struck again but had to take a step back to catch the mutant's next attack first so he wouldn't break his fingers.

When the mutant came for him, Nikolai managed to pierce his side with full force, but the mutant nevertheless managed to push him straight through the wall.

The crunching of Nikolai's ribs sent bile up his throat, and he felt an unbelievable stabbing pain in his chest, which seemed to become sharper and more dominant with each breath.

"*General?*" he heard through his earpiece. "*General, what happened?*" They'd probably seen red-hot signals flashing on their monitors.

"I'm okay," he replied curtly and broke off contact, leaving him on his own. They couldn't do anything for him now anyway.

He struggled to his knees and slit the dying mutant's throat to stop the shrill noise it was producing, but Nikolai knew the damage had already been done.

The other team ran towards them, and Brigadier General Lucas helped him to his feet. Nikolai pointed towards the mutants' quarters. "Throw the gas bomb and get those young mutants. Both of them."

The Brigadier General nodded and ordered the other team to grab the mutants while continuing to support Nikolai.

"Help them," Nikolai rasped.

"But General—"

"*Now,*" he ordered.

His Brigadier General released him, and Nikolai felt

unsteady on his feet. He tried to take a deep breath, but that only made the stabbing pain worse and made him see stars.

With one hand pressed to his chest, he saw Lieutenant Renée come out, followed by Kent. The moment Raven stepped through the hole, the already ruined outer walls gave way. Lieutenant Renée dove forward and landed on her hands and knees, but Lieutenant Colonel Kent was too late. As he jumped, one of his legs was caught under the collapsed concrete and got crushed entirely. Kent clenched his teeth and began to moan inwardly. His eyes almost popped out of their sockets, and the man was doing his best to make as little noise as possible—even though the effort was futile.

Nikolai was sure that if the other mutants hadn't retreated already, they would surely come this way now.

While the other group was busy grabbing the young mutants, Nikolai got up and walked over to Kent, with the Lieutenant already on her knees before him. She had contact with the monitoring room.

Together they tried with all their might to pull Lieutenant Colonel Kent out from under the rubble but soon found it was to no avail. His leg was stuck under hundreds of pounds of concrete, and from Kent's reaction, there wasn't a lot left of it.

The other group came up with the two little mutants in their arms, and they pointed back hastily. "The other mutants won't stay away for long, so we need to get out of here as soon as possible."

Nikolai nodded and looked at Lieutenant Renée, who had fallen silent. "I've never done that," she said into her earpiece.

"Done what?" Nikolai asked.

She looked up, her face covered in dirt. "His leg needs to be amputated."

Brigadier General Lucas looked gravely at Kent. "We don't have long."

"We're not leaving anyone behind," Nikolai said decisively. "I'll do it."

Lieutenant Renée's eyes widened, but she said nothing as she began to rummage through her tools for the right materials.

"No!" Lieutenant Colonel Kent groaned, realizing what was about to happen and pushing Lieutenant Renée's hands away as she tried to tie a rubber band around his leg to stop his blood circulation and prevent arterial bleeding.

Nikolai grabbed Kent's face and looked him straight in the eye. "It's your only chance of survival. You're going to lose your leg anyway."

Kent's eyes flooded with fear, but he nodded at his general. Nikolai gave him a piece of leather to bite on. The alcohol they carried was used to sterilize the large knife and Kent's leg. After Lieutenant Renée prepared his leg, and Brigadier General Lucas wrapped his arms around Kent, Nikolai put the blade firmly into the flesh and began to saw. It didn't help that Kent started screaming as Nikolai sliced through the leathery muscle tissue. Everyone had held their breath until Kent finally vomited and passed out from the pain.

Nikolai's face twisted from the wound in his side when he finally cut through the bone. His rib cage was protesting with every move he made. It hadn't taken long in the end, and the moment Kent's leg came loose, he wiped off the sweat on his forehead with his sleeve.

Lieutenant Renée had made sure that the rubber band was kept tight around the Lieutenant Colonel's leg, minimizing the blood loss, and his Brigadier General hoisted the unconscious Kent onto his shoulders without Nikolai having to ask.

He still heard a buzzing in his ear, indicating that they were trying to reach him from the monitoring room, but since he and his group had no time to lose, he left it unanswered. Besides, he didn't have to answer to hear how bad it was—he knew. The damp patch under his clothes had already spread far and wide, giving him enough indication to know that things weren't going well. He didn't also need to hear it.

He would have it looked at when they were safe, but since his trauma surgeon was now life-threateningly injured, this could wait. He would push through, Nikolai promised himself, and he thought of Hunter waiting for him on the other side.

* * *

The first place, as this bunker was called, finally came into view, and a weight was lifted off his shoulders. The two mutants could be shipped off to the capital, and then… His heart nearly burst, thinking about that future.

Nikolai was jolted from his thoughts by a sound from behind them.

Mutants.

Even if the mutants hadn't had good hearing, they could have tracked the path. They would have been able to track them by the blood that leaked from Kent's wound alone, leaving a dark red trail. And now they were heading straight for them—purposefully, as it was clear that they were focusing on the individuals with the young mutants in their arms.

Shit.

Nikolai had trailed behind and was now the only barricade between the mutants and their targets. He instinctively reached for the swords on his back but cringed at the movement. It caused the wound in his chest to tear even deeper.

He ran out of time. The mutants reached him and slammed him hard to the side, causing his ribs to scream out as he fell to the ground and hit his head against a rock. His head was spinning, and one of the glasses of his night-vision goggles was cracked, causing his vision to regain its sight slowly and for him to breathe again.

Meanwhile, the soldiers holding the child mutants were attacked, and he saw Brigadier General Lucas, carrying a still-unconscious Kent on his shoulders, collapse to the ground.

Nikolai had lost too much blood, but still tried to place his arms at his sides and push himself up. He had to do something—wanted to do something to protect his soldiers. The wound in his chest allowed him to reach only one side of his body, which gave him just enough room to pry his gun free from its holster.

Don't ever shoot, he was told during his first military training, *only if there is no other option.*

Well, Nikolai thought as he flicked the weapon's safety, *here goes nothing.*

He waited for his head to stop spinning and steadied his arm. Taking a deep breath, he closed one eye and aimed at his target.

Nikolai shot two of the three mutants straight through the head—dead in one shot. He missed the third because his breathing had jerked its way out. But the next shot hit the mark, and the last mutant, who had approached the sound, fell dead to the ground.

His hands trembled as he watched Lieutenant Renée run up and down, helping several people, whom he could no longer see clearly, into the bunker.

Nikolai exhaled and lowered his head onto the cold, damp ground.

Then the world turned black.

CHAPTER 22

"I expect to be done in a month," I told my parents, rocking the chair I was sitting on with my legs. It was the first time I called them and I had promised them I could give them five minutes later in the day after my shift that morning. So, when my pager signaled *communication problem field* from the monitoring room, I gritted my teeth and ignored it. There regularly were connectivity issues with the field, but they were often resolved quickly, and it wasn't like *I* could do a lot about that.

If it was urgent, they would alert me.

"Here, they don't talk about mission 3B on the news anymore—like it's inactive," my father replied dubiously.

I frowned. "It's more active than ever, actually."

"There's even a rumor that the mission is already over because the scientists think they've found the solution," my father said.

Sighing, I frowned even deeper and looked down at my stack of paper—which in no way indicated an ending mission. "Those kinds of rumors go around every year."

My mother sighed in agreement. "Just be careful there,

Hunter." She looked up with a small smile. "In any case, we are very proud of you."

I smiled back. "Thank you. Being interim medical head is less intense than it sounds, but a huge responsibility—and a big step in my career."

"We just want you to be happy," my mother smiled more broadly, "and if that means your career, then that's completely fine." She looked up, suddenly putting a hand on her chest, and exclaimed, "Oh yes! By the way, at my work, they asked if you've met General Zaregova yet?"

"Of course I met him," I replied quickly, feeling my cheeks turn red. I hoped my parents couldn't see it. "He's my general."

"*And?*" my mother continued, intrigued, her curiosity peaked by something in my voice. "What's he like in real life?"

Before I could answer, my beeper went off again. This time with an emergency signal from the monitoring room: *multiple critical functions.*

Startled, I looked up. "Mom, dad. I have to go. Love you!" And I disconnected before they could say anything back.

My chair bounced against the wall behind me so hard it rattled the filing cabinets as I shot from the desk and sprinted to the monitoring room.

* * *

Arriving in the monitoring room, I heard various voices, beeps, and signals going off. One by one, the conversations with the field seemed to come to a halt until only one microphone was still active—Raven's.

I looked up at the screens and scanned the information to

determine what I was already afraid of: the various members of the group, except for Raven, were all injured or unconscious—or completely critical, in Nigel's case. And—I realized, watching the last screen as my heart split in two—in the case of Nikolai.

"Major Jameson, Lieutenant Renée is asking for you."

I took a seat at a table and connected with Raven, reviewing her stats. Except for a very high heart rate and external wounds, she appeared to be okay. "Raven?"

"Hunter," her voice broke, "my god."

"What's going on?"

Raven seemed to be panting with exertion and puffed, "The mutants."

Someone else tried to get her camera to work, but the lens appeared to be broken. *Of course.*

"I'm trying to get everyone in, but they're all injured."

Everyone? I bit my tongue before blurting out the question.

"It's too much," Raven continued. "I can't do this alone."

"Make sure everyone is inside first, Raven. Then we'll get an overview," I said calmly. "You're doing well. We are here, and we are all listening. You are not alone."

"I'm afraid there'll be more coming," she squeaked anxiously on the other end of the line, exerting her already sore muscles. In her condition, she was forcing too much.

"You can do this," was all I could say.

After a while, we all heard a door slide shut with a loud suctioning sound, indicating that the room where Raven and the rest were in was hermetically sealed.

"Okay, Raven," I said firmly. "Next step; how many injured are there?"

Raven was still panting. "Five wounded: three slightly

injured, one seriously—that's Kent," Raven said. "And the General…" Her voice trembled a little, but she sounded brave. "Gods."

I held my breath.

"*General Zaregova.* Keep your eyes open, General," I heard Raven say through the microphone. "It doesn't look good," she concluded to us softly.

My eyes scanned the monitors and came to the same conclusion. It was clear that there were two critical cases, neither of which had much time. But two critical patients at the same time—while only one person could help—would definitely end up in two life-threatening situations.

I opened my mouth again and pushed away my panic, "Is everyone else stabilized?"

"Yeah, but…" Raven gasped, and there was silence on the other end of the line. I heard fabric tear before her voice came back. "Kent has lost too much blood. I've already tied off his leg, but I don't think he's going to make it." She breathed jerkily. "The General has a head wound and multiple broken ribs, it seems. He may also have a collapsed lung, but I can't say anything about the condition of his other organs." She was silent for a moment. "Hunter, I can't do this alone. I'm going to lose him if I tend to the rest first."

"The other organs seem intact for now, Raven," I replied calmly, looking at Nikolai's body scan, cogs turning in my brain.

There was only one thing to do.

"Stabilize him as best as you can, then focus on Kent with our help."

"Then I won't be able to help the General, Hunter. He dies if I help Kent."

"No, he won't die," I replied firmly. "Kent needs your help more right now."

"I can't save them both, Hunter." Raven's heart rate picked up again. "I don't even know if I can save *one*. Please don't make me choose."

Raven was right, of course—she couldn't do this alone.

"You don't have to choose, Raven. Keep the General as steady as you can for as long as you can and gain time for *me*."

Again, there was silence on the other end of the line, and I looked up at the team behind me. "How long does it take to reach the first place?"

They looked at me in shock but replied, "One hour, on foot."

"Is there another way to get there?"

They stared at me, shaking their heads.

I moved my focus back to the screen. "Raven, leave the rest if they're stable, but keep an eye on them. We'll be helping you from here, every step of the way."

The people in the monitoring room nodded my way, and I spoke into my microphone again, "Do everything you can to stabilize the situation for an hour. I'm coming."

Raven wouldn't have to go through this alone, and I would do everything I could to save the group members. But above all, I wouldn't leave Nikolai's life to chance. He couldn't just disappear out of my life now. He simply couldn't. I refused to believe that.

I threw the headset on the table and grabbed a new communication and first aid kit from the shelves. Someone ran with me through the medical ward to get the necessary supplies, which I needed for the various procedures.

There was no time to do anything else before I pushed

open the doors of the building and sprinted onto the grounds. On the way, I passed Jordan, who was talking to someone, but looked up at me as I raced by. A second later, I heard two footsteps fall in step with me, and he ran beside me.

"What's going on, Hunter?" Jordan asked, frowning, with worry in his eyes.

I answered in a hurry. "Zaregova's team has problems. Only Lieutenant Renée is uninjured. Lieutenant Colonel Kent's leg has been amputated, and the General…" I swallowed and gathered myself. "It's an emergency."

Jordan grabbed my arm and tried to stop me. "And you're going *there now*?"

Nodding, I tore myself free. "I can't let Raven do this alone." And sprinted again.

"*Who?*" he asked.

"Lieutenant Renée," I snapped impatiently, but he didn't seem to listen.

"You can't do this alone, Hunter; it's too dangerous," he called after me.

"Come with me then," I replied.

Jordan swore and then ran ahead of me. On the way, he opened a room where he took out two pairs of night-vision goggles and a rifle.

"Where are they?"

"The first place."

He nodded. "Do you know the way?"

"No." I clenched my jaws in frustration.

Jordan shook his head and ran with me to the wall, where he typed in the access code. Someone came running and waved her arms wildly to where we were standing by the wall.

"They're coming," I hissed.

Jordan grunted. "I'm doing everything I can."

Finally, the door opened, and Jordan pulled me inside. He quickly closed it again, making it impossible for them to open it on the other side. He'd unlocked the next door before there was a loud banging on the first and muffled voices sounded. We were unauthorized to go through the wall at the moment, and there was too little time to explain.

I realized that, without Jordan, I would have literally gotten nowhere. "Thank you, Locke."

Jordan looked at me, but didn't smile. His face was solemn as he strapped the weapon to his body. "I owe you this one, Hunter, but I hope you know what you're doing. I don't want to lose my position for nothing—if we survive at all."

I nodded, and put on my night vision goggles to hide the tears in my eyes.

Jordan gave me a thoughtful look before he also put on his night-vision goggles, and together, we stepped out of the open door—onto the shadow plains.

CHAPTER 23

After walking rapidly for almost an hour, we finally arrived at the bunker. Jordan had pulled me behind him before I could walk out of the dense forest, and he quietly explained that we had to make sure there were no more mutants around before we could go to the team that needed our help.

I had never been here before, and it took me a moment to realize that the bunker was built in a mossy hill. Around it, I saw nothing that showed any sign of life, but I trusted Jordan's insight and willingly placed my life in his hands. After a while, Jordan gestured for me to follow.

We crept to the entrance, where we passed the ravages of the battle. Several dead mutants were lying around, and I was amazed at how lucky the group had been. How had they taken out those mutants? Jordan swore and answered my thoughts.

"Bullets…" he muttered, turning a mutant's head toward us with his foot, revealing a small, dark hole where his eye had been.

At the door, he typed in the access code, and it sprang open with a sigh. A disk of light appeared through the opening, and I slipped inside.

"Raven?" I called after the door had closed and we were cut off from the outside world. I hurried across the room, taking in the scene, which seemed to be reasonably stable for now. A soldier with an arm in a brace was cleaning the wounds of a person lying on a table. There was another soldier on the couch with both arms over his face. And...

My eyes glided anxiously over the white sheet in the corner of the room, which clearly covered a human body. I bit my tongue so hard that I tasted blood and continued my way through the bunker.

"Raven?" *Where is Nikolai?*

"Hunter, here," I heard Raven reply wearily.

At the end of the hall, I ran into the room from which Raven's hoarse voice had sounded and saw her standing over Nikolai's body. My breath caught as I walked over to his other side. Nikolai's face was contorted with pain, and his breath came in short, erratic bursts. But he was still breathing.

He was still alive.

"Nigel?" I just asked Raven as I pictured the white sheet again.

She shook her head and swallowed loudly. Her eyes filled with an emotion she couldn't deal with, and unresolved panic engulfed her face.

I ran my hands over Nikolai's chest. "How much anesthetic have you given him?"

"Everything that was left." Raven shook her head, and her voice trembled. "I used the last syringe before cleaning his wounds and drilling a hole in his skull to relieve pressure on his brain."

"You did well," I said and grabbed her arm. I made sure

she looked straight at me. "You made the difference between life and death for so many people today, Raven."

She looked away, and I saw her bite back the tiredness out of her eyes. "The General went back for Kent. He got caught with his leg under a large chunk of concrete that we couldn't lift. We soon learned we had to amputate his leg if we wanted to save his life, and General Zaregova was not going to leave him—so he performed the procedure despite his own injuries." Raven swallowed and I, too, looked at Nikolai now.

Brave, stubborn Nikolai.

"But the collapse of the building attracted even more mutants to the sound, so we took Kent along, and it slowed us down a lot. We had come a long way until the mutants caught up with us. That last fight would have been the end if the General hadn't drawn his gun."

Raven blinked and focused on my hand, with which I tried to keep Nikolai awake by tapping his chest under a protesting murmur from him.

"Nigel died half an hour after I spoke to you," she explained. "He had lost too much blood."

"You gave everything, Lieutenant. You couldn't have done more," I heard Jordan say behind me, and Raven looked up at him, her eyes filling with tears again.

"Everything wasn't enough," she simply said.

I looked straight at Raven. "Clean yourself and try to get some rest. I'll take over."

Jordan nodded at me when I met his gaze, and he walked over to Raven, who had turned her eyes back to Nikolai. He gently placed a hand on her shoulder, causing her to look up at him again and blink. For a moment, she seemed about to say something, but after one more look at me, she nodded and walked out of the room with Jordan.

My hands slid over Nikolai's bare chest, and I gently applied pressure in several places. Some of his ribs were—as Raven had concluded—broken. His fourth, fifth, and sixth ribs hadn't been able to withstand the force of the blow he'd received, and one of the ribs had split his skin open.

There wasn't much I could do about broken ribs, but I had to make sure the wound was closed quickly to stop the bleeding. The fracture had indeed caused a collapsed lung, which meant that I had to place a drain. It had to be there for at least a few days to let all the fluids and air out.

My fingers continued on the path to his abdomen, and there I put pressure again in different places. When his face didn't twitch in pain, as he had done when checking his broken ribs, I released my retained breath with relief. For now, everything seemed to indicate that the rest of his organs were not damaged. His chest didn't feel unstable either, which meant I didn't have to open it unnecessarily.

Kent's death probably saved Nikolai's life. If Raven hadn't had time to relieve the pressure on his head, he could have succumbed to it. But the consequences of brain damage due to the pressure on his head would have to be revealed later.

I opened the small case I was carrying and prepared some pain relief in a syringe. It would subdue the pain from his broken ribs and collapsed lung, reducing the risk of pneumonia. He couldn't physically handle that right now.

"Hunter?" Nikolai rasped confusedly, and he turned his head to me as I put the syringe in his arm. "What are you doing here?"

I put my hand on his cheek and rubbed my thumb over the corner of his mouth. "Try not to talk, Nik; I'm going to help you."

* * *

After Nikolai lost consciousness from the anesthetic, Jordan entered the room with the rest of my things.

"How is she doing?" I asked him.

"She's holding up."

Jordan then fixed his concerned gaze on Nikolai, who already seemed quite out of it. He would mumble something every now and then, but I couldn't make anything cohesive out of it. An uneasy feeling washed over me.

This was exactly why they wouldn't let you operate on family or loved ones as a surgeon.

My hands automatically started completing the standard tasks: disinfecting, sterilizing, and clearing the surgical site of any resistance or obstacles.

The hole Raven had made in Nikolai's skull was clean and had done its job. She had delivered great work. Typically, his lungs would have been treated before his head—but since Raven hadn't been trained in complex medical procedures, it was a good thing she hadn't done anything differently.

I, on the other hand, *had* been trained for it, and now it was my turn.

Finishing up his head, closing his wounds, and installing the drain in his chest for the collapsed lung, was doable. I would place the drain in an incision between two ribs and suture it in place. In theory, this should provide quick relief, but the drain should be left in for a few days, and his broken ribs also needed time to heal. For this process to run smoothly and prevent inflammation, Nikolai needed advanced drugs. I had taken a few shots of this increased cell growth medication with me, but it wouldn't be enough to get him back on his feet in a few days—especially not with the drain.

Jordan did everything I told him to do, which made things run a lot smoother. When I had finished all the steps and finally closed Nikolai's wound as far as possible with the drain, I looked up and saw Jordan stare at me.

His gaze spoke volumes, and I turned around to the faucet to rinse my hands. When I finished, I saw that he was still looking.

"What is it?" I asked Jordan carefully.

He stared at me, smiling a little, and narrowing his eyes—like he realized something. "You love him."

"What?" I felt my heart shoot into my throat.

"You love him." He gestured with his head at Nikolai.

I looked away and felt the blood rush to my face but said nothing.

Then he laughed out loud. It was a surprisingly happy sound. "You really love him, don't you?"

My eyes darted to Nikolai, and I blinked a few times. I rubbed my arms and nodded slowly.

I did love him.

My hand moved over my cheek unintentionally and came back moist. My feelings for him didn't make me weak, I realized. They had enabled me to help him against all odds. It had made me strong enough to step onto the shadow plains—for him.

"Don't cry, Hunter," Jordan said softly, walking over to me, and wiping away my tears. "It'll be okay."

I shook my head, laughing. "I'm not crying from

sadness."

"Does he know about your feelings then?"

My eyes closed for a moment, and I shrugged. "I have no idea."

Jordan cleared his throat. "Let me rephrase that, because we, men, require a certain degree of clarity." He raised an eyebrow in emphasis. "Have you *told* him about your feelings yet?"

I looked up. "No."

His other eyebrow raised too. "Maybe that's a good place to start *when* he wakes up."

"But—"

"He's the General," Jordan finished, nodding. "That's right. *So?*"

"So, he's *the General.*"

"What does it matter?" Jordan asked, shaking his head.

"My career is important to me, and this mission is important to him, so—"

"Things *only* have the meaning you give them," Jordan roughly interrupted me. "If I had given the fact that I am Kenneth's son any power—at any point in my career—it would have become a power that could be used against me. Ignore the things you don't want to affect you, because if you make a point of something, it eventually *becomes* one."

I bit my lip and repeated his words in my head. Of course, he was right.

Jordan laughed again. "What if you get a promotion and people question it? Then what? Do you think they're going to reverse that promotion, Hunter? *No.*" He shook his head. "You accept that *fucking* promotion and get on with your life. Don't give it any meaning, and then people won't have reasons to pay attention to it. Only the people who don't want to face their own shortcomings will find something in others to blame—to make themselves feel 'better'."

He ran a hand through his hair. "The question is, would you rather want the approval of *those* people or be with the man you love? If it were up to me, it would be a damn easy choice."

It *was* an easy choice, but one that scared the living hell out of me. I was afraid to lose control of my life if I gave a little too much of myself to someone else.

"Don't try to reason yourself out of this, Hunter. We do enough of that in life." Jordan took my hand and placed it over my heart. "Get out of your head and *feel*. What do you *really* want?" He shook his head again and looked at me. "Life is too short to not follow your heart, Hunter. Listen to what it has to say."

Before he walked away, I opened my mouth. "Thank you, Jordan—for everything today."

He only winked at me before he walked out into the hallway.

Bewildered, I sat down next to Nikolai and let the tears flow. I couldn't bring myself to leave him and go to the sleeping quarters. I also wasn't ready to face the white sheet in the central room yet.

Now that Nikolai was relatively stable and calm, I clasped his hand and held him tight. I hoped he could sense I was there and instinctively reached for the dog tags I wore around my neck. Nikolai should have worn his necklace on this mission.

I let my tears run wild as the adrenaline was running out. I took his necklace off and put it back around his own neck.

Today there had been a possibility that Nikolai could have died, and that tag belonged around the neck of a living person.

Dead. He could have been *dead*.

Pressing my forehead against his hand, I felt its warmth— a sign that Nikolai was still here. And I would personally ensure that it would stay warm.

Nikolai would make it because he was not rid of me yet. He couldn't be rid of me yet.

Our story had only just begun.

CHAPTER 24

NIKOLAI

Nikolai opened his eyes but had to immediately shield his face against a blinding light. His eyes adjusted, and he slowly became aware of the warmth on his skin.

The bright, warm light came from the sun.

Nikolai looked around and noticed that he was lying in a field of tall, green grass. He carefully pulled himself up and smoothed his clothes. He looked down and saw that he was wearing his official, formal army uniform, including decorations and medals.

Strange… He couldn't remember putting it on.

Nikolai shook his head briefly and looked to the right, where a beautiful white house stood in the open field. Not just any house, he noticed—it was the house he'd grown up in. Where his mother still lived.

He began to walk toward the house as if some unseen force was pulling him there, and he noticed that the sky was completely blue, except for a few soft white clouds. That made Nikolai frown, though he couldn't quite place why.

He heard a loud laugh and immediately saw a woman running around the corner of the house with a child trailing after her. His gaze sharpened, and he registered the way she moved—the color of her wild curls. Hunter.

He would recognize her anywhere.

He automatically adjusted his path and walked towards her. Suddenly, she turned her head his way, and everything in him focused on the woman in front of him. Hunter Jameson was the answer to a question that had haunted him all his life. She took his breath away, unleashed something in him, and she'd been doing that since the first moment he'd rested his eyes on her.

She placed a hand above her eyebrows against the sunlight and squinted her eyes. When she saw who he was, her eyes widened, and she lowered her arm, dumb-struck.

Hunter gently knelt in front of the child and said something to him softly, running a hand through his hair. The child ran inside, and she began walking towards Nikolai. She was wearing a long, loose dress with a floral pattern. Her long dark blonde curls hung free, and swayed slightly in the gentle breeze.

When she reached him, she smiled slightly, but the corners of her mouth twitched as if she tried to resist the motion.

"Hello, Nikolai," she said, sounding so remote that it could have been a whisper. Her cheeks turned a little pink. "It has been a long time."

Something wasn't right, Nikolai realized. They had just seen each other. But where?

"Hunter," he said, grinning at her pink blush. "What are you doing here?"

She planted her hands on her hips. "What are *you* doing here, Nikolai?"

"This is my childhood home."

Hunter tilted her head. "I didn't know that."

"How could you have known?" he simply asked.

She lowered her gaze to the ground, giving him a full view of her long, dark lashes.

"Do you want to come in?"

Into his own house? But he nodded and followed her. He noticed that her back stayed tense the entire way.

"What do you think of it?" he asked, pointing to the house when she looked at him.

She smiled and looked up. "It's perfect. That's why we bought it."

"Bought it?" he muttered in surprise and frowned. He couldn't imagine his mother ever selling it. Except, perhaps, to him.

Hunter led him into the house, and he took a seat on a couch she gestured to. "Tea?"

Nikolai dipped his chin and ran a hand through his hair, trying to organize his thoughts.

She went to the open kitchen and made tea. He kept looking at her and noticed that her cheeks were still a little flushed. Nikolai had to resist the urge not to get up from the couch and approach her—or hoist her on top of the kitchen table and slowly roll up her dress until he was able to trail a path upwards with his mouth.

Instead, he sat frozen on the couch. And, somehow, he sensed a distance between them… He felt like an outsider in this room, which made no sense at all, since it was exactly as he remembered it.

Hunter sat down next to him on the sofa, a bit further away, and smiled a little wider now, letting her amber eyes join in. "How are you?"

"Good."

"I'm pleased to hear that." *It's been a while*, her eyes seemed to echo.

Nikolai frowned and regarded her thoughtfully. Then his eyes wandered to her hands. He captured one from her lap and ran his thumb over the ring she was wearing on her finger. She stiffened. He let go of her hand after turning it over and inspecting it.

"No calluses." Nikolai slightly bowed his head, and his eyes met hers again. "When was the last time you worked?"

He let his eyes slide past his own hands and noticed that he was not wearing a ring. Hunter's throat moved up and down, and he saw that her gaze had followed his. She let her eyes land on the mug of tea in her lap and opened her mouth as the small child burst into the room with a toy plane in hand.

"Mom, look what I found!"

Mom?

Hunter gave him an apologetic look and shifted her attention to the boy "Robin, can't you see Mommy has a guest?"

Mommy? Nikolai thought again, feeling his heart pound frantically inside of his chest. He looked at the little boy—Robin—again and noticed that he had freckles, as well as brown hair and dark eyes.

"Who is this?" he asked Hunter, disregarding the child for a moment.

He wanted answers. Was this his child? She had said they hadn't spoken in a long time. But… he couldn't imagine not seeing her for years. A knot formed in his stomach at the certainty that something was off.

Hunter looked at him and raised an eyebrow. The boy approached him cautiously. She grabbed the little boy's hand and smiled sweetly at him. "This is General Zaregova, Robin."

"Wow…" The boy's eyes widened. "Cool."

Nikolai couldn't help but grin at the little boy, who resembled Hunter in so many ways that he immediately liked him. But when he shifted his gaze to Hunter, the smile disappeared. Her gaze was filled with such pain that for a moment, he didn't know what to do.

"Robin, can you let me talk to the General, please? I'll come back outside as soon as possible."

The boy shrugged indifferently and ran out of the door with the plane high in the sky.

"Why are you here, Nikolai?" she then asked him directly, a severe look in her eyes.

Nikolai frowned again and swallowed. "What do you mean?"

She stood abruptly and fisted the fabric of her loose dress. "You can't suddenly show up out of nowhere after all these years."

"What are you talking about, Hunter?" He rose too, extending his hand to her, and rubbed his thumb over her cheek. *So soft.* "Is Robin mine?"

She took a step backward and looked at him with wide eyes as if she had burned herself on his touch. "*How dare you,*" she hissed furiously.

He could see the flames igniting behind her eyes. "If we've somehow seen each other in the past ten years—let

206

alone slept together—then this is the first time I've heard about it." She shook her head.

Ten years? What was she talking about? His brain couldn't complete the increasingly complex calculation.

"That's *not* my child?" he asked.

She turned red. "No, *Robin* is *not* your child."

"And he's not yours either?" he insisted, hoping she could explain this bizarre situation.

Hunter's mouth dropped open as if he'd slapped her in the face. "He *is*. I'm sorry to disappoint you, Nikolai. I was present during the birth of *my own son*." She said the last three words with a tight voice.

"And you haven't seen me for ten years?" he repeated, incredulously.

The words *own son* echoed through his head. That son had a father, and he wasn't it. Nikolai wanted to smash something.

"No," she replied, frustrated. "*Where is your head?*"

He ignored her biting remark. "How did that happen?"

"What?"

"That we didn't see each other for so long."

She laughed cynically. "Why are you asking me? You thought your work was more important than looking at a life beyond the army."

He scanned her face, pausing for a moment to wait for her to burst out laughing, to admit that she was fooling him. But he'd never seen her look so pained before. "I've let you walk out of my life? I don't think so."

"Ten years too late, Nikolai," she muttered, blinking back tears. "You're *ten years* too late."

His heart was beating like crazy as he looked at the unshed tears in her eyes. Clearly, it wasn't too late. She apparently still had feelings for him. How could he have ever let her walk out of his life? What was more *important* than her?

"Hunter…" He wanted to pull her to him, but then the front door in the hall opened, and a deep voice filled the house.

"I'm home!"

A tall man with brown hair, brown eyes, and a muscular build stepped into the room. Nikolai had no idea who this man was, but he immediately moved a little closer to Hunter and let his eyes drift to him. "Oh, do we have a visitor?"

We? Nikolai's frown seemed to be part of his regular expression from now on.

The man raised his eyebrows as he cast his gaze on Hunter. "What's going on, Hunt?" He walked over to her and took her hands in his.

Nikolai took a few steps back, as if the two of them had stepped into a bubble, from which he was unceremoniously banned.

"Nothing." Hunter shook her head. "I'm just surprised. General Zaregova brings back so many memories."

She didn't want to meet Nikolai's eye.

The man's head turned to him. "General Nikolai Zaregova?" the man asked in disbelief. "It's an honor." He shook his hand in appreciation, and Nikolai could only stare at the man.

"Is it?" he asked Hunter, who was still avoiding his gaze.

The man burst out laughing, clearly unable to read the situation, and clapped him on the shoulder. "Modest, too. No, my wife has nothing but good things to say about her time at mission 3B." He smiled and looked back curiously at Nikolai. "To what do we owe the pleasure?"

Wife. At the word, Nikolai's entire body had stiffened. *Was this Hunter's husband? The boy's father?*

"Oh." He cleared his throat, but it only seemed to tighten further. "I just came to see how she was doing. I do that with everyone who has been so crucial to the mission."

The man smiled admiringly at Hunter, *his wife*. "We are all very proud of her here."

"Naturally," Nikolai muttered softly, trying to catch Hunter's eye, but she apparently only had eyes for the man next to her. He felt the start of a stabbing headache.

The man beamed down at her and seemed to have forgotten entirely about Nikolai—which he couldn't blame him for. Not *entirely*.

"Has Robin met him already? I'm sure he would love meeting a real general."

Hunter nodded. "He thought it was *cool*," she laughed. Relatively weak, Nikolai thought.

The man—*her* husband—looked up at Nikolai again with a friendly, conspiratorial grin. "He'll tell all his classmates about it. What a lucky guy."

Nikolai gave him a crooked smile, but felt ice running through his veins. *This man was the lucky guy.*

The man gently placed his hand on Hunter's stomach, and Nikolai had to hold everything together not to frustratingly sink on his knees in front of them at the intimate gesture.

"And how's this little one?" he heard the man mumble softly.

Nikolai's smile faltered, and only now did he notice that the belly under her loose dress was slightly swollen. When he looked up from the hand, at Hunter's broad smile, he saw red.

The man leaned over and planted a kiss on her mouth, which she returned.

Nikolai couldn't stand it anymore and shot out of the house without another word. He walked quickly past the little boy, who looked up at him, startled.

He started to run—leaving it all behind until he saw the sun go down. Nikolai finally dropped to his knees and let out a loud sob.

The sun reached out, closed his eyes, and bathed him in a warm light that flashed electric blue behind his lids.

Nikolai cried out. He wanted to turn back time. He had to—he had to—he…

* * *

Nikolai opened his eyes with some effort as if both sockets had been beaten black and blue. He had felt and seen the sun on his skin, he realized—the old sun, the real blue sky, and… *Hunter.*

His heart was beating wildly. Painfully wild, as he felt a sharp pain rip through his chest.

Nikolai gazed at a dark ceiling, then lowered his chin a little to look out into the room. His head was still pounding, hard.

When his hand also woke from sleep, he felt that someone was holding it. He let his head roll slightly to the side and saw dark blonde hair in a messy braid. The hair that had moved so freely in the wind, just a moment ago.

Hunter.

She slept on the table he was lying on with her head leaning on her folded arms. She clutched his hand tightly with her own as if she couldn't bear to let go of him.

Nikolai still felt the stings of the distant dream in his heart.
He wouldn't let go of her either.
He would fight for her.

CHAPTER 25

Nikolai's recovery went well—the first night. But because I didn't bring enough of the medication he needed, it wasn't going fast enough. His healing process needs to be quicker so that he could be transported back to base, and because I had a feeling that a defenseless Nikolai equated a defenseless world. It made *me* feel defenseless.

He needed to move independently as soon as possible, and be taken back to the base, where he could fully heal and regain strength. But the drain first had to do its job. That took at least two days.

The following day, Nikolai had awakened and had been completely lucid. He immediately resumed communication with the base and the capital from his bed. Because he had '*a lot to discuss*'. He was also able to eat a little, which was a big step, especially in the absence of the advanced medication. He needed all the extra strength he could get.

We hadn't been able to talk one-on-one yet, as the only times I could be alone with him were at night when I sat beside him while he was sleeping. The courage I needed for that conversation was somewhat absent. It didn't help that

Nikolai had looked at me a few times with so much emotion that I had the urge to sew his eyes shut. It felt like a mirror was constantly being put in front of me, making me hear Jordan's words again: *what does it matter?*

But my feelings and reaction to everything that had happened in the past few days were extremely new to me. Never before had I felt this way or cared so much about another person. The line between life and death on this mission was so thin that I was afraid of shooting myself in the foot. And assuming he returned my feelings... It would only complicate things further.

I knew I had to face my feelings soon—but not yet. Now, Nikolai's recovery was the priority. He had made clear with his looks that he wanted to be alone with me for a while, but I had pretended not to pick up the signal. Of course, he knew that, because Nikolai was always aware of *everything*. So, his looks had turned into small, calculating smiles when no one was watching, which resulted in me trying to avoid him as much as possible.

But that wouldn't last, as Jordan and the others had decided to go back to base. It was important that the wounded received the care they needed, and there was no point in staying here if the majority of the group could return. Nikolai also had to get back to base as soon as possible. There, the right help, medicine, and equipment were available to make his healing process as smooth and fast as possible.

But *surely*, Nikolai had immediately agreed and told Jordan that he just needed *me* to last a few more days in the bunker. And when Jordan turned his back to Nikolai, the look he gave me spoke volumes.

* * *

Before the rest of the soldiers were due to leave, I found Raven in the central room late in the night. She sat on the floor, her legs folded underneath her and with her back against the wall.

I sat down next to her and rolled my head to her. "How are you?"

"All things considered… okay." Raven shrugged. "Major General Locke helps."

We were quiet again for a moment before Raven clasped her hands together and continued, "We'll take Nigel back to base tomorrow so he can be taken to his family and have a decent burial."

I nodded, and she looked my way.

"Do you think they want to know who was responsible for his death?"

"You are not."

"I wasn't able to help him in the end," she immediately countered. "*You* could have saved him."

I sighed and turned my body toward her so I could look her straight in the eye. "With everything that happened, I couldn't have saved him either. An amputation in the field, without additional medical care, is, in most cases, a death sentence. The only way he would have survived was if mutants hadn't attacked you."

For a moment, Raven was silent again, then nodded almost imperceptibly. She seemed to blink away her tears but then smiled at me. "I'm glad you came."

"Me too."

"The General will be very grateful to you, too," she continued.

Nodding, I turned back against the wall and stretched my

legs out in front of me. I looked at the ceiling and avoided her gaze. "He's grateful to you, too."

Raven bit her cheek as she continued to look at me and she grinned. "It explains *so much*."

I held my breath and looked up at her, but her smile only widened. When I was about to open my mouth, she raised her hand and shook her head. "Don't even try to deny it."

My laugh caught in my throat. "I wasn't about to. I wanted to ask what made it so obvious." She was now the second person who had noticed my feelings in a short time. "Did you hear it from Locke?"

Raven raised her eyebrows and shook her head. "He knows?"

I nodded, and she shrugged. "Not bad. But no, I didn't get it from him. Since you spent most of your time on base with me, I just noticed that you were often distracted with staring at the General." She laughed again. "Which is not shocking since you are certainly not the only one who has ever stared at him. But you're the only one he's ever stared back at. It was obvious once I started paying attention."

"My god." I put my hands in front of my face. "Do you think the others know?"

Raven shrugged. "People only think that the General finds you physically attractive, as Kelian mentioned, but no one else suspects that you actually have something going on. And it's not like word would spread around the base if anyone did suspect it. They're all scared of the General."

I nodded in agreement. "Hopefully, it stays that way."

"They won't hear it from me," she promised.

"You're a good friend."

"*And* an accomplice," she said, with a devilish smile on

her lips. "Under *one* condition."

I raised my brows at her.

"Tell me everything that happened between you two." She sighed deeply and put her hands over her heart. "As a hopeless romantic, I want to know everything, and I'm almost desperately welcoming the distraction at the moment."

My laugh had already escaped my body before I realized I was holding it back. I'd never shared these kinds of feelings with anyone before. Raven was the first person in my life I spoke to about this sort of thing, and now that I thought about it, she was also the first real friend I'd ever had. So, I told her everything.

Eventually, the conversation turned into sharing more stories with each other. We talked about relationships, our childhoods, and family, until we both yawned loudly and went to bed, still smiling.

* * *

The soldiers had left early that morning, led by Jordan. Before they left, I had pulled Raven into a big hug, and she'd given me another wink before putting on her night vision goggles.

When they were officially gone, I contacted the base, who could tell me when the group had safely cleared the wall. I got in touch with Jordan shortly after their safe return to base, and he said I had two days to get Nikolai to strengthen— before switching over to another plan. He also told me that I should probably have a *good conversation* with him about his recovery.

I suspected that Nikolai would not be strong enough in time for the journey back. Not without the capital's meds running out, but I still wanted to give it a little bit of time—

give his body a little more grace to fight on its own. You have a lot of control in the medical field, but not over everything.

My heart was beating wildly as the realization that I was now alone with Nikolai sunk in. I walked down the hall to the room set up for him and knocked.

"Hunter," he sighed as I entered and immediately extended his hand to me. A gesture of affection. Maybe even more than that.

I grabbed his hand and lowered myself into the seat next to him.

Nikolai frowned in concern. "Your hands are cold."

They were not.

I put one of my hands on his forehead, and he hissed in relief.

"You're hot with fever, Nik. It's your body's way of warding off disease and healing."

But that wasn't very beneficial in his case. Now that my meds had run out, and I had to make do with the last dose of pain medication, I started to worry about his other lung. If his aching ribs interfered with his breathing too much, he could still develop pneumonia and—

Nikolai squeezed my hand and drew my attention back to his face, where a smile had appeared. "You dragged me back from hell again, Hunter."

"You weren't in hell," I replied.

He sighed painfully. "Then, at least I was very close."

After we looked at each other for a while without speaking, I felt tears welling up in my eyes. Tears that had been fighting their way out for two days now.

Nikolai's gaze softened to the point of tenderness, and he ran his hand over my face to wipe them away. "Oh, Hunter.

Don't cry."

I sniffed in frustration. "I understand now, Nik—what you tried to warn me about in the beginning."

He said nothing, but continued to stroke my cheek comfortingly.

"It's so damn hard to love someone who keeps throwing themselves into the heat of battle, and it's so damn hard to have feelings for someone who isn't even assured of the next day."

Nikolai smiled. "No one's assured of that."

I rubbed my hands over my eyes. One of my great strengths has always been to reason in times of great stress and panic. But when it came to Nikolai—his life and his health—I didn't even want to face the most obvious. There was no possible scenario for me in which he didn't make it.

He clutched my hand again and ran his thumb over the back. "So, you love me?"

I looked up and met his penetrating gaze. "I've rushed onto the shadow plains like a moron to keep you alive—what do you think?"

"Good." Nikolai squeezed my hand. "Because I love you too."

"You do?" I asked.

He nodded and released my hand to tuck some escaping hair behind my ear. I smiled and leaned forward gently, then pressed my lips against his, being careful not to get close to his chest.

Nikolai smiled against my lips and put his hand at the nape of my neck to pull me closer. He deepened the kiss before breaking away and ran his fingers over my face. "About after this—"

I shook my head. "We'll talk about that later. You have to rest and recuperate first."

He nodded wearily, and his eyes softened before he closed them again, quickly sinking into a deep slumber.

* * *

Nikolai had slept the rest of the day and night, and only woke up when I brought him food and drinks or came to check on him. He smiled at the childhood stories I told him over dinner.

I told him about the afternoons when I often went to get ice cream with my father after school. That my parents sometimes danced together in the living room at night when they thought I was asleep. How I would lay down at the top of the stairs in the hallway to look down at them through the railing. I'd told him that it was one of the reasons I joined the army. To put an end to all horrors, to all despair. To give people the peace that my parents had found in each other and to keep it.

But hours afterward, when Nikolai stopped responding cohesively to questions and only grew warmer, I knew his body was losing the fight. I'd walked out of the room and called Jordan. He had said that the monitoring room had also expressed their concerns a moment before and was just about to contact me when I called him. Jordan was going to consult the capital about the next step, and would immediately get back to me.

Not even half an hour had passed before Jordan called.

"Hunter, I'm coming straight from the meeting. We have permission to come by hover heli. To make sure they fly well, I'm coming too. Be ready with Nikolai in half an hour."

Overwhelmed with relief, I took a deep breath. "Thank

you, Jordan."

To come with a hover heli meant they were serious: there was an important reason why the only model present on the base was never used. It was common knowledge that the helicopters and planes could not navigate above the shadow plains, so using them would have been pointless. The signal from the equipment and receivers seemed to be somehow disrupted by the presence of the mutants, causing you to fly blind. However, they could use the vehicle for short distances because navigation could be done manually, especially now that Nikolai's situation was critical and he desperately needed the help of medication.

It was rare for it to be deployed, but General Nikolai Zaregova was extremely important to the mission—they had no choice. He'd done so much for Ardenza that Ardenza owed him something in return.

Once I'd packed everything and prepared for departure, I began the task of getting Nikolai ready for transport. I made sure to keep the drain in his chest, and strapped his body to the stretcher I had moved him onto, checking that his head and ribcage were free from pressure.

I heard the bunker door slide open and footsteps coming my way. Jordan entered in a clean uniform and glanced over to Nikolai. He looked solemn as we lifted the stretcher together and took it to the helicopter. This happened at a rapid pace, with Jordan keeping a close eye on the environment for any signs of danger.

I sat down on the chair next to the stretcher to keep an eye on Nikolai. After we sat down and fastened the seat belts, I checked the buckles around Nikolai's body and saw his eyelids flutter.

"Too tight?" I asked him and watched him swallow with effort.

His eyes sparkled as he shook his head with difficulty.

"All right," I said, and grabbed his hand.

Nikolai turned his head in my direction and whispered, "Thank you."

"For what?"

"*Everything.*"

The word carried so much meaning that I could only stare at him. He held his breath as I leaned forward and ran my lips over his cheek. His whiskers pricked me, and I sat up straight again. I could still feel the spots where the hairs had touched me tingle after the hover heli was finally ready to go and took off.

Nikolai exhaled weakly and let his eyes fall shut, but I did not look away.

CHAPTER 26

At the medical center the next day, I was quickly updated and started on the piled-up paperwork. Of course, I immediately had to account for the spontaneous rescue mission to the main base in Barak, but due to the success and circumstances, no sanctions were imposed.

After the hover heli had landed behind the wall yesterday, we were met by a team ready to help. I'd recognized most of the faces of the medical staff, and immediately knew that I could leave Nikolai in their capable hands—where he could finally receive the help he needed.

Jordan had been talking to the pilot when he glanced down at me and told me to rest for a couple of hours before going back to work—and that I would be the first to get notified if anything changed with the General.

After a few hours of sleep, I'd gone to the medical building to see if I could be of any help. At first, I had used the hustle and bustle of work as an excuse to avoid my feelings for Nikolai *and* Nikolai himself, so I still hadn't seen him since we got back. I knew there was nothing I could do anyway—and that he needed rest to let the meds do their work. But when someone came to tell me that Nikolai was awake at the end of the afternoon, I didn't quite know what was holding me back.

I walked into a hallway and saw Raven coming my way. The moment she saw me, her eyes widened. I beckoned her, and together we quickly slipped into my office. Raven hugged me the moment the door closed.

"I'm so happy to see you again." She sighed as she let go of me, and lowered herself into one of the chairs. "That was a hell of a week."

I took a seat behind my desk where I folded my arms and tapped one of them with a finger. "You wouldn't say," I said sarcastically.

Raven looked up and grinned. "How was it?" Her eyebrows arched and spoke volumes. "Between you two?"

The corners of my mouth subconsciously trailed a path upwards. "Good." My smile disappeared again. "But his condition quickly got worse."

She nodded. "We all held our breath over in the monitoring room, as his data kept fluctuating."

"And how are you doing?" I asked, eager to change the subject.

Raven's face fell, and she looked away.

"Is it Kent?" I asked, clearing my throat, and watched her stiffen completely at the mention of his name.

"Raven, if you feel the need to talk about what happened, or what you might be blaming yourself for, I'm here for you."

Naturally, I knew what it felt like to lose a patient, but losing someone in the field due to limited resources was a tough pill to swallow. You would always keep pondering the 'what if,' and doubting whether your abilities were to blame.

I could only be there for her.

Raven swallowed, and I saw that she was doing her best to keep control over her emotions. Red crawled from her chest up to her neck.

"Raven," I said softly, "it's not your fault."

She shook her head, and her gaze moved to her hands. "No. I know that. It's just that I felt so helpless." She looked up again. "I just can't help but wonder if I couldn't have done more. Whether the whole situation could've been avoided."

"You did everything you could, right?"

Raven shrugged and took a deep breath. "That's just it. What if I can't do enough? What if we were better educated in self-protection?"

I thought about this for a while. "Then a lot of injuries could be prevented, and the number of medical crises reduced," I replied, and she nodded firmly.

She ran a hand through her dark curls. "I've never suffered from a dual function in my career. But in this situation, I *was*. I no longer knew what I stood for. It would have been nice if I hadn't had to carry each responsibility on just *one* shoulder—if you know what I mean.

"It certainly helped a lot that you and Major General Locke came. That you didn't leave me alone." She rolled her eyes but smiled broadly. "Not that I suddenly want to become a surgeon or anything—gods no. I've seen enough medical shit for a while. It's also far too much studying, and I'm more of the doing type. But I'll see. I'll be home in a week, and then I can rearrange my life."

I let her words sink in and smiled. "Friends don't abandon each other, right?"

"No." Raven got up and smiled back at me in a way only

she could. "Friends don't abandon each other."

* * *

Nikolai was somewhere on the floor above, and I felt his presence as if he were tethered to me. Without overthinking it, I got up and walked quickly toward the surgical complex. There was only one separate sickroom in the whole medical building, as the space did not allow for much more luxuries.

I saw that there were no people in his room at the moment, so I decided to sneak in, quickly shutting the door behind me. Nikolai immediately looked up from his tablet, and I saw a light twinkle in his eyes. He was still in bed, connected to various devices.

"Hunter."

I tilted my head and inspected him. "How are you feeling?"

He didn't answer right away, as he was still looking at me. "They removed the drain and closed my chest again. My lung function is quickly returning, thanks to the medication, and my head is no longer bothering me." He took a deep breath. "Another operation isn't necessary."

"That's good," I said, more lightly than I felt. I didn't know what to do with my hands.

His eyes shone admiringly. "And that's what you can do under pressure. Imagine what you would be capable of if you had more time."

I let out a breath and sat on the edge of his bed. "I think the reason I perform well is because of the pressure. I've always been that way, with everything."

"Is that why you joined the army?"

"It is useful," I agreed.

After a beat of silence, I looked up at him, trying not to make my smile too cocky. "By now, you must be glad they sent me since this is the…" I pretended to be deep in thought, counting my fingers, "*third* time I've saved your life?"

His face twisted into an honest grin. "I'm very grateful to you, Hunter."

I put my hand on his leg and tried to lighten the mood. "I suggest you put your money where your mouth is."

His eyebrows raised. "You don't want to know what you've just set in motion, Jameson," he replied with a sly smile.

"I missed you," I said. "These past weeks."

He nodded and took my hand. "So much was happening at once that I had to focus on the assignment. *For us.*" His thumb stroked the back of my hand soothingly. "I'm not officially allowed to talk about it yet, but a lot is going on behind the scenes."

"You don't owe me an explanation, Nik. You were just doing your job," I responded firmly. My heart still had to recover from his words: *for us.*

"I do," he started again. "I'm extremely lucky that you were sent here. I was an asshole in the beginning…" The corners of his mouth curled up when I didn't contradict him. "But I thank the gods on my knees every night that you're here."

I casually waved the gesture away. "You are so dramatic." But I felt the effect of his confession settle deep inside my heart.

He winked. "That's what a near-death experience does to a man, Hunter. Get used to it."

This time I didn't laugh.

'Get used to it.'

I wanted to, so badly.

I felt myself crawl back into my shell, to not have to deal with the emotion, and as if Nikolai realized what was happening, he took my hand and held it close to his heart—which I felt beating, steady and strong.

Slowly, I stood, without meeting his eyes, and focused on a point on the wall. The conversation of a few days ago flowed between us like electricity.

He squeezed the hand he was holding lightly. "Hunter…"

I shifted my gaze to his and smiled weakly. "Try to get some rest, Nikolai."

With that, I slipped my hand from his and walked out of the room.

A few days ago, when he said he loved me too, I'd never felt happier. But the further I walked away from him now, the emptier I seemed to feel.

* * *

The next morning, I went back to the surgical center because I couldn't resist visiting him.

A night of advanced medicine and cures that we had at our disposal had ensured that he could walk on his own again—making him fully dressed at the table in his room when I entered.

"Major Jameson," he just said, gesturing to a male nurse standing in the room.

"General. I wanted to check in and see how the recovery is going."

The nurse looked up and saluted me. "As it stands now,

the General can get back to work in two days. His body is responding well to the drugs, and his wounds have almost completely healed. The lung is also almost back at seventy-five percent of its original capacity."

"That's good to hear," I replied dully, and smiled at the nurse, who had finished preparing the correct medication and gave Nikolai an injection. Then he left the room.

Nikolai took a sip of his drink and looked up at me. He was wearing a black, short-sleeved shirt that hugged his muscular body. The dog tag I'd given him back, now hung on top of his clothes. He saw me looking at it and turned his head to the side for a moment, studying me. Then he got up and walked to the door, closing it gently.

"It's yours, Hunter," he said from behind me, and carefully walked towards me, curling his arms around me. "But I'll keep it with me for now."

I swallowed and turned around in his embrace. It felt good to be held by him.

"I'm relieved to hear that you're responding well to the medication. This mission cannot do without you."

One corner of his mouth curled up. "What about you?"

I swallowed. "Me?"

"Yes, you?"

My mouth went dry. "I don't know what you mean."

"Oh, please, Hunter. We both know you know *exactly* what I mean." He seemed almost impatient. "Didn't we already have this conversation?"

"Then you already have your answer."

"What has changed, Hunter? What happened between then and now, except that you got scared?"

I clenched my jaw tightly, and I let him think what he

wanted. I hadn't *gotten* scared; I'd never *stopped*—it had only gotten worse after I'd come face to face with his mortality.

Nikolai let go of me and took a step back. "Hunter, I honestly don't feel like circling each other forever."

I folded my arms and looked at the ground.

"Did it mean nothing to you, then?" he asked.

"Of course, it did," I replied, but I didn't want to think about the conversation we'd had. The man I loved had the most dangerous profession in all of Ardenza—he'd almost given his life for it. I was *terrified*.

Nikolai frowned. "What has changed then?"

"Nothing." *Everything.* My feelings were growing by the second.

"Hunter—"

"Is there anything else I can help you with?" I asked, wanting to remove myself from the situation. I couldn't— didn't want to feel that pain.

Before he could react, the door opened again, and another nurse came in to scan his lung.

Judging by Nikolai's frustrated look, he was not done talking.

I saluted him as he looked at me through narrowed eyes. "I'm interested in the result, General," I muttered, and slipped out of the room before he could say anything else.

CHAPTER 27

I was woken in the middle of the night by a thunderous bang and sat up straight. At the next charge, I rolled off the bed and immediately lowered myself with my stomach on the floor, protecting my head with my hands.

When a second later proved that nothing was breaking down around me, I slowly let myself come back to my feet and opened the curtains. I rubbed the sleep from my eyes in a hurry.

Far away, near the wall, the sky was filled with embers and lit up by flames. There was another loud bang, and I saw fragments crashing down the wall. It was only a small part of the large wall, but the sight of it sent shivers down my body.

What the hell was going on?

All over the base, people came running out of buildings towards the wall. I could even hear them scream outside— and there was *never* any screaming.

I ignored the panic I felt bubbling up and dressed quickly. Outside, I started running toward the wall to see what was going on, only to be stopped on the way by someone else— Jordan—who pointed the other way. *Back.*

"What's going on?" I asked him.

"The hover heli exploded, and destroyed part of the wall. It attracted mutants," he yelled at me over the noise and biting wind, ordering other people to turn around.

Shit. *Nikolai.*

I zipped up my coat and ran toward the medical building, under protest from Jordan. I rushed to the surgical center with everything I had in me. And as I sprinted into the hallway and opened a door, I bumped into someone.

Nikolai.

"Shit, sorry. Are you okay?" I cursed as I ran my hands over his chest, looking for injuries. "There has been an explosion at the wall. The mutants are here."

"Yes, I know." He quickly placed his hands on mine and bent down a little so that he could look straight into my eyes. "Hunter, whatever happens, do *not* leave this building—under any circumstances."

I looked at him and felt something hideous bubbling up.

He certainly didn't, because he shook me hard. "Swear that you won't leave this building."

My eyes opened wide, and I could feel the blood rushing through my ears. "Who gave you permission to leave your room?"

Nikolai sighed deeply. "We don't have time for this." He started to walk past me. "Promise me you won't leave."

I let out a loud, indignant breath. "I won't promise that."

"*Hunter*…" he warned, and a dark shadow crossed his face. "This isn't the time to be rebellious."

"Exactly!" I yelled at him. "You aren't fully healed yet. What the hell made you decide to throw yourself into this fight?"

Nikolai's ears turned red. "You can help me by staying inside."

"*No*," I exclaimed. "You can help *yourself* by staying inside."

"Why won't you just listen to me, for once in your life?" he fired back.

I shook my head with wide eyes. "You can't tell me what to do, Nikolai. I have to help the wounded—inside and out. That's my job! I'm a goddamned *soldier*, not a defenseless person who doesn't know what she's doing."

"It's my profession, too, *Hunter*—and I'm the *fucking* General, as you've made so abundantly clear. *My* job is to keep everyone safe here. Including you! If I don't do that now, there may be no one left to help."

I grabbed his arm as he started to walk again. "And I'm your doctor, telling you you're not recovered enough to fight."

He shook his head and tightened his jaw. I saw that he was shaking. "Then it's a good thing I outrank you."

My mouth fell open. He pulled his arm out of mine and walked away. "Nikolai!" Panic clouded my vision as he walked on, and I ran after him. "*Nikolai*, don't go outside. *Please*."

He turned abruptly and grabbed my hands. "Don't you understand? The scientists believe they have found a serum, Hunter—a *solution* to the mutation. I'm not going to stand by while everything I've worked for crumbles, now that we're this close."

I felt my throat tighten as my head tried to register his words. The scientists thought they had found a solution?

Nikolai didn't look back as he walked on, leaving me

behind, stunned. "Stay inside, Hunter."

It was a command.

"*Damnit.*" I sprinted after him.

I didn't have time to get the medical staff together because the world as I knew it was in chaos. Outside the building, I could see Nikolai running away toward the wall ahead, and before I made up my mind what my next action would be, there was a cry for help.

"Doctor!"

I love you too; I suddenly remembered the words he had spoken not long ago. The switch in my head flipped, and I rushed toward the screaming. It came from soldiers closer to the wall, where the hover heli had been the day before. The material scattered over the site by the explosion had evidently caused casualties.

The soldier who had yelled at me was barely intelligible above the sound of another explosion and the screeching of the mutants. The group of soldiers near the wall threw explosives over it, hoping to incapacitate most of the mutants—and there were many, judging by the shrill sound of their shrieks. But I knew they couldn't keep this up for long. The sound was way too loud and would attract even more mutants.

I helped the soldier, whose thigh had been pierced by a piece of metal, and did my best to stop the bleeding. I quickly tied off his leg and hooked my arms under his armpits. Under the loud wailing of other wounded, I pulled the soldier as fast as I could towards the building behind me. And as if the gods themselves had answered my prayers, the doors opened, and someone from the staff rushed over to take him from me.

That was one.

I immediately ran back to where I'd seen more wounded. I checked soldier after soldier, administering first aid, until more medical personnel arrived, leaving no body untouched.

After checking every person on the ground, I did my best to ignore the bodies that had stopped responding. I couldn't do anything for the dead right now. I went from wounded to wounded, helping to cover injuries and getting the seriously injured to the medical center when needed—but luckily, a lot of soldiers were still able to keep fighting.

I love you too, Nikolai's words echoed through my mind as I breathlessly wiped the sweat and dirt off my forehead with the back of my arm. The closer I got to the wall, the more wounded I seemed to encounter. Here too, a few were already dead. They were so close to the wall that I didn't want to go there because a bit further along, mutants were trying to climb through the broken part of the wall.

I remembered that the wall had been very thick, since six of us had easily fit inside. And since the hover heli was completely destroyed, it must have been a very violent explosion.

So powerful, it seemed, that it had been able to blow through at least ten feet of a thick concrete wall.

Ten feet of *concrete* wall?

Nothing was impossible, of course, and a hover heli explosion wasn't just anything either. But so violent that it went through a ten-foot-thick and thirty-three-foot-high wall? It didn't make sense.

This wall, I realized, was not like the rest of the wall in Ardenza. Not only because this was the third built, but because it was built more quickly. They'd *really* been in a hurry if I were to believe the stories about that time. I moved closer to some of the debris and picked it up with much more ease than I should, confirming my suspicion.

This wall wasn't made of concrete at all; it was made of plasterboard.

When I heard a shot being fired, I looked up and saw Nikolai standing in one of the watchtowers with a rifle pointed at the wall.

Had he been aware that plasterboard had been used instead of concrete? The Nikolai I knew would want to nip any weakness in the bud right away. Then why had they never built a fourth wall around it?

There was only one possible answer: because Nikolai didn't know.

And as if he realized I was watching him, his head turned my way as he reloaded his rifle. I quickly tore my gaze away and refocused on the wounded around me.

* * *

Most of the injured were now stable or being treated at the medical center. Staying outside was no longer an option, and I'd even seen Nikolai leave his sentry to run to the hole with other soldiers.

After a while, the sound of explosions and shots finally stopped, after which only the screams of mutants remained. That might have been worse, but it was a good thing the noise stopped, since sound was something the mutants gravitated toward like moths to a flame.

Inside the medical center, I rushed to my office and typed in the number of my direct line to the capital with trembling and dirt-crusted fingers.

"*Major Jameson.*"

I gasped. "Yes, hello. I understand that we've called dozens of times already, but where's the backup?"

The man on the other end of the line mumbled something incoherent to someone. "*It'll be a while before they are there*," he finally said.

"We called three hours ago. It's an hour's flight for hover planes—they should have been here already."

"*A hover heli has been sent.*"

"*A hover heli?*" Were they stupid? Didn't they realize what was going on?

"*Was there anything else, Major Jameson?*"

"How many hover heli's?"

Silence. "*One.*"

And then it hit me. They had no intention of helping us at all. We were already written off as a lost cause. The fall of the first wall had caused countless victims, and now they probably didn't dare take the risk anymore. In addition, there was a third wall somehow, which was too weak. Someone must've known and hadn't done anything about it.

Who the hell would have thought it was a good idea to have politicians in an office make decisions about topics they had no idea about?

I love you too; I heard Nikolai's voice again and clenched my jaw.

"*Major?*"

"Has the area been surrounded yet?" I asked quickly, calculating. I held my breath.

"*Yes, we've*—" His answer was cut short with a lot of noise on the other end of the phone. I heard another loud 'idiot' being hissed, and then the line went dead.

They had cordoned off the area.

I knew it.

That meant they would literally leave us here. We were officially labeled collateral damage. They probably already had the official press statement in black and white ready to be published.

After *everything* that mission 3B and General Zaregova had done for Ardenza, they would drop them. Here, people risked their lives day and night to help the world. Why didn't the world help them? Help *us*.

I dialed another number and held the phone to my ear.

* * *

Back outside, I saw that more of the wall had come down, and several mutants were emerging from behind it. It took many soldiers to push them back, and Nikolai, among others, hacked away with his swords before they could put their claws into someone.

The number of mutants that emerged seemed less than a few hours ago, and there was no more loud noise. The chance that another stream of mutants would come their way from far in the shadow plains was getting smaller and smaller. My heart made a hopeful leap.

But it was short-lived.

The hairs on the back of my neck raised as I spotted movement at another part of the wall—the one that was still standing. A few mutants let themselves fall from thirty-three feet high, and dropped to the ground like bags of bones. For a moment, they didn't seem to move, as if they were dead. No one on the damaged, but military-protected side, realized what was happening until the mutants scrambled to their feet and straightened.

More mutants from the top of the wall dropped down, and I realized, like the rest of the soldiers, that there were not fewer mutants. The mutants had just moved and were trying from a different place.

The soldiers standing nearby were overpowered and brutally murdered within seconds. There were no more obstacles between the mutants that had now crossed the wall and the base. The path was clear.

Their sinewy and rickety bodies were a distraction from the strength they possessed. They were wearing torn clothes— if they were wearing anything—and some had a few strands of hair left on their heads. Their white, bloodshot eyes turned toward me, and my breath caught in my throat. I was the next human in their path.

The moment the mutants came my way was also the moment everyone else sprang into action. Part of the group of soldiers stayed behind at the broken wall, and another part sprinted to the side of the wall from which mutants were dripping down. The last part—Nikolai's group—chased the mutants who rushed to the medical center and me.

Nikolai motioned for me to go inside with frantic movements. His group was too far away to catch up with the mutants, and he was focused entirely on me. I got the hell out of there, ran back into the medical building, and closed the doors behind me.

"Barricade all windows and doors!" I yelled, pushing the nearest table to the large doors myself. I heard my command echo through the building once, before everyone sprang into action.

Raven came running. "Hunter?"

"Mutants crossed the wall. They're coming here," I

reacted.

"*How?*" Her mouth formed a big 'o'.

"They came from another side of the wall."

The clattering of a smashed window filled the room, and everyone cringed collectively.

"Weapons," I asked her, panicking, "where are the weapons?"

"In the back," Raven replied calmly, then grabbed my arm and pulled me after her. I gestured for more soldiers to follow us, and we were on our way with a group to the cabinet where the necessary weapons were stored. With a few people, we divided the guns over the group that was inside and listened in silence to what was going on outside. The sounds of shouting humans and crying mutants mixed.

A moment later, another window shattered, and a sinewy hand shot inside. The armed soldiers unlocked their rifles while the rest continued to tend to the wounded in the building.

Just as the mutant's head appeared through the window and two people aimed their guns, the end of a long knife protruded from the mutant's wide-open mouth. The blade was pulled back roughly, sending a stream of blood gushing from the mutant's mouth, and causing him to slide limply out of the opening. Through the broken window, I could see Nikolai's bloodstained and contorted face before he, too, disappeared from view.

There was more banging against the outer metal walls, and the glass clattered. I suddenly remembered that there was a car in the basement of the medical building.

With great strides, I walked up to Raven and said, "Barak had the area cordoned off."

"Where are they then?" she asked dubiously, her head flipping to the side as another loud bang sounded against the door.

"To make sure that nothing or no one can *escape*," I clarified.

Raven's head shot back, and she gasped. "What?"

We had to duck to avoid glass shards as another large window broke, and I returned my gaze to Raven, who was shaking her head.

"Damnit," she roared. "*Goddamnit.* I would have been done in two days."

I looked up at her and grabbed her hand. "I'm going to try and make sure you still are, but I have to get out of here for that."

"Those filthy, conniving——" Raven clenched her fists furiously. "They're going to let us die here?" she asked, flames blazing in her eyes.

"Not if it's up to me," I replied, squeezing her hand. "You're in charge now."

Raven nodded at me once, her gaze relentlessly blank, and pulled me into a brief hug. "See you on the other side."

I nodded back.

Until now, I'd done everything in my life by myself, so this was going to work, too.

Because I wasn't ready to die, certainly not alone, and certainly not today. There was still too much I wanted to experience—a whole life I wanted to share with someone.

I love you too.

So that day hadn't arrived yet.

CHAPTER 28

NIKOLAI

Nikolai had completely lost sense of time.

He didn't know for how long the fight had been going on when he saw the mutants rushing toward Hunter from the other side of the wall. He didn't know how long it had taken him to spur into action, and he didn't know for how long they'd been protecting the medical center now.

High in the air, Nikolai crossed his long blades and braced himself for the impact of the frail body that could hit him at any moment. He'd already raised the alarm at the capital right after the first explosion awakened him. And again, after news of the broken wall had reached his room at the medical center. The last time he'd sounded the alarm was when he'd seen the first stream of mutants emerge from the wall. So, it was clear that if the capital had wanted to help, they would have done so already. He knew they could. But after the incident of the first wall, it had become crystal clear that they wanted to avoid such a situation at all costs, and had now taken precautions.

The moment he shoved his knife between the ribs of a mutant on the ground, the earth began to vibrate. Nikolai put his foot on the rib cage and wrenched his blade free from the sinewy body. It wasn't until he separated the mutant's head from its torso that Nikolai dared to pry his gaze from the sight in front of him.

With as many soldiers as they were now, they could handle one or two mutants at a time. But not for long, because it was extremely tiring. When a mutant hit you, you were *really* hit. They dealt bone-breaking blows.

The shaking of the ground intensified, and Nikolai looked around, keeping an eye out for another mutant. A humming sound came from the woods, and a car raced down the path, straight at them. The car stopped a few feet in front of him, and he turned so the headlights wouldn't blind him. The bright glow now completely enveloped the mutants and overstimulated their hypersensitive nerves.

A soldier stabbed one of his knives through the eye of a momentarily distracted mutant, deep into the skull. Nikolai slit the throat of a mutant lying on the floor, groaning in pain, but the movement sent a deep burst of pain through his own chest. Instinctively, he reached for it and felt wet, warm liquid slide down his chest. He cursed.

The light from the car behind him dimmed, and he heard doors slam open and shut. He turned to see Hunter step out from behind the wheel with a man he vaguely recognized. It wasn't, however, one of his soldiers.

A moment later, more cars drove down from the trail, and dozens of soldiers got out and charged onto the site, led by several men and women.

He saw Hunter say something to the man and pointed to

Nikolai, causing the man to rush toward him with determination. Nikolai watched the fight as he, too, faced the man, suppressing the urge to go after Hunter.

"General Zaregova." The man saluted urgently. "Colonel Cress. Major Jameson has me inform you that the third wall is made of plasterboard, and that we're here to reinforce you." He gestured around him. "Where can we best assist you?"

Plasterboard? Nikolai's brain was working overtime, but he suddenly remembered where he knew the man from. While the Special Shadow Unit was in the set-up phase, and the plan for mission 3B was getting finalized, Nikolai had attended several meetings to learn more about the wall and the shadow plains beyond. The various sentries near the new base had given him many insights into how best to set up the base. Colonel Cress had been one of those present.

"At the collapsed wall. That's where the new ones come out." Nikolai pointed down the path toward the wall, which was still crumbling. "Try to limit sound as much as possible."

The Colonel nodded, then ran over to the other soldiers who had entered the base. He gathered the leaders of the groups and quickly explained what had to be done.

Nikolai began to breathe shallowly, his mind still catching up, as he digested the new information.

The wall was made of plasterboard? *Of course*, a voice in his head said, *otherwise the wall would have still been standing.*

He immediately realized who was behind this.

Chief General Domasc.

Two years ago, after the first wall fell, and the third wall had been built in a short time, Nikolai proposed to construct an additional fortification. Just to be on the safe side—

reducing the chance of another disaster even more. But General Domasc had declined his request, saying that the wall was as strong as necessary.

As strong as it took to discredit Nikolai, yes. As strong as it took to question Nikolai's integrity, and have a reason to depose him. Or better yet—get rid of him completely.

From the moment he was put in charge of mission 3B, and his popularity in the military became apparent, Domasc had opposed him. He'd wanted to put other people forward as generals, but the delegates hadn't wanted that. They had wanted the best of the best—which he was. But as Nikolai's popularity spread among the population, it was rumored that he might become the youngest chief general ever. From that moment on, Domasc had officially felt threatened.

Somehow Hunter had managed to bring in extra troops after all. He wanted to hear all about how she'd managed to do this, but that came later. *Later*, because it had made a significant turning point in the current struggle, so there even was a later in the first place. Nikolai felt a sense of immense pride as he saw her rush back inside and immersed himself back into the fight.

* * *

With the extra help, it soon became apparent that they had a chance to win this fight. The support forces under Colonel Cress had ensured that the influx of mutants had dwindled until none of them could enter the grounds through the wall anymore. They had then worked very hard to rebuild the wall as far as possible with the remains of the plasterboards.

But there had been casualties. The largest number came from the explosions near the wall. The hover heli used to get him and Hunter out of the shadow plains had seen little use in recent years. So little, it seemed, that there had been a short circuit while charging the battery, and it had completely melted. This, in turn, had started a fire, which eventually led to an explosion.

Nikolai was of the opinion that the government and army leaders had the deaths on their conscience. If they had sent help sooner, no, if they had sent support at all, it would have made an enormous difference. He would see to it that this information would be made public and that they would pay for it. And then, there was the wall, which, had it been made of concrete, could have stopped the attack even better. After all the effort Nikolai put into keeping his people safe, the capital had acted as if their lives didn't matter.

Near the end of the battle, Jordan had approached him, completely exhausted. "The situation at the wall is calm, and back in order again." He pointed his thumb at the smoke that filled the air far away. "The dead mutants are now being collected and burned."

Nikolai nodded. "Good."

"Shouldn't you get yourself checked out?" Jordan had asked with concern, as he noticed his soaked shirt.

Nikolai decided that it was a good idea. His people were safe for now, so he could take a moment to get himself checked.

He walked into the medical center and looked through the building, checking the crowd for Hunter. She had been stubborn today. So, besides wanting to thank her, he wanted to scold her even more. He grunted in irritation and looked around impatiently, his eyes scanning the building for her.

But she wasn't there, so Nikolai let Lieutenant Renée

treat him, and thanked her for what she'd done. Jordan had told him in great detail what the Lieutenant had done for him in the field when she was on her own. How she had to give up Lieutenant Colonel Kent, and then tried to keep him alive until Hunter arrived. Nikolai would personally see to it that the Lieutenant would receive the promotion she deserved.

He also knew, from observation, that the Lieutenant spent a lot of time with Hunter. But the moment he'd asked the Lieutenant where Hunter was, she'd indicated that she didn't know, and the sparkle in her eyes had made clear that she and Hunter told each other more than he'd initially thought. Then she had quietly cleaned his wounds. After a while, Jordan walked in and signaled to speak to Lieutenant Renée. She had followed after him when she finished up wrapping new bandages around Nikolai's clean wounds.

Nikolai swallowed his impatience and helped with clearing out and burning the mutants. Because once he found Hunter, he wasn't sure he'd ever let her go.

CHAPTER 29

It was late in the evening when I lowered myself against the wall and leaned my head backward. The fight had been over for a few hours, and this time had quickly ticked away as I oversaw the help that was needed—both for the injured and the dead.

Immediately after the battle, I'd made my way along the wall to map the dead and wounded and had run into Colonel Cress. The Colonel, who had been in charge of the surrounding of the area, had immediately come to the base with me and deployed all his soldiers when he found out that the fighting was still in full swing. The capital had told them that there had been a major battle and that they had to cordon off the area. They weren't allowed to enter the premises until further instructions.

I had thanked him for his hard work at the wall. That extra help had made a big difference. Despite that, the death toll was slowly adding up. There had been no soldiers included that I knew personally—except for Sergeant Wellington, whose skull was crushed entirely on one side—but I knew each of them was leaving loved ones behind.

I watched the soldiers walk by, taking the last mutants to burn. My head throbbed as I hung it against the cold wall and closed my tired eyes. I had also seen Nikolai in action. The stories about him weren't wrong: he was an expert with weapons and could move his body like no one else. According to Raven, he had briefly popped into the medical center after the fight, looking for me. She'd indicated that he had nothing serious, except for a few stitches that had burst open again. At the time, I'd been working with one of the other surgeons in the operating room, removing a piece of metal stuck in a soldier's lower back.

I let out a breath and felt the air warm around me. We could all have died—*Nikolai* could have died again.

My hands trembled with exhaustion, and I folded them in front of my mouth, blowing heat into them.

"Hunter," came a voice from a distance, followed by a pair of footsteps coming my way.

I opened my eyes and saw Nikolai standing in front of me. He was dressed in all black, and his eyes seemed to glow. He looked as if he'd come to deliver death on a tray.

A *damn beautiful* death, though.

He stood at my feet and effortlessly hoisted me up, after which I smiled weakly at him. How did he still have the strength for such things? The man was a machine, that was for sure.

The spoken and unspoken words of that morning hung between us like crackling tension. The moment I got back on my feet, he ran his thumb down my cheek, leaving behind a static, tingling sensation.

I hadn't said a word before I wrapped my arms around his neck and pulled him closer—until our lips met. Nikolai allowed my eagerness and pressed his mouth back on mine just as diligently. I didn't care that all the soldiers could see it—I didn't care at all anymore. They were allowed to think whatever they wanted.

I opened my lips to him and pulled him closer. All I wanted to feel was his skin against mine. But Nikolai's mouth remained unopened and hardened, after which he created some distance between us and looked down at me darkly.

"You need rest."

"And you don't?" I replied, running my teeth lightly down his neck.

This seemed to break the leash he had on himself, and he pressed me against the wall with a sigh, opening his mouth for me. His hands made their way over my body as if I were the most precious thing in the world. Nikolai's hand swallowed mine entirely, and I squeezed it lightly. A sigh escaped his throat as I broke the contact of our lips. His pupils were dilated, and he was breathing deeply.

I pushed us off the wall and grabbed his hand, leading us over the grounds toward his rooms. My body trembled with excitement.

When we finally got inside, he softly closed the door and turned around, his eyes grave—inspecting my body. He took off my dirty clothes and threw them in the corner of the room. I stared from my clothes to my body, then back to him while he also took off his.

Nikolai put his hands in my neck, planted a kiss on my lips, and carefully guided me to the bathroom. There he gently turned on the shower and began to wash my hair and body. All the while, I stared at him, tired but alert at the same time. I've never had someone look after me so… intimately.

"I don't want to keep it a secret anymore, Hunter," he suddenly said. "Not for anything or anyone."

I opened my mouth to say something, but Nikolai held up a finger. "Please let me say this."

Droplets hung from his dark lashes, and his wet hair was stuck to his forehead, but his eyes were on me. "All day today, my thoughts were with you. I wondered if you were all right, if you weren't in any danger, and if I'd get another chance to touch you or hear your voice."

I swallowed as he fell silent again, searching for words.

Nikolai closed his eyes and let his head fall back under the stream. "I had a dream when I was injured." He opened his eyes again and looked at me. "I dreamed of the sun—the old sun—and I dreamed of you."

Nikolai ran a hand down my shoulder until he curled his fingers around mine and pulled me closer. He put his other hand on my face. I leaned my head into his touch and continued to look at him as he stroked my cheek with his thumb.

"You were so very *real*, and you weren't with me." He shook his head, and water trickled down his face. "You had built a life of your own that I wasn't a part of, and I couldn't understand how I'd let it get to that."

I breathed softly, and my heart beat madly in my chest. Was it just me, or did the water get a bit warmer?

"But then I understood, Hunter," he laughed. "This mission, the military, all of this… it doesn't matter. It doesn't matter because this mission in itself isn't life. This only means something if you actually have something or someone to fight for."

I exhaled. He looked into my eyes, which were slowly

clouding with more than just water.

"This is what I never understood—until you came along. I always thought I was stronger than others because I didn't let anyone get close. I thought *loving someone* meant becoming more vulnerable." He ran a warm hand over my bare chest, where my heart was still pounding wildly, and the corners of his mouth curled up. "But loving someone makes you stronger. When I was injured in the field, I could've died. My body would normally have given up, too, but everything in me *knew* you would be on the other side. You, and the life I could have with you. It kept me going, fighting for you and that future. *You're* the reason I didn't give up—why I'm still fighting." He whispered the latter.

It sounded so fragile that I raised a hand to his face. "You are my reason too," I said.

Nikolai squeezed my hand again, and his eyes smiled. He kissed my forehead, then leaned his head against mine for a moment. I nestled my face into the crook of his neck, and focused on the rise and fall of his chest as we stood together under the shower.

"Marry me," he said hoarsely.

Goosebumps spread over my body, and I froze. "What?"

I felt his lips pull into a smile against my forehead. "Marry me—after all of this."

My hands regained feeling and encircled his neck. I raised my face to him.

"Marry me," he said again, turning off the shower.

My heart was beating in my throat, and my mouth went dry. I blinked. "But—"

"*Marry me*, Hunter Jameson," he interrupted, still smiling broadly.

A small hysterical laugh escaped my throat, and I felt my face start to glow. My whole body seemed to suddenly wake up. I knew what I was going to say—had always known what I was going to say—before the words left my mouth.

"*Okay.*"

It came out like a sigh, almost as if everything inside me experienced deep relief.

"Is that a yes?" His eyes darted across my face in wonder, as if searching for a sign that seemed to contradict my answer.

I nodded. "Yes."

The rational part of my brain protested in disbelief, but my heart couldn't stop dancing.

I didn't know who moved first, but before long, we were claiming each other with an urgency so far unmatched. Nikolai pressed me against the shower wall and kissed me as if I was the only thing that could keep him alive in that moment—as if I were the beginning, middle, and end of his world.

It felt so natural to be with him—to touch him. Like we were made for each other. As if we had already done this countless of lives. And everything in me attested to that.

He ran his fingers over the tender spot between my legs and cursed when he found me already wet. I placed my hands on either side of his head and kissed him deeply. *Now*, I tried to tell him, or maybe I said it out loud.

He massaged my nipple with a thumb and forefinger, and then lifted me against the wall until my legs were clamped around his waist. He slowly guided himself inside, holding my gaze the entire time, until he was fully seated, and my breath came in short bursts. There were eons in his eyes, and I was overcome with an emotion I didn't know how to handle.

Nikolai clearly felt the same, and moved closer to repossess my mouth with his.

He withdrew slowly and thrust deep into me again.

A muffled moan sounded from deep within my chest, and reverberated in the bathroom, making him move even harder and faster. I felt myself stretch further under the pressure he was exerting, and I grabbed his shoulders to brace myself. He moved his lips to my neck and licked down over the curve of my breast before taking my nipple in his mouth and sucking gently. My hips tilted up in desperation, and I tried to take in more of him, to satisfy the longing that was building inside of me.

It would never be enough with Nikolai, I realized. I would never get enough of him. He moved a hand under my butt and tilted me slightly, reaching more places than I had ever gotten to with my fingers. His hips met mine at a relentless pace, making it difficult for both of us to maintain a rhythm.

The moment I reached my climax was also the moment Nikolai let himself finish inside me, clutching my trembling legs. He slowed down and met my gaze.

I saw his pupils constrict slowly as he looked at me and wound a lock of my hair around his finger.

"I love you," I whispered.

He smiled in a way that was just for me. "I love you, too."

I pulled him closer to kiss him, and he let go of my hair to wrap his hand completely around the back of my head.

When I put some distance between us and he slowly lowered me, I saw him gazing at my mouth and back to my eyes. "I guess that's convenient, if we're getting married."

I swallowed my surprise and said, almost shyly, "I guess so."

Taking a deep breath, I studied him. *Marriage.* Nikolai Zaregova—the most wonderful, brave, strong, and intelligent man in the world—would become *my* husband. My heart skipped a beat at the idea.

"I don't know if I want kids," I suddenly blurted. I had no idea if it was important to him, but he should know that before committing to me, right?

"Me neither."

"At least," I rattled on, "I always thought I didn't want them in the world we live in. But now that a solution may have been found, I don't know anymore."

"Me neither," he agreed again. "But we're going to figure that out together. And whatever the outcome is going to be—it will be okay—because we have each other."

"We would have really great kids," I added quietly, deep in thought about the idea of children resembling a younger Nikolai. That was a future—something I'd never dared dream about before.

Nikolai smiled, planting a kiss in the corner of my mouth. "Without a doubt."

CHAPTER 38

It was early morning when a knock sounded.

"General Zaregova?" someone said from the other side of the door.

Sighing, Nikolai trailed his lips lightly over my forehead and rolled out of bed, with a slight crease between his brows. On his way to the door, he put on some pants, making his muscles tense carelessly under his skin.

I bit my lip.

"Yes?" he asked, opening the door.

The voices at the door were hushed for a moment, and I couldn't quite catch what was being said. A moment later, the door slammed shut again, and Nikolai walked back into the room with a telephone to his ear. His gaze was thunderous.

"Yes." He sighed, wearily rubbing a hand over his face. "So are we."

Nikolai leaned against the wall by the stove. "Jordan's fine."

I raised my eyebrows. Was he on the phone with *Kenneth Locke*?

"You're not serious," Nikolai growled, pinching the

bridge of his nose. He sounded like he had to suppress the urge to throw the phone out of the window with a frustrated battle cry.

I suppressed a laugh, and he let his gaze drift to me. The wrinkles between his brows smoothed a little.

Nikolai walked over to the bed and sat on the edge so he could place a hand on my leg, making guttural sounds of agreement through the phone.

The hand on my leg stopped moving, and he raised his eyebrows at me.

"Which article are you talking about?" he asked, inspecting my face. Nikolai pointed his finger at me in question.

I shook my head and shrugged innocently.

The twinkle in his eye reappeared, and one corner of his mouth lifted. "I don't know, but I can't say that I mind."

The man on the other side said something that made Nikolai chuckle. A short, sincere chuckle.

"Thanks," he said after a while.

Another moment passed when I heard the man talking on the other end, but couldn't make out any of the words.

"I'll pass it on," Nikolai said, before he hung up.

He was silent for a moment as he looked at me. "That was delegate Kenneth Locke."

I nodded. "I figured. Why did he call?"

Nikolai wrinkled his nose. "To apologize. He was obviously seething."

"Does he know who was responsible?"

He nodded. "They had an emergency meeting, but due to the panic and fear that was spread over the first wall crisis, the majority *by one vote* had decided not to send aid, but to

256

cordon off the area."

"Cowards," I growled.

"Agreed," he said, leaning back on his arms. "But," he continued, "of course, delegate Locke had voted for help and he was extremely pissed. He disclosed the voting information so I could do with it whatever I wanted. Guess who had the deciding vote."

My breath caught. "Chief General Domasc?"

Nikolai nodded. "He was the one who, according to delegate Locke, was stirring up unrest before the vote was due. And since everyone has him on a pedestal and trusts him completely when it comes to crises, he'd been able to manipulate some of the delegates."

"And all because he sees you as a threat?"

"Even I didn't expect he'd rather see me dead… but," his eyes narrowed, "Locke had mentioned an article published last night. It said that the government and military abandoned us during a serious breach of the wall yesterday. But also, that some high-ranking military personnel at the main base were aware that the wall wasn't made of concrete, and deliberately covered it up."

I pursed my mouth. "That's a good thing then. At least the government and military are held accountable for their actions."

"Yes, it is." Nikolai nodded thoughtfully and moved closer. "All *extremely* coincidental."

I nodded solemnly. "What did he think about it?"

"He said that if the article hadn't been published, he would have gone to the press himself. But he also mentioned that there's already a group talking about a replacement for Domasc—and that I have his vote if I want to take over in a few years."

"Wow," I sighed. "Would you consider that?"

He shrugged. "It's not my priority right now, but I'm certainly not writing it off. Not after everything Domasc has done."

I nodded and leaned over him after he dropped himself back on the bed and opened his mouth again. "I also had to pass on that the scientists agreed yesterday: they found a solution against the mutation—a serum that they'd been working on. Locke has had a few test serums sent to us to try on some mutants, if we had any left."

All thoughts left my head.

"So it's true?"

He nodded.

"Officially?" My eyes had widened, and I had to clench my jaws tightly to contain the hope that had begun to surface.

"Yes."

I looked at Nikolai and felt a wide smile take over my face. He smiled back as he took my hand and kissed it.

There was a light at the end of the tunnel. After almost fifty years with a weak sun. Twenty-five years without natural sunlight. Twenty years after the first mutation, and fifteen years with a world half cloaked in darkness—they'd finally found a solution.

I put my hands to my mouth and cried.

* * *

Exactly one day later, the serum arrived at the medical center in an airtight, sealed container. It held five glass tubes, of which the lab technician unpacked one to prepare for the trial. Explicit instruction had been given during that morning's briefing, where we had spoken to some of the scientists. They had explained that the effect of the serum was based on the fact that the mutation gene can be deactivated, and then removed from the DNA definitively.

The syringes containing the serum had to be placed in the bone marrow to stimulate stem cells to generate new cells. These new cells could disable the mutation and remove this piece of genetic material. In turn, it would be reversing the mutation in the mutants, as far as their bodies could take it.

We had a living mutant from the fight two days ago that we'd kept in the medical center. The mutant was already strapped to the operating table and completely sedated while we connected the chest and head to several devices.

The scientists and a few delegates from Barak watched on a large screen, and were also shown the mutant's vital signs live. The technician thawed the serum and liquefied it, so that it could be administered. She poked right through the top of the glass vial with a syringe, and extracted several milliliters of liquid. We watched breathlessly as the syringe now filled with an ocher sustenance, which seemed to have a neon green glint that reflected the light.

While she was working, I saw Nikolai standing behind the glass wall of the locked operating room. He winked, and a warm feeling coursed through me.

I cleared my throat and looked at the screen, where those present from the capital were watching. "We're ready to administer the shot."

The lab technician nodded at me, and she inserted the needle into the mutant's leathery skin before further lowering it. The mutant's body twitched for a moment as the serum slowly dissipated from the syringe. We all looked breathlessly at the data on the monitors.

A mutant's heart rate was the same as that of a 'normal' human. But the heart rate raised drastically as the serum made its way through the mutated body, searching for the places it was supposed to attack. It worsened, and it went against my nature not to intervene. But I tried to watch as calmly as possible as the scientists had already indicated that this could happen. We were all still in uncharted territory, working on something that would change the world—change the future, forever.

That realization almost brought me to my knees.

When the heart rate was so high that an average person wouldn't survive, it slowly dropped again. The mutant's chest, which was still jerking up and down a moment ago, returned to a normal rhythm.

As predicted, the brain activity of the mutant brain gradually increased. Where previously only a kind of blue cloud floated through the reptilian brain, it now slowly spread like an ink stain over the entire brain. The further the inkblot spread, the more the heart rate dropped, and the slower the chest rose and fell. After a few minutes, the mutant even began to squeak as if gasping for air.

He made such panicky noises that I stepped over and put a hand on his arm to soothe him. The serum seemed to rush straight through the anesthetic, and the brain got overloaded with stimuli. Because the brain had worked in such a singular way for so long, it didn't immediately know what to do with the other, now active parts.

As if instinct told him that I was standing next to him, the mutant moved his head towards me and gurgled slightly. The mutant opened his eyes and looked straight at me. Pure panic clouded his vision. His mouth opened as he tried to squeeze out a sound, but only distorted guttural moans came out. Tears ran down his gaunt cheeks, but he didn't understand what was happening or what was going on. And judging by the flared areas in his brain activity, his brain also didn't have enough strength to figure it out on its own—to understand any of it at all.

The mutant had to be in a lot of pain.

But…

He experienced feelings and emotions. He had tried to speak, and his pupils were no longer dilated, as they usually were with mutants. Even the way he'd turned his head toward me had been calm—not like a skittish animal.

Now he was gasping for air, and it was apparent he was dying. Not from his injuries of the fight, but because his brain and body couldn't make the switch back.

As a doctor, I didn't want anyone to suffer unnecessarily, especially when it was evident that he wouldn't survive the day—perhaps even the next hour.

I looked up silently and grabbed the anesthetic, which I injected into his arm under protest from the scientists. A cloudy look seeped into his eyes, and the panic vanished from his features as the pain slowly subsided. Only a serene expression remained.

Ten minutes later, he was dead.

But he had died a *human*.

* * *

Later we spoke to the scientists, and they said this was the first time they had seen the effect on an adult mutant. They weren't happy about my early abortion of the process, but they also recognized he wouldn't have made it.

As with regular, healthy humans, the adult mutants were already past their developing phase. At this point, the body struggled to adapt to the significant changes. It was similar to when someone had been walking on his feet for forty years and now had to suddenly walk on his hands for the rest of his life. That would never become first nature again. Children can still cope with such changes, though, which means that young mutants could have a chance at survival. What the quality of their life would be was, naturally, still unknown. We would have to find out in the coming years through further research.

In the meeting that morning, it also became clear that the serum would be developed into a vaccine so that everyone's genes could be modified to prevent this mutation. Sunlight therapy would therefore no longer be a necessity but more of a leisurely activity.

We still had to figure out a way to quickly spread the serum across the shadow plains and thus erase the mutant problem, root, and branch from the world.

But at least we had a *chance* at a normal life.

CHAPTER 31

NIKOLAI

Three weeks after the serum trial, which the Barak science group had pronounced a 'success', the corpse of the *mutant man*, as Hunter had called it—was buried. It was the first mutant that had died as a human. At least, Nikolai thought, something that resembled one.

He had then attended a meeting with a handful of delegates, who had once again apologized. The absence of Chief General Domasc had not gone unnoticed, but Nikolai couldn't blame him. If he'd been in his shoes, he wouldn't have dared to show his face either. For now, he'd lay it aside— at least for a while, as he could better use his energy toward rebuilding the wall, and arranging construction for decent protection around it. He would even have a completely new wall built, if necessary.

He went back to civilization for the first time in three years, and he had no intention of coming back anytime soon.

Now that the mission was officially a success, and they had accomplished their goal, there was a lot of work waiting for him in Barak. His job was to pick it up, and ensure that the following steps taken were the right ones. But he certainly wouldn't forget that the military and government had abandoned him and his soldiers when it came to their political gain. Despite their apologies, Nikolai just couldn't accept it. If they thought that he did, they were in for a big surprise.

Nikolai had lost fifteen people in the attack. Fifteen hardworking, courageous people who had supported a mission others had no idea about. Every day, *they* sat behind shiny desks in their smart suits, making decisions about a world they weren't even really part of.

No, Nikolai thought, *I certainly won't drop it.*

But first, two other things required his attention. The first: wrapping up this mission. Making sure the next general to take over had the smoothest possible start. His second focus was Hunter. Now that he had her in his life, he no longer wanted to be separated from her. He didn't want to be sent to any part of the world other than where she was. He wanted to adjust his life to Hunter. His future wife.

Nikolai leaned back in his chair and decided to do something he hadn't done in a while. He called his mother.

The line rang twice before she answered.

"Zaregova," she chirped.

"Mom," he said, and the woman on the other end of the line fell silent. "It's me."

"Of course it's you, Nik." She chuckled. "I was wondering when you would call."

His heart was beating in his throat. "We're wrapping up the current mission, so I just wanted to let you know I'll be coming back."

There was a moment of silence on the other end of the

264

line. "You're coming home?"

"Yes."

"What have you done to my son?" She laughed. "As far as I can remember, he would never leave his work behind."

Nikolai bit the inside of his cheek. "I'm done with this place after three years."

"*Really*," she replied sarcastically.

"And…" Nikolai continued.

"I knew there was more to it," his mother chimed in. "You've met someone, haven't you?"

He sighed. "Yeah."

"Why do you make it sound so complicated, Nik? Spit it out," she said.

"Do you think Dad would have been disappointed?"

"Disappointed?"

"In me?"

His mother was silent for a moment and then asked, incredulously, "Why would he be *disappointed* in you?"

Nikolai cleared his throat. "I caught feelings for someone during my mission."

"So?"

"Well," Nikolai moistened his lips, "he always said it was dangerous to get distracted at work. That it was better if you loved no one. He's the prime example."

The other end the line crackled, and his mother barked, "Nikolai Zaregova, what the hell are you talking about?"

"If he hadn't thought of us that day, he might not have been hit by a bomb."

"Nik," his mother said sternly, "your father didn't die because he was distracted. He died because he wanted to help another man—after which they were both hit by a bomb."

"Helping someone?"

"Yes." His mother sighed. "Oh, Nik, this is all my fault. I should've talked to you more about it, but you were always so closed off when it came to your father. Somehow, I always thought you'd come to me if you wanted to talk about it. If I had known you were telling yourself these kinds of stories, I would've cleared things up much earlier."

Nikolai smiled to himself. "I'd like to talk about him sometime."

"Then we'll do that," she said. "He would be proud of the man you are today, Nik, and would have loved to meet the woman you want to build a future with."

"He would have liked her," he replied with a grin.

His mother laughed, too. "She must be very special."

Nikolai let go of his breath. "She is."

* * *

The night before he was due to leave his home of the past three years, he walked into the bar for the last time, where he had to get his sunlight therapy. He greeted the generals who were still there, and smiled at them as they arranged a round of drinks.

In the months leading up to the mission that had started three years ago, he'd drawn up a list of the soldiers he wanted as generals. Jordan, who was now grinning at him, had been on top, and had been with him from the start. The others poured in over the years, returning from their previous missions and being notified that they were wanted here. All the soldiers on his list eventually came. Not one of them had turned down his offer, even when he'd given them plenty of room to do so.

But that was also the reason they had been on his list. Not because they all hoped for the glory that Nikolai had had in his career, but because they knew that he had requested them for a reason. That this mission was important.

They were good men and women with integrity, and they were the most capable soldiers he had encountered in his career.

They, too, had now completed their mission, and would be replaced in the coming months. The base would be turned into a sentry for a transitional period, until they knew how to proceed, apply the serum, and set up the next mission. In addition, there probably would be several groups going onto the shadow plains to push them back, hopefully starting the process of making the other half of the planet habitable again.

That morning, he'd packed up the last things and prepared his rooms for departure. It was a crazy idea to leave his rooms behind, especially now that so many new memories had been made in them.

Three weeks earlier, immediately after the serum was injected, he'd been asked if he could come back to Barak. Everyone suddenly seemed to want his attention, or to ask his opinion on the next steps. Nikolai had replied that he would not come for three more weeks and would first take leave—after three years of continuous work on this mission.

No one had contradicted him.

Nikolai took a sip of his drink, and looked across the room to see Hunter sitting alone at the bar. There wasn't a chance that he would leave without her. Not that she wouldn't manage without him—no, Nikolai didn't know if he'd make it without *her*. He wanted to face the outside world with her beside him. If he thought about what it would be like out there, now that the news about the serum had spread, they were going to need each other.

A while passed before he stood and shook hands with the generals at the table. They had supported him immensely over the years, and had been the only constant factor in his life before Hunter. He was extremely grateful for them.

Nikolai walked to the bar after a wink from Jordan. He didn't care what people thought about it anymore—although the soldiers here seemed to accept it. He didn't care at all about what would be said in the capital. *The capital*, he thought, *had other things to worry about.*

He and Hunter had done a lot together in the past two weeks. After Lieutenant Renée—Raven, as he was supposed to call her now—left, they'd slept together every night. It had become the most natural thing in the world to wake up next to her, and he thought it was crazy to think that he had been without her for years. Nikolai never wanted to sleep without her again. Not because they could lay together—since they got so turned on that they weren't able to sleep at all—but because he would wake up now and then in the middle of the night and listen to her breathing. That satisfied him more than anything had ever done.

Carefully, he placed his hand on Hunter's shoulder and squeezed it gently. She turned her head to him, and the second seemed to stretch out as a smile spread over her face.

"Are you all packed?"

She nodded, and he leaned against the bar. "I didn't have much to pack. You?"

"As far as possible, yes. It's only now that I realize how little I've lived with these years." He tilted his head back. *With how little value I've gone with through life.*

"I've also completed work for the next medical head—if one even comes." Hunter drained her glass and set it on the counter, then got up and put on her coat. "Of which, by the way, the administrative work always sucked, so thank you for that."

He laughed out loud and followed her outside. "Remember when I told you Arepto asked for you to be his replacement?"

"Yes." She looked up. "But now you're going to tell me that you chose me because you felt guilty about your misplaced view of me?"

Nikolai smiled but shook his head. "No, Arepto had made his wish crystal clear, in a message expressing his anger—at me."

Hunter's brows raised.

"He was furious about what had happened to his wife, which is very understandable. But he may have been angrier about you. And after writing a whole letter full of complaints about having such an incredibly young talent thrown to the lions for my endless and pointless mission, he asked— demanded—that I give his position to you."

"Oh, *no*," Hunter groaned, realizing what he meant.

Nikolai expressed her suspicion. "So you didn't have to go into the field anymore."

"And you *agreed* to that?" She narrowed her eyes to him. "*What?* So that I could stay safely behind the wall, and you wouldn't have to worry about me?"

"No." Nikolai pursed his lips and tried not to laugh. That would only make her anger worse.

"Because I saved your life?" she pushed out, upset.

"No."

Hunter raised an eyebrow. "What then?"

"Because I had never seen a surgeon with so much potential in my entire career."

She jerked her gaze away and looked to the ground, but not before he saw the response to his compliment in her eyes. "So, you decided to reward me with paperwork?"

"No." Nikolai shook his head, laughing. "That was a bonus."

He put an arm around her shoulders and pulled her closer, pressing a kiss on top of her head. "I gave you the position," he said, "because I wanted the world to see it too."

CHAPTER 32

In the car on the way to the ceremony, I rested my head on Nikolai's shoulder. He grabbed my hand tightly and kissed my forehead. The presence of his hand's calluses was a reminder of the mission and everything that had happened there. Everything he'd been doing for the last couple of years.

The return to Ardenza had been peaceful: instead of going straight to Barak, we decided to retreat for a while. We wanted to be together for a few weeks—*alone*. My parents didn't mind, and the government nor the army dared to refuse after the shitshow they pulled.

It had been heavenly, the weeks together. We witnessed each other outside of a critical and restless situation. We'd cooked together every day—in which Nikolai also proved to be exceptionally good—and we'd always had conversations late into the night. These nights usually turned into something more, which ended with both of us exhausted in each other's arms. Usually in bed, but regularly on the couch, the floor, the bathroom, or against the nearest wall, too. There had even been a morning when I'd walked into the kitchen, and he'd already pulled me onto the counter before I could reach for the fridge.

But above all, I had grown to love him even more. I now dared to speak the words freely and express my love for him, which I did as often as I could—and in as many ways as possible.

"When you become a lieutenant colonel in a moment, you'll be even more unbearable, won't you?" Nikolai smiled broadly.

I opened my mouth with fake indignation. "It's just a title, *Nikolai*." A title that gave me goosebumps all over my body, yes. Only not nearly as much as Nikolai did.

"I think they should give you more than an award," I said. "A statue, an official apology—you name it." I snapped and rolled my eyes.

He snorted and pinched my side, causing me to slide over to the other side of the back seat. "I'm serious, Nik. How long have *I* been there?" My eyebrows puckered. "You were there for *three years*. You're the main reason the scientists were able to find a solution. Because of you—"

Nikolai cut the words off by kissing me. "As much as I like to be glorified—"

"You don't like that at all," I interrupted.

"—I can't overlook the fact that I wouldn't even be here if it wasn't for you. In more than one way."

I kissed him back and whispered to his lips, "I don't want you to overlook that fact."

Lazily, he ran a hand up my spine to my neck, where he rested his fingers. "And now you're going to be my wife."

"Whoa." I stretched out my hands in front of me and

looked pointedly at my ringless fingers. "Nothing's set in stone yet."

Nikolai laughed. "Forget it, Hunter. You can't get rid of me anymore."

My cheeks warmed from the determination in his words. I grabbed his hand and gently squeezed it. It was an extraordinary experience to have so many and such deep feelings for a single person. Nikolai definitely was the most intense lover I'd ever had—ever would have, if it were up to me. There was absolutely nothing that he only did halfway.

After a while, the car came to a halt, and the door was opened by a soldier dressed in black. He saluted. "Major Jameson." His words were drowned out by the cheers of the crowd along the sides. I nodded at him, trying to calm my nerves before taking in the masses.

His gaze then shot to Nikolai, and he held his salute when an admiring gleam entered his eyes. "General Zaregova."

Nikolai's reputation seemed to follow him wherever he went. Then again, Nikolai hadn't been spotted outside the mission for three years, and most people hadn't seen him properly anyway. I looked at Nikolai sideways, who nodded to the soldier, and placed a hand in the small of my back.

It had been quite a change for me to see Nikolai under a bright sky. He had always been beautiful, but after the gold had seeped back into his golden-brown skin... It seemed as if new life had been breathed into him.

We walked towards the stairs past the crowd, who were taking pictures and shouting names. *Our* names. Nikolai was known, of course, as the general of the most crucial mission in the world, but it took some getting used to hearing my name from so many mouths at the same time. The press rejoiced, now that they could finally shoot Nikolai's photos—the ones all his admirers in Ardenza had been waiting for. They would probably cut me off if they got their hands on them.

That thought made me grin, because I just couldn't blame them. I'd always been too busy with myself and my ambitions to concern myself with anything else—like how wonderful General Zaregova was. But I had finally joined his fan club.

"Hunter! Nikolai!" the people yelled.

"Major! General!" the press shouted.

It was all quite overwhelming.

"Did you know it would be this busy?"

"No," he replied, lightly pinching my side. "But I'm not surprised."

"Should we have gone separately?" I bit my lip and smiled at the people on the side.

"*No*," he replied firmly.

I had suggested to Nikolai to walk into the building separately, but he had said he was proud of what we had and wanted to show off his engagement. The press had heard that we were a couple even before we got back to the capital. Soon, stories of our time in the mission had circulated.

We had talked beforehand about how we wanted to share the news. This was, of course, a complicated situation for the military, and normally one of us would have been forced to resign. But since they'd made such a colossal error of judgment, and the people were on our side, they now hid behind our popularity.

"Major Jameson!" came a high-pitched child's voice that caught my attention.

I saw a little girl sitting on a man's shoulders, who was

274

holding her tightly, and she waved a piece of paper and a marker. She was so young that I had no choice but to approach her.

"Did you call me?" I asked her.

The girl nodded shyly, after which her father gave me a proud look. "What did you want to ask Major Jameson, Zoey?"

She looked at her father for a moment and then at me again, her cheeks red. "Did you really save the General's life?"

"Yes." I nodded and gave her an encouraging smile.

"Could I become a doctor, too?"

The question made me grin. "I'm sure you can, Zoey. You can become anything you want."

The girl beamed and asked me to sign her paper before I continued.

Nikolai was already waiting at the top of the stairs, and he only had eyes for me, a proud smile spreading over his face. Together, we walked into the building.

* * *

The hall where the official ceremonies were held was large, and already packed with an audience: family, friends, and journalists filled the rows as we entered and walked towards the stage.

I could see my parents sitting in the center of the room, and I smiled at them, watching my mother wipe away a tear, and my father smiling back. He pointed to the center of the stage, where Nikolai had sat down among the other generals, and silently formed the words: *Is that him?* Beaming, I nodded, and my father gave me a thumbs up.

Of course, my parents had heard about General

Zaregova, but like for the rest of the world, he'd been a mystery to them. When I called them with the news that I was coming back in a relationship, they'd been bewildered for a few moments after hearing with who precisely.

Upon entering, I spotted Raven and Jordan, who had not yet taken a seat on the stage. They had been talking when I waved at them and walked over. It was the first time I saw them outside the mission, and I'd missed my friends.

Jordan was to receive an award for his assistance during the final battle, and Raven would be promoted to major for her work in the field. They'd seemingly grown closer over the past few weeks, as they seemed wholly relaxed with one another, laughing together. Raven had told me that Jordan had helped her in the field when she hit rock bottom, and they'd clearly developed a friendship outside of the mission.

The moment I got close, Raven nudged his shoulder, making him smile as he walked towards the stage to take his place next to Nikolai. On the way there, Jordan stopped to kiss me on the cheek, and Raven rolled her eyes at me before she pulled me into a hug moments later. She looked great.

There was an announcement for everyone to sit down, and together we walked to the stage, where we sat down beside each other. A moment later, the buzz died down, and the room fell silent.

I was the first to stand, and saw Major General Hawke walk onto the stage. I couldn't resist the surprised smile that my lips curved into. The Major General nodded at me, and went to stand before the lectern.

"Major Jameson came into my office a few months ago because I wanted to offer her a position in mission 3B." The Major General cleared her throat and looked around the room. "She was young, had no field experience, and had only graduated a year before. Despite that, I had the utmost confidence in her abilities for this mission. But even Major Jameson, who has no lack of self-esteem, showed a slight crack in her spirit when I explained what I was offering her.

"Nevertheless, she accepted the mission and—from what I've gathered—entered into an experience that would change her life in more than one way. I also heard that she was widely underestimated on arrival."

I scanned the line of soldiers on the stage, and Raven shook her head. She pointed to herself, mouthing the words *I didn't*, making me smile.

The audience laughed, too, and my gaze met Colonel Arepto's, who stood at the back of the room, grinning. I nodded gratefully at him as he winked back. Colonel Arepto had done precisely what I asked of him: *he* had leaked the story about the attack and the plasterboard wall to the press right after I informed him about it. During the conversation, He'd said that he'd liked to get revenge—but I had a feeling it went deeper for him. It was an opportunity to help the soldiers in the field this time around.

"She showed initiative, and took the lead when the mission needed it most. And with her choice to take on the mission, she saved the lives of several people present here, today." She glanced back and looked intently at Nikolai. "Of some even *several* times."

He grinned wolfishly.

"She did all this at the risk of her own life. Hence, Major Doctor Jameson has been promoted to Lieutenant Colonel Doctor Jameson."

The Major General walked up to me, shook my hand,

fastened the golden pin with the three horizontal stripes, and handed over my new epaulets. "Congratulations, Lieutenant Colonel."

I saluted, smiling. "Thank you, Major General."

* * *

Nikolai was the last to be awarded, and a loud buzz arose in the hall. I saw his gaze slide to the stairs, hands clenching, as Chief General Domasc walked onto the stage.

Chief General Domasc took place on the stage and addressed the audience. "It's the first time in three years that General Zaregova is back amongst us in civilization." He turned to Nikolai and nodded at him. Nikolai nodded back, but the icy look in his eyes promised violence.

The cameras captured all of it.

"And," Domasc continued, looking out solemnly over the audience, "in those three years, he has worked tirelessly for the good of our world. Under his leadership, hundreds of mutants have been extracted from behind the wall, which all contributed to the research for a solution to the problem. A solution that is finally here."

The crowd applauded.

Oh, the Chief General was a cunning man.

Nikolai kept his eyes on the General's back, who didn't realize he was digging his own grave that much deeper. Or he had figured it out, which would mean he was seriously underestimating Nikolai.

"General Zaregova has been a key figure in creating this new chapter of hope, and for that, we will all be eternally grateful to him. But since he cannot get any higher rank—"

Except for Chief General, I thought cynically.

"—we would like to award him with the highest order for his service and commitment to mission 3B."

Nikolai stood to receive his ribbon, and I finally caught his eye. He nodded at me with a look that said exactly what I'd been thinking. I clenched my teeth to keep from smiling. General Domasc had better enjoy his time being Chief General, as he'd just given Nikolai the motivation for that which he so desperately wanted to keep him from.

* * *

I found my parents at the back of the hall, where they had been patiently waiting. When they saw me coming, two broad smiles appeared on their faces. My mother ran up to me and drew me to her. My father also seemed emotional and hugged me tightly.

It felt good to be home again.

"We're so happy to see you, Hunter," my mother said, wiping away another tear. "That last month was still a long one, but it helped that this time we were sure that you were safe."

"*Lieutenant Colonel* Jameson," my father said. "Sounds pretty good."

"It does, doesn't it?" I replied with a grin, and scanned the room.

I found Nikolai on the other side of the hall, talking to a tall woman—his mother, no doubt. Suddenly, he turned his head and looked straight at me. I motioned for him to come and looked back at my parents.

"Mom, Dad, there's someone I want you to meet."

EPILOGUE

I opened my eyes and pulled the duvet higher over my naked body to keep the heat inside. Instinctively, my hand slid to the other side of the bed, where Nikolai had been. It was still a little warm, which meant he couldn't have gone far. I turned to the nightstand and reached for my wedding ring. Just as I was about to grab it and put it on my finger, the duvet knocked the ring right off the cabinet.

The ring had a thin band with a small oval amber diamond, which I had picked out two years ago. Nikolai had said I could choose anything I wanted, but my choice was made when I saw his eyes land on this one. For himself, he chose a simple golden band.

I wanted to contribute to the rings, too, but Nikolai had insisted on paying for them. It turned out that he could buy all the diamonds in the world. Compared to my savings account, which was by *no* means small, his seemed fit for a king.

After we got married, our finances had merged, and I

nearly had a heart attack when I wanted to check the accounts one morning. I had asked him why the hell he'd never told me before that he was rich, and why he didn't keep his account separate. To which he had only replied that everything that belonged to him was also mine.

I quickly got out of bed to pick up my ring from the floor, slid it on my finger, and got back up. Probably a little too fast because my head started spinning wildly, and I saw stars dance before my eyes. To regain my balance, I had to lean on the bed for a while. I hastily picked up my dressing gown from the chair next to my bed and wrapped it around my body.

As I pushed myself off the bed again, a wave of nausea hit me, and I braced myself against the walls as I ran for the bathroom. There, I quickly dropped to my knees and threw up in the toilet.

Not a moment later, I heard Nikolai rush upstairs to find me hunched over. "Hunter," he said soothingly, gathering my curls and holding them out of my face. "Do you need anything?"

I nodded, but continued to lean over the bowl on my elbows. "Water," I gasped.

He took a cup from the cupboard and filled it with cold water. Then he also prepared a cold washcloth, with which he dabbed the sweat off my face and throat.

After a while, the nausea subsided, and I lowered myself against the wall behind me.

Nikolai filled up the cup again and sat down next to me. "Is everything all right?"

I nodded.

"What happened?"

"Nothing special. I got out of bed and I didn't feel good."

I gently shook my head.

"I was preparing breakfast, but I don't know if that's useful to mention right now?"

No, it wasn't, but I happily tilted my head his way. "What were you making?"

"Your favorite."

My stomach turned in protest. "Then, yes," I said. I really had to get him out of here.

He kissed me on the forehead and walked back downstairs, where he went to try and save some food from burning. When I heard the door to the living room close, I slowly got up and walked over to my wardrobe.

* * *

A little while later, I arrived in the kitchen already dressed, and put my hands behind my back as I sat down at the kitchen island.

I had fallen in love with the large white mansion that stood in the meadow, close to Nikolai's childhood home, and he hadn't protested for a moment when I said I wanted to live here. He had immediately arranged the purchase agreement with an abnormally quiet determination.

We had finished the renovations a year ago, and it turned out beautifully. The house was located in the middle of nature, surrounded by tall grain and grass fields. But it was also close enough to easily visit my parents or go to Barak, where I could be within half an hour. It was spacious and white, with lots of natural materials like wood and marble. Again, Nikolai let me choose all of it, as he told me that he would be satisfied with whatever I wanted.

Thus, I created my dream home.

I also thought it was imperative not to depend on someone else, so Nikolai and I shared the rest of the costs.

Obviously, I still had my job as a surgeon, and, as I expanded my specialization, I had enough time to figure out what I could do for the military in the future. It had taken some time to convince the hospital that I couldn't be there for an emergency within ten minutes, but in the end, they went on board, and we made some excellent agreements.

"Nik," I said, as he threw a tea towel over his shoulder and arranged the food on the plates, "I have a present for you."

He looked up suspiciously from the plates and narrowed his eyes. "Okay…"

Nikolai brought the plates and put them on the table, after which he took a seat in the chair opposite me.

Suddenly he stood back up again. "What do you want to drink, by the way?"

"Wait a minute," I responded impatiently, and grabbed his wrist. "Close your eyes."

He didn't.

"*Close* them, Zaregova."

He closed his eyes.

"Hold out your hand."

He did, and he laughed. "You'd better not—"

I kissed his mouth and put the present in his hand. "Open your eyes."

Nikolai looked at what was in his hand. It was priceless to see his face change when he realized what he was holding—what it meant.

He blinked a few times and then looked up at me in amazement. "Are you…?"

Shyly, I bit my lip and nodded. "Apparently."

Nikolai shook his head in disbelief at the pregnancy test. He opened his mouth and closed it again, then looked back up at me.

I shrugged. "I thought it was weird that I was nauseous, *given that I'm never nauseous*, and wanted to take the test, just in case. Because I know morning sickness exists," I rattled on. "And I thought, *who knows?* But yes, I am pregnant."

"You're pregnant," he repeated, and a smile slowly took over his face.

I nodded. "Now, you really can't get rid of me anymore."

Nikolai got up and walked towards me. He pulled me off the stool into an intimate embrace and kissed me.

He grabbed my face with both hands and looked at me intently. "We're going to be parents?"

"Yeah," I laughed.

"Goddamnit," he said, love lacing the words.

I beamed and smiled broadly at him. *Goddamnit.*

ACKNOWLEDGMENTS

Nothing has ever given me more satisfaction than writing this book. Never have I felt so strongly that this is what I'm supposed to be doing. The past few years haven't been easy, but books have been a lifeline. So, first of all, I'm grateful to all the authors who make an effort to write their stories and books. Thank you!

I also want to thank myself. Like Hunter, I always tried to reason my way through life instead of trusting my heart. So, it has taken some time and effort to get to this point in my life—where I'm truly happy. I'm thankful I didn't give up when it seemed the easiest option. I'm glad I've always kept faith in myself, even when I had many question marks running through my head. My personal growth, from someone who began to doubt she would ever finish anything in her life to someone who has written a book in two languages and is self-publishing it, is… wow. I'm quite proud of her.

Ares, you don't want to know how grateful I am for you. You have held my hand over the past few years—even when those weren't always easy for you too. It doesn't matter what time it is or where we are; you always listen to all of my ideas.

You support me in everything I do, anchor me when I need it most, and always make me laugh. I don't think most people realize how much light you bring to my life and how incredibly sweet, funny, creative, and intelligent you are. You're my person. Thank you for letting me be such a big part of your life.

Mom and Dad, I know the past few years haven't been easy for you either. I can't imagine what it's like to see your child struggle and feel powerless. Your priority is that your children are happy, so I'm very grateful that you had my back when I decided to quit my degree and follow my dreams. I can't imagine doing this without you.

Dad, I couldn't have wished for a better father. You're my biggest supporter: whatever idea or dream I share with you, you believe I'll succeed.

And Mom, I can't think of a better best friend as a mom. No one can match your enthusiasm for my book, probably not even me.

I love you both.

Stan, no one else has such blind faith in my success as you do. You don't need to hear my plans or know the details—you just believe I'm going to make it. You know I have just as much faith in you. You don't care what people think of you and what you do. You raise your middle finger to the status quo and do whatever you feel like—and in my eyes, that's admirable.

I want to thank my beta readers; Alexandra, Papa, Mama, Ares, Marit, Iris, Cor, and Marieke. With your help, I was able to improve my book, and your feedback meant a lot to me and the story.

I also want to thank my Patrons; Rob Beset, Evi van den

Elzen, Thera van den Elzen, Irene Werner, Carlo Muller, Stan van den Elzen, Ares Keuning, Renate van den Elzen and Marcel van den Elzen. I am super, super, super grateful for your support—again, more than you will ever know.

Then, my friends: I've known many of you for a long time, but some maybe not. It means a lot to me that you really care and that you encourage me. Thank you for your tireless enthusiasm about everything I'm doing, even when it isn't always possible to keep track. True friends support each other, no matter what. You showed me that.

For my other people and family: you know who you are, even the people I don't talk to that much (anymore). Your kind words and encouragement mean a lot to me and stay with me.

And for the people I don't know well, but who do respond enthusiastically to what I'm doing—you are part of this, too. Kindness knows no limits!

Finally, you, the reader of my book. You'll never know how special it is to me that you read my book. That you filled a few hours of your time on Earth with my work. This first book is very special to me and marks a new phase in my life, so thank you for being a part of it. And anyone who also takes the time to post a review online, anywhere, or recommend my book to friends, family, strangers… Thank you a thousand times.

BRITT VAN DEN ELZEN ALWAYS WANTED TO EXPLORE OUR SOLAR
SYSTEM BUT INSTEAD DECIDED TO CREATE HER OWN UNIVERSES.
WHEN SHE'S NOT TRAVELING, SHE RESIDES IN THE
NETHERLANDS, WHERE SHE LIVES WITH HER FAMILY.

WWW.BRITTVANDENELZEN.COM
INSTAGRAM @BRITTVANDENELZEN
FACEBOOK, TWITTER & TIKTOK
@BRITTVDELZEN

IN 2023

THE STORY OF
RAVEN AND JORDAN

WANT TO KNOW HOW THE STORY CONTINUES?

FOLLOW ME ONLINE OR JOIN MY NEWSLETTER (THROUGH MY
WEBSITE) AND BE THE FIRST TO RECEIVE UPDATES.

WWW.BRITTVANDENELZEN.COM

Printed in Great Britain
by Amazon